# Rogue

*Curse of the Hybrids*

*Book 1*

# LISA LAGALY

PUBLISHING

Published in the United States of America

First Printing, 2024

ISBN

paperback: 978-1-966455-04-2

ebook: 978-1-966455-05-9

LL Publishing

Lisa1.author@gmail.com

To my　　　　daughter

Artist, organizer, athlete, student.

Lover of cats and hater of spider-crickets.

My reference for all things teenager,

Listener of woes,

Muse.

# 1

## *Honey*

She shouldn't have come. All the people here were old and shabby looking. She stood out because she was young and shabby looking.

"You're new here, aren't you dear?" the short, older woman in line in front of her asked.

The woman's fine silver hair was chopped close to her head, exposing delicately wrinkled earlobes weighed down with dangling purple beads. Her over-sized T-shirt and dark blue leggings were a little worn, but she looked and smelled clean, at least compared to all the other people Honey could smell.

"Yes."

"Thought so. I would have remembered those eyes. Are you here alone?"

"Stop flirting with her, Sheila," the old man behind Honey groused.

He had a smoky smell, like a campfire, not cigarettes, a wrinkled face, dark hair peppered with gray, and a jacket even though it was summer warm.

"It's called being nice Bob. You should try it sometime."

"I'm nice; when the situation calls for it."

Sheila shook her head. "Never mind him, Dear. Where are you from?"

"Um, around."

Sheila nodded like 'around' was a real place. She probably heard it often given where they were. "Have you been camping?"

That was a nice way to put it, but it wasn't the reason the long-sleeve plaid shirt that had been almost new a few days ago now looked and smelled like Honey had rolled in a pile of ashes and run a couple of marathons. Thinking about the reason nearly made her break down again.

"Yes."

"They have beds here. Showers too if you want to get cleaned up. It's pretty safe."

"Thank you." Could the woman smell her? Was her air shield not working? Honey quickly inspected the thin layer of air she'd pulled to herself to hold her scent in. It still looked and felt complete.

The showers and the beds were the reason she'd chosen to come to this shelter. Whether she stayed depended on who else was at the shelter. So far, she hadn't smelled any wolves or magic, but they weren't inside yet. Honey looked around again like she was curious but really she was pulling more scents from the air. Her nose caught a whiff of fried food from somewhere down the street and her stomach immediately rumbled so loudly a woman three spots ahead of them turned to look.

"When was the last time you ate?" Sheila asked.

5

Honey rubbed her belly. "Not that long ago." She had eaten her last energy bar at noon, but that was before she'd run fifteen miles.

"They should open the doors soon," Sheila said kindly.

"Good."

"I hope they have bologna sandwiches again," Bob said.

"You're the only one," Sheila scoffed. "Do you know how unhealthy those are?"

"Pfft. I've been eating them my whole life." He patted his rotund belly. "There's nothing wrong with me but old age."

"Oh look, they've opened the doors a minute early today," Sheila said.

"Will wonders never cease," Bob mumbled.

It took several minutes to get into the building, but once they were inside, Honey acquired a sandwich (not bologna), a bag of chips, a banana, and a bottle of water within two minutes of passing through the doorway.

She sniffed the air again to be sure, but no wolf smell other than her own assaulted her. It should be safe to drop her air shield – she wasn't sure how much longer she could hold it anyway. As a kindness to her fellow diners, Honey took her smoky, sweaty self to an isolated table far away from everyone else.

It was the first real meal she'd had since *that* day if a slice of mystery meat and processed cheese between two floppy white pieces of bread could be considered a meal, not that she was complaining. Her tears did not improve the texture.

A shadow fell over her plate just as she stuffed the last bite into her mouth – a wolf if her nose wasn't mistaken – several of them. Darn. She should have been paying more attention to her surroundings. She should have left up her air shield. What a stupid mistake. Her parents would be disappointed in her.

She didn't look up until she'd picked up her napkin and opened it wide enough to wipe her cheeks and mouth at the same time. A boy in his late teens with dark blond hair and blue-gray eyes was looking down on her with one side of his lip curled up like she'd been rolling in manure. She could feel more people standing around her on her side of the table, but she didn't turn her head to look. She wouldn't let them intimidate her.

"Do you need something?"

"Where are you from?" the blond boy demanded.

"Just passing through."

"Do you have a pack?"

"Not your business."

"Rogues are my business."

"Glad I'm not a rogue then."

Phooey. Phooey. Phooey. Her dad had warned her about this. This was exactly why she had to avoid other wolves. Rogues were wolves who had been rejected from the pack. At best, packs chased rogues away, but some packs killed rogues outright. Because of who her mother was, she'd never been part of a pack, nor did she need to be.

He sat down in front of her, leaned forward, and sniffed the air. "You smell, and not in a good way."

"Thanks for pointing that out."

7

"You don't smell like you belong to a pack."

She leaned forward and sniffed at him. She didn't know you could tell wolves belonged to a pack by sniffing them, but the only other wolf she'd ever been around was her dad.

"You smell like detergent, body spray, sweat, and did you have garlic earlier?" She actually liked his body spray, but she wasn't about to tell him that. There were scents from multiple wolves on him too. Maybe that's what he meant by pack. He backed away with a look of disgust.

"If you have a pack why are you in a soup kitchen?"

"I'm just passing through and the food is free. Why wouldn't I be in a soup kitchen?"

"Where are you going?"

"Not your business."

"How old are you?"

"Again, not your business. Excuse me. I need to bus my table." She pushed her chair back, but as she'd half-expected, something blocked her from backing up entirely.

"You need to what?" the boy queried.

"Bus my table." She pointed at the sign on the wall behind him that was several tables away.

"You can read?"

"Of course. Didn't *your* pack teach *you*?" She made sure he heard the emphasis on your and you.

While he was thinking that over, Honey glanced at the wolves behind her. Two more males and a female. All were about the same age. All of them had beautiful faces and condescending looks. She felt like one of those nerdy kids surrounded by the bullish 'in' crowd in a bad high-school movie. Not that she had watched many of those since Mom found high-school movies irritating.

"I just want to throw my trash away. Will you let me up please?"

"You're not done," the male on her right said, pointing to the unopened bag of chips.

"I'm saving it for later."

To prove her point, she grabbed the bag of chips and stuffed it into the top of the backpack leaning on her feet.

"Let's see what else you're saving for later."

The wolf leaned forward and grabbed her bag. Honey nearly froze him but stopped herself in time. Freezing him would be bad. If she was going to make a clean getaway, she'd have to freeze all of them at once and hope there weren't any other wolves around to notice the scent of her magic or witches to notice something odd. Besides, as long as he didn't find any of the cash cards or the birth certificate or the burner phone she had sewn in the bottom of the bag, it would be fine.

The bully dumped all the stuff in the main pocket on the table with a flourish. It was hard to keep herself still while he unfolded and tossed her spare clothes to the side and flipped through the pretty red notebook she'd purchased in honor of her first day of public school. It was still empty except for the one day of notes she'd taken. He rummaged through the smaller pocket on the front of her bag next, haphazardly tossing her two pens, two pencils, favorite eraser, and her new house key onto the worn table.

The key. She'd forgotten it was there. She suddenly had a vivid memory of the wall of keys at the hardware store. Her Mom was to her right smiling and pointing and suggesting they splurge on the pretty ones. They'd inspected them all together before settling on the blue one with a sword and a flower. Her mom had seemed excited to get Honey her own key. Honey had been equally excited to use it, but when she got home the door was not only unlocked, it was wide open.

The key disappeared. The noises in the cafeteria crashed in on her and she realized the blond boy had pounced on the key and was now holding it right in front of her nose. "Where is this to?"

She tried to snatch it from him, but he jerked it out of her reach. "My house."

"Where is your house?"

"Not your business. Give it back."

She held out her hand. When he didn't return it after a couple of seconds, she gave up. It was just a key. It might be the last present her mother had ever given her but holding onto it wouldn't bring her back. Honey retracted her hand and started stuffing the rest of her meager belongings back into her bag. There was no way to hide how upset she was. She could smell the waves of distress rolling off herself even over all her other funk. The tears trying to drip down her cheeks cinched it.

"Look, we're here to help. Come with us quietly and you won't get hurt," blond boy lied, dropping the key on the table.

She snatched it and tucked it back where it belonged. "This is neutral territory. I can be here if I want."

"Only a rogue would say that."

"Only a rogue would know a rogue would say that," she countered. Perhaps not the best comeback, but she'd at least confused him a little, based on his frown.

"There you are Ava." A round body slid into the seat beside her and another beside blond boy across the table. Sheila handed Honey another sandwich with a wink. "I had an extra."

Honey took it with relief, not just because her tormentors were already backing away, but because she was still hungry, and she didn't think it would be polite to go back for seconds in a soup kitchen when there was still a line. "Thank you, Sheila."

Bob offered her a bag of chips from across the table. "I saved these for you. I'm supposed to be watching my cholesterol. Enjoy eating chips while you can."

"Thank you, Bob."

The blond boy's glare was sharp enough to drill into the skulls of the two older people, but they paid him no mind. They started chatting to each other and Honey as if the four wolves weren't even there. Honey focused on Bob and methodically eating her second sandwich one slow bite at a time.

The two humans stayed with her until a volunteer appeared to tell them it was time to leave unless they were staying overnight. Since she was certain the bullies wouldn't lower themselves to stay in a homeless shelter, Honey told the volunteer she was staying. Based on the look the blond boy gave her when he pushed open the door to leave, it was only a temporary reprieve.

# 2

## Honey

The questions they asked at the shelter made no sense. Did they really expect criminals or people who were trying to get away like she was to answer honestly? She didn't like lying, but the only true thing she felt it was safe to tell the volunteer was that she was homeless, and that's because it was a given. Why else would she be in homeless shelter?

After they'd finished questioning her, the shelter people gave Honey a much-appreciated, free, one-time use toothbrush and a comb. The comb was about as effective against her tangled curls as a pair of kids' safety scissors against a holly hedge, but for the first time in days she was clean. She even got to wash her clothes.

She wasn't sure what to expect in the women's dormitory. Would they be loud? Would it be crowded? Would she be able to sleep amid a bunch of strangers? The only people she'd ever slept in a room or a tent with were her mom and dad. To her immense relief, everybody, except one lady who clearly had some mental issues, completely ignored her. After walking carefully around the glaring woman who was gripping her natty bag like Honey would snatch it at any moment, Honey found a cot on the other side of the room and fell asleep almost the moment her head hit the pillow.

The next morning came too soon. She stripped her cot as instructed, then collected and quickly ate the prepackaged breakfast the shelter offered and brushed her teeth. There wasn't time to do anything else before they forced everyone out of the shelter for the day.

Were the wolf-bullies waiting? Now that she was rested and had a clearer head, she didn't understand why they had approached her. Her dad had listed all the neutral territories for her a long time ago and Indianapolis had definitely been on the list. Was it a normal thing to pick on rogues in Indianapolis? Dad had never mentioned it, but maybe it was a new development. Should she go to another town?

She collected her bag from the front desk and joined the men and women exiting out the front door. Outside, the car fumes had already begun to collect between the buildings in the early morning air, but the sun was shining, and the sky was a clear blue. It was a perfect day to explore the city.

Should she?

She'd been so focused on running and accomplishing step 1 – get away, she hadn't thought much beyond it except to temporarily manage step 2 – find food and shelter. She needed a more permanent solution to step 2 and for that, she needed a job or a computer to start an online store like her mother had. There was an idea – maybe she could continue the store. No, the killer might know about it. Besides, she wasn't a healer. She wouldn't be able to add the magic her mother did.

She discretely wiped her tears before stepping out into the sunshine. Where could she find a good job at her age? Maybe there was a book in the library, or better, maybe they'd hire her! Now which way was the one she'd visited yesterday? Everything looked different in the morning light. She took a deep breath of fresh air and quickly reversed course. Stupid bullies were still around.

Back inside the shelter, Honey dodged the volunteer who was herding people out and made a beeline for the front desk. "Is there a back way out?"

The woman at the desk didn't even look up. "No. Everyone must leave through the front."

Which meant there was a backdoor but she wasn't allowed to use it. "There are some mean kids waiting to beat me up," she tried.

This time the woman did look up. She wasn't that old, maybe forty, but her face was already starting to wrinkle and her eyes were sad and tired. "I'm sorry. It's against policy. Besides, it wouldn't do you much good. The back door leads to an alley that leads right back to the front of the building."

"Okay."

She was going to have to use her magic and get away before they could catch her and figure out the magic was coming from her.

"Hey Claire," the lady at the desk called, "did you get your car fixed?"

A skinny older lady with wispy white hair, a bright pink shirt, and a long tan skirt who was about to step outside the door nodded.

The front desk lady jerked her head towards Honey. "This one needs a ride."

Claire backed up to stand by the door and looked at Honey expectantly. Honey ran to her side before she changed her mind.

"Where to?" Claire asked.

"Library."

"Ten dollars."

"I don't have ten dollars."

"Can't help you then."

Honey grabbed the woman's arm when she started to move away, but quickly let go when Claire glowered at her. "I have a cash card. If you stop at a quick stop on the way, I will buy you something."

"Buy me gas."

"Okay." Ten dollars was a lot for a short trip, but if she could get away without revealing herself, it would be worth it.

She followed Claire outside with two other homeless people after making sure the wolves weren't waiting by the door to grab her. Claire crossed the street and stopped at an old, dusty, beat-up two door car that surprisingly managed a beep when she pushed her key fob. "Which library do you want to go to?"

"There's more than one?" Honey asked as she opened the passenger door.

"Of course. There are at least five public ones that I know of. None of them open before ten though."

"Oh." It didn't matter. She just needed to get away and conveniently, she'd be able to look up bus schedules in any library and hopefully get away from the bullies permanently. "Whatever is most convenient for you."

Claire slid into the driver seat and started moving books and papers off the passenger seat into the already cluttered back seat. The car smelled like old vinyl and oil and gas and food, but it was better than wolves. Honey slid into the seat as soon as it was clear and firmly shut the door. Something dark moved just beyond the corner of the homeless shelter, but it was too fast for her to get a good look.

Claire nodded. "Gas first though."

"Yes. Gas first."

It took a couple of tries for the car to start. The engine coughed. Honey didn't know engines could cough. She wished her dad was there so he could diagnose it. Huh. How had she never made the connection before? Her mom was a healer of people and her dad was a healer of cars. He would have laughed when she told him that. She missed them so much.

The gas station was only a couple of blocks away. With the exhaust Claire's car was spewing and the speed of traffic, the wolves wouldn't be far behind. Honey jumped out of the car before Claire had come to a complete stop and ran inside the station to pay. How many times had she done the same thing from her mom? Wasn't the last time only a few days ago?

"Which pump?"

Honey shook her head. She couldn't afford to start crying right now. "Two. Ten dollars." She handed over her cash card then gave Claire two thumbs-up through the window before grabbing and paying for a few of the healthier snacks to restock her bag.

Claire had just put the hose back on the pump when Honey returned to the car. She looked around again and took a deep breath of fuel-laden air. No wolf smell, but if they were smart, they'd be standing downwind. She slid into the passenger seat and shut the door before handing Claire the coffee she'd bought her.

"Cream, no sugar."

Claire sniffed at it, then took a sip. "I like sugar, no cream, but this will do."

For 7 a.m. in the morning, there was a lot of traffic. They drove a few blocks before they got stuck in a line of cars several blocks long.

Claire cussed under her breath. "I forgot they were working on this road."

"How far away is the library?" At this rate the wolves would make it before she did, if they'd heard the destination, which they probably had.

"About another mile to the east."

That wasn't right. The library she'd found yesterday had been much closer to the shelter. "I will just get out here."

"We'll get there eventually."

"That's okay. Thanks Claire."

She opened the door and hopped out of the car and onto the sidewalk. If Claire was right, libraries were plentiful. Right now though, she had to make sure the bullies couldn't find her. She pulled up her air shield and

17

ran north, away from the shelter and away from wherever Claire had been taking her.

# 3

## Honey

It took her an hour and a short conversation with a woman packing her kids into her van, but she eventually found a library. To kill time while she waited for it to open, she wandered around the block. She didn't smell any wolves, but she was pretty sure one of the small shopping centers had stores that catered to witches. None of them were open yet, but the smell of magic was unmistakable. She'd never been inside a witch-owned store before. Would it be safe for her to visit? If she dropped her air shield, she should just feel like a wolf to them, but would they let her in? Maybe she could try after the library.

The librarian was human and very helpful. She gave Honey a guest pass to use the computer and directed her to a shelf of books with job opportunities for teens. The books weren't helpful, but the bus schedule was. She could be on her way to another town and away from the bullies in just a few hours. Leaving had the added advantage of putting more distance between herself and where everything had happened. If anyone was looking for her, they'd likely look in the nearest city first.

The bus she selected left from the bus terminal in the center of town. It wasn't *that* far to walk, which she started to do, but running was much faster. Plus, she liked to run. Despite the overabundance of car exhaust from the busy street, she enjoyed the feel of the breeze in her hair and the sun on her face. The only thing that would have made it better is if her mom were there. Her mom, her wonderful, beautiful mom, would never run with her again.

Tears blurred Honey's sight, but not enough to keep her from recognizing the big green blob of a bus that passed her. She was here.

She slammed into something hard and dark and bounced back onto her rear. Small bits of gravel dug themselves into her palms. She didn't have to look up to know the bullies had found her. She recognized the smell of the body spray their leader used.

"Where are you going so quickly?" he demanded.

She ignored him and started flicking the gravel off her palms. They were already starting to heal, but the dirt needed to be washed off. She opened the bottle of water she'd refilled at the shelter and poured water over the worst of it.

Bully leader didn't say anything else while she flicked the water off and took several sips from her bottle. The bag-dumping bully grabbed the bottle out of her hands and threw it. "He asked you a question."

She looked around instead of up. The other two bullies were behind her and to her left. She didn't see anyone else who was obviously associated with them and none of the few people coming and going from the station were paying attention. She really wanted to freeze them. They deserved it. The problem was, it would only give her maybe thirty seconds to disappear and she still had a couple of hours until her bus to Columbus left. On the other hand, if she could hide her scent and find a good hiding place, maybe they'd leave before the bus left.

She closed her eyes and put her head down. Mom had taught her to do magic without any tells like that witch on the old TV show who wiggled her nose, but it was a lot easier to envision what was happening if she closed her eyes. Also, she'd never tried to freeze four people at once before.

She imagined the shapes of their bodies with wiggling balls inside, then stopped the balls. Slowly, she opened her eyes and inspected her work. Lead bully was watching her with his mouth partially opened like he was about to say something. She didn't think he could see her – her dad said he couldn't remember anything when she practiced freezing him – still, it was creepy. She popped to her feet and squeezed past him. After scooping up her still partially-filled water bottle, she sprinted away. She didn't have time to walk, not if she wanted to find a hiding place before they thawed. To keep the bullies from finding her trail, she pulled every molecule of her scent to her skin and held it tight.

The area around the bus terminal and transit station was not a good place to seek a hiding place. One side of the busy, one-way road was lined with bus stop signs. The other side offered a row of cars, some small trees, and a long building. Ducking down behind a car would only give her a few minutes at best and the trees were too small to climb. She ran across the street to the long building.

As soon as she stepped inside, she knew that was a bad choice. It was a well-lit, airy place with two big front desks – one with a guard – and lots of seats. The only places to hide were under the seats or behind the guard's desk.

She was desperate enough to try and convince the guard to let her sit on the floor behind the desk next to him until she got a whiff of him. A wolf, of course. He wouldn't hide her from other wolves. She spun around on her heel and ran back out the door.

The bullies would be nearly thawed by now. Her options were a construction site across the street from the terminal, and a row of tall buildings a block away. She turned to the buildings. They offered multiple levels where she could hide if she could gain entrance. She ran past a county building and a Japanese restaurant that didn't look open and turned into a parking garage. Maybe she'd get lucky and find a truck with a tarp.

Her dad had told her once to always hide in a place where she had multiple exits, so she ran up the stairs to the second-to the top floor to give herself two exits, one up and one down. It probably wasn't what he meant since both ways were accessed through one door, but she could also climb to the outside of the building if she had to. She squatted behind a car by the low wall that ran all around the parking garage floor and peered up the street towards the bus stop. Barely a minute passed before the four bullies collected in front of the transit station. By the shaking of heads and the waving of hands, she guessed the other three bullies were telling the blond bully they hadn't found her and the blond was ordering them to split up. The male bully who hadn't talked and the female headed down the street toward her. The female went toward the Japanese restaurant while the male continued on to the garage. He looked all around, although not up, sniffed the air, then walked toward the garage.

She'd never tried to hold on to her scent while running. Had it not worked? She pulled the layer of air in tighter to her body and jogged around the edge of the garage until she found a van parked close enough to the wall that she could lay on top of the bumper and lean on the wall. If anyone looked under the vehicles, they wouldn't see her feet.

It felt like half-an-hour passed before she heard the scuffle of a shoe and caught the scent of wolf. She slowly breathed in and out to keep her heart rate calm, not because wolves could hear heartbeats a car away like she'd seen in a movie once – that was ridiculous – but they could hear breathing and she needed to be calm.

For someone who was trying to find someone, the bully made a lot of noise. Was that…was he humming? If she hadn't smelled wolf, she would have thought it was someone coming to get their car. The humming got louder, then faded. He didn't even pause. Ha!

The humming disappeared. She waited for what seemed like another half-an-hour before she felt safe enough to peer around the van. She half-expected him to be sitting in front of it, waiting for her. He wasn't. Keeping close to the wall, she scuttled back to the front of the garage to look down at the street, right at head bully.

She jerked back, then peered down more carefully. Head bully was on the sidewalk across the street waving his arms at the humming bully who was shaking his head. After a few moments, head bully stomped back toward the bus stop and humming bully went further up the street.

Honey sank down into the corner behind a parked car feeling like she'd just escaped from a pack of wild animals, which, if she thought about it, was exactly what had happened. How had they known she was going to go to the bus stop or was it just a coincidence? Should she give up and try again another day? Maybe she could sleep on the roof of the garage or find an unlocked vehicle over at the construction site. Would it be safe to do that? She'd understood that neutral territory meant wolves from anywhere, even those without a pack, could wander around without worrying about stepping into another pack's territory. Was she wrong? Where was she supposed to live if all the wolves she met thought she was a rogue? She didn't want to join a pack. That was dangerous, being what she was, and she couldn't exactly join a coven. What she needed was a place where only humans lived.

As far as she knew though, that didn't exist.

Maybe she could go to a really big city like New York. Big cities didn't have very many wolves because wolves didn't like them, but it probably had a lot of witches. She'd have to keep her powers secret so they'd have no reason to bother her.

Ugh. She didn't want to live in a big city. On the other hand, there would be plenty of places where she could go to school and find a job or start an online business.

Her heart hurt at the thought of doing everything alone. She'd find some friends, some human friends, maybe even some roommates. Perhaps she could apply for a scholarship somewhere.

She'd come two hours early so she could grab a lunch and look around, but the bullies had ruined that plan. Surely, they would get tired of looking for her before the bus came. It wasn't like they knew which bus she planned to take or even that she planned to take one. Once she got on the bus, she'd do a better job at keeping her scent hidden. If, for some unfathomable reason the wolf-bullies were still around and she couldn't get on the bus, she'd find a place to stay overnight, then catch a train in the morning.

After all the preparation her parents had done and training they'd given her, she'd thought she was ready. She was wrong. How was she going to live without them?

# 4

## Honey

Two hours in a parking garage sitting behind a car was probably the most boring thing she'd ever done. Fifteen minutes before her bus was due, she started making her way back to the bus stop. She'd never ridden in a bus before, so she wasn't sure how early or late to expect it. All she knew was that it was green according to the pictures online where she'd paid for and printed the ticket at the library. It was only $30 one way, due to a discount she'd found, which she thought was pretty good. She'd heard her dad complain about airplane ticket prices enough to know those usually cost at least $100 for even short distances. She'd never been on a plane either.

She went out the back of the parking garage and ended up near the buildings that lined the open construction area just behind the bus stop. If she had any luck the bullies had gotten bored and left, but she kept her nose and ears open and her scent close while she worked her way around the construction site. She was half-way there when she caught the first whiff of wolf. Before she could even turn, there was a sharp pain in her shoulder.

She looked back to see an orange tube with feathers at the end jutting out from her skin.

She was so stupid. She should have waited another day or found another bus stop. Still, it wasn't fair. She hadn't done anything to them. She envisioned the tranquilizer molecules pushing themselves back into the dart and jerked it from her shoulder. It was too late to capture all of them, but she got enough that when she turned and threw it into head bully's prominent pec and pushed the fluid back out with a little help from her magic, he got at least half a dose.

His smug look faded into surprise, then anger as he jerked it from his chest and threw it to the ground. The humming bully picked the dart up and put in his pocket even as head bully stomped her way. He raised his hands and came at her like he was going to shove her. She ducked and elbowed him in the back so that he stumbled past her and tripped over the edge of the curve. Sadly, he didn't fall. He caught himself on the orange construction fence and turned with an even angrier look on his handsome face. She tensed in preparation when he came at her again but didn't have a chance to get into position because someone grabbed her arms from behind.

Head bully stopped right in front of her and poked her in the shoulder with one finger. "Stupid rogue. I'm trying to help you."

Her head was already starting to feel woozy, but there was still a chance she could get away. She pictured the molecules in the people around her and froze them. Now she just needed the bus. If she could get on the bus in the next thirty seconds, she might have a chance.

She jogged toward the bus stop and past the work truck that was blocking her view. The bus wasn't there yet, but it had to be soon. All she had to do was get there. She jogged one, two, three steps, then the world faded away.

# 5

## Honey

The first thing she noticed when she woke was the smell. Instead of exhaust and dust and warm cement, it smelled like a house and wolves and a little like flowers. The second thing was that her neck hurt from leaning forward and that she was sitting in a chair, no, tied to a chair, but it wasn't a cheap chair. It was made out of wood with padding on the seat and the back and the arms. She lifted her head to ease her neck, then realized she should have probably pretended to sleep for a while and listen for clues. To her surprise, she was in a nice room. It had rose and cream tones involving wainscoting, a highly polished wooden desk, a comfortable-looking couch, thick carpet, and heavy drapes elegantly drawn back to frame full-length windows. It she didn't know better, she'd think she was in a room at the White House.

It took her a few moments to remember why she was there. How long had she been unconscious? The sun was still shining outside the window behind the desk, but it didn't look as bright. A few feet away, on a small, round table her mom would have described as mahogany, the cash cards, burner phone, notebook, bus ticket, key, and her destroyed backpack were displayed in an oddly pleasing design.

She closed her eyes. Someone had discovered the hidden pocket in the bottom of her bag. Despite all her mom's efforts, she'd only lasted four days on her own. She was a failure.

No. She blinked away her tears. She couldn't give up yet. As long as she was alive, she had to keep trying. She'd no doubt missed the bus, but there would be other busses. She just had to figure out where she was and how to get to a bus stop.

Movement in front of the bright window drew her attention. A slim, elegantly coiffured woman with blond hair rose gracefully from a chair Honey hadn't noticed in front of the tall window and stepped around the desk. The woman looked about the same age as her mom, but whereas her mom was soft and beautiful, this woman was sharp and handsome.

The light from the window hit the piece of paper in the woman's hand, making it glow. The worn creases and slight browning on one edge were familiar. It didn't belong in her hand. Honey clenched her fists behind her back. How dare the woman tear up her backpack and read her private things.

The woman passed by another very tall, very muscular woman standing so still near the drapes that Honey had mistakenly dismissed her as a statue at first glance. Honey kept her eyes on her instead of looking at the blond woman who had stopped in front of her.

"Your name is Ava Smith?" she asked.

Honey didn't answer. The woman didn't deserve the courtesy. Not to mention, she wasn't sure she could. Her head was starting to hurt and she was dreadfully thirsty. It felt like she'd been sucking on cotton balls for a couple of hours. The statue raised an eyebrow at her. Honey turned away from her too and looked toward the other side of the room.

"Is this your birth certificate?"

How was she supposed to get out of this? She tugged at whatever was holding her hands together. It wasn't hard like handcuffs nor was it scratchy like rope. It was too tight to slip her hands out, but maybe she could cut it off with a claw. She sent a silent thanks to her dad for insisting she practice partial transformation every night. Even better would be to partially transform and slip her paw out, but would that work? Would whatever it was just reappear on her wrist like clothes always did when she transformed back to human? What if the cord reappeared in the middle of her arm or something? Could that happen?

The woman was still standing in front of her. She might have been waiting expectantly. Honey didn't know. She refused to look up.

"Maybe I should introduce myself first," the woman said.

She was too close for Honey to partially transform and pull her arm free. The woman would notice.

"I'm Adalynn Mooney, Luna of the Mooney pack, but everyone calls me Luna Lynn."

Loony Lynn. Honey could almost hear her mom telling her it wasn't nice to even think things like that, but

31

the woman had her tied to a chair. Maybe she could freeze her and the statue, slip her arms out, and escape. If the woman was a pack Luna though, there was a good chance they were on pack grounds. It might take more than thirty seconds to find her way out of the building and once they unfroze, the women would sound an alarm and set everyone to looking for her. Honey would have to find a car or better, a motorcycle, if she wanted to escape a whole pack. Unless, Honey focused on the shelves along the wall, she could find the woman's purse and keys.

"There's no need to be frightened. I'm not going to hurt you. I'm trying to help you."

Honey made a show of wiggled her arms, then shot a glare upward.

"We only constrained you because we weren't sure how you'd react when you woke. If you promise not to attack, we'll untie you.

She wasn't going to promise anything, not when she was already half-way through whatever was binding her thanks to her claw.

The woman squatted in front of her. Honey looked away from her, toward the door again.

"How long have you been a rogue?" the woman asked softly. "All your cash cards are full, so I know it can't have been long. What happened? Why did your pack kick you out?"

Honey wanted to tell her that she hadn't been kicked out of anywhere and it wasn't her business anyway, but that would have required talking to her, and that she refused to do.

"It didn't just happen. You were prepared." Honey saw a flicker of movement out of the corner of her eye but she wasn't sure from what. "Kids don't usually carry their birth certificates around. Was it something you did or something your parents did?"

Other than having her, her parents hadn't done anything wrong, and definitely not anything deserving of death. A big fat tear decided at that moment to creep out of the corner of her eye and run down her cheek.

"Did something else happen? Cici said you reeked of smoke when they found you, and it wasn't just wood smoke. She said you smelled like burning plastic and meat."

"Not meat," Honey whispered. The source of the smell, her parents' bodies lying burnt and blackened on the floor of the rented house in the midst of the flames raging over and around them, jumped to the forefront of her mind. Her dad, her big, strong funny dad, had been so burned she'd only known it was him from his hair and the chain he always wore around his neck. Her mom, her beautiful, smart, loving mom had died with her blackened hand reaching for him.

She didn't remember finally cutting through whatever bound her or having her feet untied, but when she finally recovered enough from the memory to be aware of her surroundings again, she was on the floor with a damp face, a dripping nose, and the Luna's arms around her.

"Tell me what happened," the woman, Lynn, said softly, pushing a damp strand of hair behind Honey's ear.

"Fire. I came home and my parents were both...they were inside."

"You saw them?"

Honey nodded.

Lynn pulled Honey into a tighter hug and rested her cheek on the top of Honey's head. "You poor girl. Do you know how it happened?"

Honey shook her head.

"Why did you run? Wasn't there someone else you could go to?"

Honey shook her head again.

"Were your parents rogues?" Lynn asked gently.

"No."

"They weren't?" she sounded surprised.

"No."

"What pack are you from?"

"We were our own pack."

"Ah, well how about we get up off this floor and sit on the couch, then we can decide what to do with you."

"Do with me?"

Lynn handed her a tissue from the box the muscular woman had passed down. "Yes, do with you. Do you have any other family anywhere?"

"I don't know." She did have a grandmother somewhere, but she didn't know her name and or where she lived or if she was even still alive. She did know she was a witch, but she couldn't say that.

"Why did you buy a ticket to Columbus?"

"To get away from the bullies."

"Bullies?"

Did the Luna truly not realize how awful her teenage pack members were? "Yeah, those four mean wolves who wouldn't leave me alone." Her voice cracked. She tried

34

clearing it but was like trying to clear glue. Lynn pushed a cold, unopened bottle of water in her hand. Where had that come from?

"They were just concerned because you're so young." The Luna said as Honey took a long sip.

"Concerned people don't rifle through other people's things and throw their opened water bottle on the ground or destroy their belongings." Honey looked pointedly at the dissected backpack on the table.

"I was only trying to learn more about you so I could help you. I'm starting a program to help rogues get back on their feet," she said with pride.

"I was on my feet until the bullies knocked me down."

"You were on the run and alone. Now you have me." The woman pushed herself up off and floor and brushed off her pastel slacks as if her rose-colored rug might be dirty. Honey stood up beside her. Lynn was at least an inch taller, unlike Honey's mom who was three inches shorter, or had been.

"Now, how old are you? The year on this birth certificate is illegible."

Because Honey had made it that way. Did it matter if she told her? She chewed her lip. It might if she needed to get a fake ID to get a job, which is what she'd been planning to do once she accomplished step 1: get away. Finding a job would help her accomplish step 2: find food and shelter. "Promise not to tell anyone?"

Lynn gave Honey a, 'children say the silliest things', look. "You are too young to be worrying about your age."

Honey looked over at the other woman. She hadn't moved or said a word since passing on the tissue box. "You have to promise too or leave."

Woman 2 snorted.

Honey shrugged and looked around. A picture on the wall beside the desk caught her attention. Lynn was in it along with a big, muscular man with light brown hair, and a boy not quite as tall as her. Even though he was several years younger in the picture, Honey still recognized him – head bully. Lynn must be his mother.

Lynn saw where she was looking and walked over and pulled the picture off the wall. She leaned casually against the desk and touched the faces with a fond smile. "My husband and my son. This was five years ago when Brayton was thirteen. It's disturbing how fast they grow up." Lynn released a long sigh, then hung the picture back on the wall.

Honey's mom had had one picture with all three of them together, but couldn't display it in case someone saw it, not that they ever had visitors. She'd kept it in the false bottom of a shoe box high up in the closet. Honey was seven in the picture and wore a green dress that her mom said matched her eyes. Her dad was smiling and had his arm draped over her mom's shoulders. Her mom hadn't quite smiled when whoever it was had taken the picture, but she'd had an amused look in her eye and a quirk to her mouth. Honey had used to beg to see it, especially when her dad was away on his business trips. Was the picture still there or had everything burned to the ground? Would it be too dangerous to go back and look?

"Fine," Lynn said, waving her hand like she was swatting at an irritating fly before jerking out the chair tucked under the desk. "I promise not to tell anyone."

Honey swiped a couple of tears from her cheeks. "What?"

"Your age. I promise not to tell anyone."

Honey forced herself to focus on the present. "Or write it down, or speak in sign language, or record it, or share it in any way."

Lynn sighed and plopped down in the chair. "Tell me already."

"You have to promise. Her too," Honey nodded at the muscular woman.

"I don't even care, but I promise not to divulge your highly secret age in any way, shape, or form," muscles said.

"Can I tell my husband?" the Luna asked.

"No."

"But I tell him everything."

"I'll tell him if he needs to know, maybe. You can tell him you promised and that you are a wonderful woman who would never dream of breaking a promise."

Lynn laughed. Despite her sharp features, she had a nice laugh. "Fine, I make the same promise that Bernadette did."

"She's Bernadette?" Honey pointed to muscles.

"There's no one else in here."

"Just making sure."

"Okay, spill. What's your age."

"Fourteen."

She lifted her hands as if she was saying a prayer, then picked up a pen. "You are a freshman then."

"Mmm, not really. I was home-schooled."

"Home-schooled?" She said it like she'd never heard of such a thing.

"Yes."

"For how long?"

"Forever." It wasn't worth mentioning that she'd gone to high school for one day. Lynn might be able to figure out where she'd come from.

Lynn put her pen down. "You've never been to a formal school?"

"No." She guessed Lynn wouldn't count gymnastics or martial arts or pottery class and she didn't need to know about those anyway.

Lynn leaned back in her chair. "I guess we'll just have to get you tested. We might have to put you with some younger kids so you can get caught up."

"But they already tested me."

"Who did?"

"The high school. My mom was going to let me go to high school but they didn't know what grade to put me in so they made me take the SAT."

"And," Lynn said, "What did you get?"

"A 1600."

"No. You. Did. Not," Bernadette stated.

"I did."

Luna Lynn got a sly look in her eye. "Prove it and I'll get you free ride to college."

College!

Honey pinned her with her eyes. "This semester?" That was only three weeks away.

Lynn's eyebrows quivered. "Yes," she said after the slightest hesitation.

"Do you have a computer?"

# 6

## Honey

Luna Lynn was flabbergasted. Honey decided she really liked that word. Bernadette was also flabbergasted.

"I can't believe this," Lynn said again, moving the mouse around the screen as if that was going to reveal the page Honey was showing her on the college board site was fake. "Brayton took the test three times and only got a 1420."

A 1420 wasn't bad, but Honey couldn't help but be a little smug that she'd done better than head bully. "Which college am I going to go to? Do I get to choose? I want one that offers a major in chemical physics."

"You want what now?" Bernadette asked.

"Chemical physics. It's the study of chemical processes while thinking like a physicist."

"Ah, well, I'm on the board of our local college where most of the wolves attend. I was thinking you could go there," Luna Lynn said. "I'm sure they have both chemistry and physics. Maybe you could do a double major?"

"That would work. It would give me something to build off of. I could always go to another college and get a masters or PhD in the field if I needed."

"O.M.G. You are serious!" That was Bernadette again.

Luna Lynn gave Bernadette a sour glance. "Why are you surprised by this? She's only fourteen and she got a perfect score on the SAT. She can do whatever she wants."

"Yeah, but she…I mean look at those eyes, and that hair."

"What?" Honey reached up to try and straighten her hair with her fingers but she knew it was a lost cause. Her curls loved to tangle and she was pretty sure there were still three comb teeth lost somewhere in the mess.

"Wait, a second. This score is for someone named Honey," Lynn said suspiciously.

"I know. That's me," Honey said.

"Cici said the people at the shelter called you Ava."

"You don't use your real name at a shelter," Honey scoffed.

"Especially with a name like Honey," Bernadette snorted. "Your mom was a hippy, wasn't she?"

"Shush, Bernadette," Lynn said. "Is your name truly Honey Smith?"

"Yes."

"And your parents were named Matt and Mindy Smith?"

Lynn must had read that on the birth certificate. Honey couldn't think of a reason to remove her parent's names since she was pretty sure they weren't their real

41

ones. She'd asked her mother once if Mindy was her real name. Mom had said it was close enough.

"Yes."

"Why does that remind me of an old TV show?" Lynn mused.

Since she and her mom didn't have a TV, Honey had no idea.

"Are you talking about Mork and Mindy?" Bernadette asked.

"Probably. Excuse me for a moment, I'll be right back."

Lynn strode purposely out the door, leaving Honey sitting in front of the computer with Bernadette standing over her. She was tempted to google how to get to the bus stop, but with Bernadette watching…actually, what difference did it make if she was watching? Honey opened a new browser window and started typing.

Bernadette slammed the laptop closed on her hands. "No."

"But I just wanted to…"

"No."

Fine, there were other things she could do to figure out where she was, like look out the window. She pushed the rolling chair backwards and spun around, then launched herself out of the chair and toward the window. She expected Bernadette to stop her, but the woman didn't move. They were on the second floor. The first thing Honey noticed was a big blue metal barn which was just across the wide drive from there window, but there were lots of other buildings and people walking between them. She didn't see any in wolf form. Far beyond the

42

barn, she saw fields and a large patch of trees stretching toward what she guessed was the west based on the position of the sun. There were a few cars parked around the buildings but no motorcycles. It was a good thing she hadn't tried to run – the cars were all too new to hot-wire. She'd have to locate a key if she was going to escape that way.

"I found it," Lynn said entering the room with a large workbook in her hand. "Have a seat, Honey." Lynn flipped through the book then set it purposely in front of her opened to a nearly blank page. "This is a practice SAT test. I've opened it to the math portion. I need you to prove to me that you are the Honey Smith whose account you pulled up. If you can get all those right, or nearly all of them, you've got your scholarship."

Honey raised her eyes just enough to see Lynn's face. "I'll need a pencil."

"Okay then," Lynn said forty minutes later after checking over Honey's answers a second time. "I am impressed. Let me show you to your room."

"My room?" Honey asked from where she was watching out the window again.

"Yes. If I'm going to sponsor a fourteen-year-old for a full ride scholarship, I'm going to keep an eye on her. You will be my ward. When the university is on holiday, you will live here, and when it's in session, you will live in the dorms. I'll ask Brayton to keep an eye on you too."

"That won't be necessary," Honey said quickly.

"I'm hoping you'll rub off on him. Mmm. What did your mother teach you about boys?"

"They like to see if they can get girls to take off their clothes, so don't drink anything they hand you and be very suspicious if they try to sweet-talk you into something," Honey recited.

Bernadette snorted.

"Your mom was not wrong," Lynn agreed, nodding sagely. "You're very young. I recommend you stay away from boys until you're eighteen at least. That will give you four years of distraction-free studying. Well, boy-caused distraction anyway. You might want to rethink telling people about your age. Most boys will behave if they know how young you are. Not all, unfortunately."

"I will take your advice under consideration if the situation warrants it."

"Maybe you should become a lawyer. Seriously, you sound like one," Bernadette mumbled.

Someone pounded on the door. "Mom, is the rogue awake yet?"

"Yes, you can come in Brayton. How do you feel?"

The door slammed open and head bully stomped in, or would have if the carpet hadn't been so thick. "Like someone shot me with a tranquilizer dart." He glared at Honey as if she'd been the one to load the gun and shoot it into his back.

"It's a good thing you weren't actually shot then, you'd be whining about the bruise too," Honey snarked.

"That's enough you two. You're both awake and it worked out for the best," Lynn said. "Come along Honey. I have some conditioner that will work wonders on your hair."

44

"I doubt anything will work on that rats' nest," Brayton scoffed.

"I guess we won't have to worry about Brayton," Bernadette commented to Lynn.

"Worry about me why?" Brayton asked suspiciously.

"I've decided to make Honey my ward. She'll be starting college with you in a few weeks. She's underage, so I want you to keep an eye on her like she's your little sister."

"You're what…You want me to what?" he sputtered.

"You heard me."

"Mom, she's a rogue. She doesn't have any money."

"She doesn't need it. She just got herself a full ride. The girl got a perfect score on her SAT in a single attempt. I've seen the scores myself."

If he'd been able to shoot laser beams with his eyes, Honey was pretty sure he would have a hole burned through her head. "It's a trick!"

"It's not a trick. She just took the math portion of your practice test and got every one of those problems right too. Bernadette was watching the whole time." Lynn nodded toward the desk. "Check them yourself if you don't believe me."

Brayton scowled at the desk, but a moment later, turned to Honey and scanned her from head to toe with what she could only classify as an evil grin. "This means she'll have to take the WOLF class with the rest of us, doesn't it?"

"WOLF class," Honey asked.

"It's part of the curriculum," Lynn explained. "Since a good proportion of the students are wolves and wolves

45

have a lot of pent-up energy, the college offers special fitness and martial arts classes for wolves. The freshmen class is at 5:30 in the morning, three days a week."

"Doesn't the name make the human students suspicious?"

"No," Luna Lynn said. "They think it stands for Wilderness Officer Land and Fitness training and the witches know better than to tell them the truth, or they should."

"There are witches at the school?" Honey asked, and then worried that she'd sounded too eager. She knew witches and wolves went to the same schools because her parents had met in college, but she had thought witches wouldn't be allowed at this college since Luna Lynn was on the board.

"Anti-discrimination laws mean we must allow everyone to attend, assuming they meet the criteria. Unfortunately, we are not allowed to use 'wolf' as a criterion," Lynn explained. "You don't need to worry. Any witches who use spells on wolves without their consent are immediately expelled."

"Oh, that's…good." Honey changed the subject before she got herself in trouble. "Do they teach Krav Maga in the WOLF class?"

She'd wanted to take a class after her dad told her how useful it was for self-defense, especially for women, but she couldn't find any classes in her area.

"What?" Brayton looked at her like she was speaking a foreign language.

"It's the technique the Israeli military uses."

He rolled his eyes. "Why do girls always fall for the latest trends?"

"It's been around since the 1940s."

"I'm sure there will be plenty there for you to learn, Honey," Luna Lynn said soothingly. "Now, come along. I'll show you to your room."

"Her room?" For a moment Brayton looked absolutely horrified, then it morphed back into anger. "She's a rogue. She belongs with the rest of them."

"She's not a rogue anymore Brayton. I have decided to take her as my ward. She's a part of our pack."

His eyes darted between Honey and his mother. "Your ward? Have you asked Dad?"

"I haven't informed him of my decision yet," she paused for a moment, then turned to Honey and extended her hand with a smile. "Come on, Honey. I'll take you to meet my husband."

Honey hesitated. She hadn't agreed to be Lynn's ward, but Lynn was going to pay for her college. It was better than trying to find a job that would pay enough to feed and clothe her at her age – much better. The only challenge would be hiding the entirety of what she was. She could do that. She'd been practicing her whole life, after all. She slid her hand into Luna's smooth one and, ignoring Brayton completely, followed Lynn out into the hallway.

Someone was yelling, although it was muffled.

"I used to have the office right next to Brandon's," Luna Lynn said back to her, "but he and his visitors get so loud, I moved down the hall. I like the lighting in my new office better too."

"Brandon is your husband?"

"Yes. Alpha Brandon Mooney, but everyone calls him Alpha Brandon."

Honey nodded as they stopped in front of a heavy wooden door with carvings of animals in each panel. It looked ancient. There were several sets of gouges that she was sure came from wolf claws. Luna Lynn knocked on a flat part in the center of the door and called out. The voices inside subsided just before the door swung open. Lynn dragged Honey inside. Brayton followed so close behind her he stepped on the heel of her shoe, or maybe that was on purpose.

The room was masculine – overwhelmingly so. Honey had always thought her dad smelled good and Brayton wasn't bad, but the combined scents of so many male wolves from who knows how many years made her feel a little nauseous. In looks the room reminded her of the bar scene in Beauty and the Beast when Gaston was singing his song. It was all leather and wood and while there weren't any antlers, there was an ancient musket hanging on the wall over an intimidating desk that was holding down one end of a large bear rug.

"What do you need, Dear," asked the man who matched the picture Lynn had in her office. He was about the same size as her dad in person. The other wolf in the room was slighter and wirier and still fuming about whatever he'd been yelling about. Honey guessed he was the one who had been yelling because Alpha Brandon didn't look upset at all.

Lynn pulled her forward. "This is Honey. She is a minor. I've decided to make her my ward. Her parents were killed and she ran away to save her life. She got a perfect score on her SAT. I'm sending her to college. Can she join our pack?"

"Honey? She told the people at the shelter that her name was Ava," Brayton said loudly.

"No one uses their real names at a shelter if they can avoid it," Lynn informed him.

Honey might have found it amusing that the Luna had repeated her words if she wasn't pinned beneath the gray-blue eyes of the big man in front of her. His eyes were like his son's except they had the beginnings of crow's feet at the corners. That meant he smiled a lot, although he wasn't smiling now. "This is the rogue you were telling me about yesterday, Brayton?"

"Yes, Sir."

"What pack are you from, er," he turned to his wife. "Her name is Honey?"

"Yes."

"All right, Honey, what pack are you from?"

She decided to tell the truth as far as she could. She wasn't good a lying – her mom always caught her and she didn't even have a wolf's nose. "I don't know."

"What do you mean you don't know?"

"She's been a rogue all her life. She doesn't have a pack," Brayton declared behind her.

Honey turned around to hammer him with a glare. He was such a know-it-all even though he knew nothing. "That's not true. My parents just never told me."

"Why would your parents have to tell you if you lived in the pack?" Brayton scoffed.

"I didn't live in the pack. I was a lovechild. No one knew I existed."

Everyone went absolutely quiet, so quiet Honey could hear children playing somewhere outside the well-insulated windows. After living in so many different places, she could recognize and appreciate well-insulated windows.

A laugh burst out of the wiry man. Alpha Brandon glanced at him and snorted. Honey didn't see Lynn's reaction, but she was smiling when Honey turned to see who was patting her shoulder. "That explains why you were home schooled and why you were ready to run at a moment's notice," Lynn declared. "Oh, my goodness, wow. I am impressed your parents kept you hidden that long. I bet your dad's mate found out. She probably killed them in a fit of jealousy. Hell hath no fury like a woman scorned."

Honey was pretty sure her mom and herself were the only women in her dad's life, but she didn't correct her.

Alpha Brandon wiped his hand down his face, then looked down at Honey with a sigh. "Well, Lynn, I had some serious doubts when you proposed your save-the-rogues program, but if we manage to save any more genius love-children, I guess it will be worth it, even if we have to rebuild the lodge a few times."

"Rebuild the lodge?" Luna Lynn asked.

"Yeah, one of the males we brought in yesterday didn't like his accommodations," the wiry man said.

"Did you tranq him too?" Honey asked.

From the look the alpha and wiry man shared, she was pretty sure they had. "He was probably afraid you were going to kill him if you approached him the same

50

way Brayton approached me." She gave Brayton a well-deserved reproachful look. "Homeless shelters attract people because the people who need it know it's a safe place to go. Maybe you should set up a shelter for rogues downtown. Once word gets out that they can come and go freely, you can help the ones that ask for it."

"You *are* a wise little thing, aren't you?" the alpha said. "Come here, Honey."

He took her hands in his big ones. "I accept you into the Mooney pack." Her skin tingled where his lips pressed against her forehead. "And I accept you as my mate's ward. Make us proud."

# 7

## *Honey*

It wasn't until she was in the shower that she remembered she had used her magic when she was darted. Had Brayton and his bully squad noticed? Surely he would have mentioned it if he had. Maybe the breeze had been strong enough to waft the smell of magic away or perhaps they thought it was something else. Her dad said magic reminded him of the ozone smell some printers made. Her mom's magic didn't smell like that though. Hers smelled like spring sunshine and warm earth when you could almost see the plants growing.

Someone banged on the door. "Hurry up in there. If you want to drown yourself, I can take you to the pond."

Sharing a bathroom with Brayton for the next two weeks was going to be an adventure. "I'm waiting for my conditioning treatment to finish," she yelled back.

"Your what?"

"Your mom gave me some conditioner to try. I have to wait two minutes before rinsing."

"It's already been thirty!"

"No it hasn't." She checked her watch. "I've only been in here ten minutes."

"Well, hurry up. I have plans tonight. I have to get ready."

"Going to torment more homeless people?" she yelled.

"None of your business."

She didn't hear him stomp away, but she was pretty sure she felt it, either that or there was an earthquake.

She got out as soon as she washed the conditioner from her hair, dried, then wrapped herself in the fluffiest towel she'd ever used. Brayton was leaning by the door of her assigned bedroom with his arms crossed when she opened the door of the bathroom with her dirty clothes scrunched tightly in one hand.

She stepped to the side. "It's all yours."

He pushed himself off the wall, but instead of going into the bathroom, he stepped right in front of her. "We need to talk."

"About what?"

"You and how you disappeared for two hours."

"Two and a half," she corrected automatically.

He didn't look impressed. "You disappeared. You were there one moment and gone the next. How did you do it?"

"I ran."

"Ugh," he pulled at his hair, then poked his finger into the bare skin above her towel. "I don't know how you won over my mom and my dad, but I know you are a rogue. Did you use a spell?"

"A spell?"

53

"Yeah, you can't play dumb. You got a freaking 1600 on your SAT, unless you somehow spelled that too." He squinted his eyes. "Did you?"

"Your score wasn't bad. I'm sure you're smart enough to know wolves can't do that kind of magic."

"But. They. Can. Buy. It." He poked her chest aggressively with each word.

"Why does that make you upset? You buy and use things from humans all the time, like tranquilizer darts."

"You admit it was a spell then. Where did you get it?"

"What difference does that make?"

"Because it's illegal to use spells on wolves!"

"Even if a wolf used it on his or herself? What about healing spells?"

"Wolves don't need healing spells. We can heal without them."

"Usually," I agreed.

"Where did you get the spell?"

"I don't know what you're talking about."

"Ugh!" He pushed her backward into the doorway with his finger, then shook it at her. "Stay away from me and my friends and I don't care what Mom says, I'm not going to be your babysitter."

"Excellent. We agree. Enjoy your night."

She stepped around him and into her new room. Lynn had tried to put her in the blue room next to Brayton but he'd protested so much she ended up putting Honey across the hall from the bathroom. She'd called it the yellow room, but other than the pale-yellow walls and slightly darker yellow pillows on the creamy bedspread, it wasn't that yellow at all. She wondered what Brayton's color theme was – black maybe?

She put on the spare clothes from her backpack and started working on her hair with the brush Lynn had given her. The conditioner did help.

There was a soft knock, clearly not Brayton's. "Are you decent?"

"Yes. Come in."

With her pastel clothes and the bright light above her head, Luna Lynn looked like she was glowing. "Feel better after the shower?"

Honey hadn't said anything about feeling bad, but maybe Lynn could see the headache on her face. Her mom had always been able to tell. "Yes. I'm much refreshed."

"Wonderful. I know it's getting late, but I was wondering if you'd like to go shopping. You need some clothes and supplies for college. Brayton is, well I love him to death, but he's about as much fun to shop with as a toddler."

A vision of an eighteen-year-old Brayton having a temper tantrum in aisle one filled her head and she burst out laughing. Brayton chose that moment to poke his head into her room with another scowl. The scowl morphed onto the Brayton in her head and made her laugh even harder. His mother looked between the two of them and smiled.

"What?"

His mother waved him away. "Go get ready for your date."

Another image popped into Honey's head. A random female and the tear-stained Brayton looked at each other,

55

then turned their heads forward in unison and started screaming together.

She had tears coming from eyes – happy ones this time.

"What is wrong with her?" Brayton asked.

"She's had a long day. Go." Honey felt a hand on her shoulder. "Are you all right?" Lynn asked, watching her with concern. "Maybe I should let you get some rest."

Honey erased the picture from her head and made herself calm down. "I'm fine." She waved randomly. "He's just so…" She almost said, 'full of himself', but decided she shouldn't say that to his mom. "I'd love to go shopping with you."

She'd never shopped with anyone other than her mom and only very occasionally her dad. It was dangerous to be in public with Dad since he might be recognized, and people would wonder about the teenage girl he was with and would definitely wonder if he was seen with a witch.

Luna Lynn took her to a mall. Honey had been in a mall maybe once in her life. She remembered endless walking and a store with some really odd but cool gadgets. She would have liked to explore another gadget store, but there wasn't time to look around at the speed Lynn visited the clothing stores.

Honey had never tried on so many outfits in her life. She was worn out after the second store, but Lynn just kept going. After the fifth store, Honey collapsed onto the first bench she saw and decided she was sleeping there for the night.

Luna Lynn sank gracefully onto the bench facing hers. "That store did leave a lot to be desired, but there are several more on the second floor we haven't hit yet."

Honey glanced beseechingly up at Bernadette. The woman had been with them the whole time, mostly standing around, but she had to be tired of shopping too. Honey hoped she was anyway.

Bernadette raised an eyebrow, then to Honey's great relief said, "Luna, I think you've worn her out."

"Nonsense. We're just getting started."

A whiff of something sweet and spicy floated under Honey's nose and her stomach let out a roar.

Lynn frowned at her like she should have controlled the noise, then looked at her dainty white and gold watch. "Oh my, look at the time. I didn't realize it was so late. Sorry. I bet you're hungry. The fare at the food court is passable at best. There's a nice restaurant down the street we could try."

Honey swallowed but it didn't do much good. Her mouth quickly refilled with saliva. She couldn't remember ever being so hungry "I don't think I can make it to the restaurant," she groaned and stumbled to her feet. Between using her magic for hours and not having a proper lunch at all, she could barely think straight.

How she got food, she couldn't recall, but when her brain started working again, there was an impressive pile of trash in the tray in front of her. She wiped her mouth with a napkin and was embarrassed to come away with a sandwich worth of mustard and ketchup. Especially when she realized Bernadette and Lynn were on the other side of the small table watching her warily.

"Sorry. I'm usually not so messy. I was really hungry."

Lynn looked around then covered Honey's hand with her own and said in a low voice. "Did you transform today?"

"No."

"Did you have lunch?"

"I had a bag of trail mix."

"Huh. Maybe you're having a growth spurt. You went ravenous and almost attacked a food court worker. That usually only happens if someone has shifted a couple of times in one day. I better sign you up for the full meal plan. We can't have you wolfing out in front of the humans at college."

Honey was pretty sure her hunger had been caused by using her magic most of the day on top of the lack of food, but she didn't tell her that.

# 8

## *Honey*

Move in day.

Honey couldn't remember ever being so excited except on her first and only day of high school.

That hadn't turned out well.

"Be careful with those Brayton. It took me years to find suitcases I liked," Lynn scolded when Brayton half-slid, half-threw one of the two large suitcases Honey had borrowed from Lynn onto the rack of the SUV.

"Yes Mom." Honey was positive Brayton rolled his eyes, even though she couldn't see his face.

"Make sure you tie them on well."

"I know what I'm doing Mom."

"Put the straps through the handles so they don't slip out."

"Mom!"

Lynn patted him on the back. "Better safe than sorry. You ready Honey?"

"Yep."

"Climb in then."

"Wait, I have another box to load first," Brayton said with his arms still holding up one of the suitcases.

"There's barely room for Honey as it is," his mother scolded.

"Well, if she didn't have so much stuff, there would be more room."

That was rich considering she only had the two suitcases and her new backpack. Everything else in the SUV was Brayton's. She didn't point it out though. There was no point in picking a fight right before they had to sit in a car with each other for an hour, especially when Brayton was driving.

About thirty minutes after the time Brayton had declared they were going to leave, they rolled out with a fleet of vehicles carrying Brayton's main bully friends and a few others who had all treated her like an annoying little kid the few times she'd run across them.

It hadn't been bad really, staying in the alpha's house. Honey hadn't seen much of anyone other than Lynn, who kept her busy shopping and doing college-related things, and the construction workers at the lodge, whom she'd volunteered to help. She'd always wanted to try her hand at home repair and the rogue had damaged a lot of drywall and flooded a bathroom when he tore out a sink. She didn't know what she was doing, but the construction workers didn't seem to mind teaching her and she was good with a hammer.

The day was clear and sunny and the drive wasn't bad because Lynn took control of the radio after Brayton played one too many rap songs, meaning one. A little over an hour later, the campus buildings rose up out of a field like the pale cores of ancient mountains. It was beautiful. Honey was so excited, if she'd been standing, she probably would have been jumping up and down. As it was, she had a hard time keeping her knees from bouncing.

"You need to take the left-most turn around the traffic circle," Lynn said.

"I remember Mom. I've driven here before."

"Yes sorry, I forgot you know everything now that you're eighteen."

To Honey's surprise, Brayton bypassed the brand-new seven-story dorms and parked in front of a much shorter, much older building just down the street – her dorm. It was even nicer in person. Unlike the smooth facade of the new dorms, her dorm had decorative brick work around the windows and the edges of the building, gabled dormer windows, and dentil molding under the edge of the roof. It was one of the oldest dorms on campus and therefore offered only shared rooms and a single, large bathroom on each floor. Lynn had apologized for not being able to find her anywhere else to stay so close to the start of the semester, but Honey had assured her it was fine. After two weeks of Brayton's off-key singing after each late-night date and whiskers all over the counter and her toothbrush, she suspected on purpose, she was looking forward to sharing a bathroom with females.

While she was gawking, Brayton unceremoniously dragged her suitcases off the SUV and dumped them beside her. She turned to thank him, but he was already driving away, leaving his mother frowning after him. Had he unloaded her too or had she unloaded herself?

"He's excited," Lynn said when she realized Honey was waiting for her. "He said he'd have his friends help him unload. We can walk over to his dorm when we're done here. It's just next door."

"You can go help him if you want. I don't have much. I know you must have been looking forward to helping him move in for a long time."

"I'll help you carry your stuff in at least. Besides, I want to inspect the dorm. There's been some discussion about tearing it down and rebuilding."

"But it's so nice. Look at all the details."

"You think? You haven't seen the inside yet. I've heard it's quite dated."

Lynn grabbed one of the suitcases and charged toward the front door. The entrance desk was only a few feet from the front door, but to the left, down a short hallway, Honey could see a large lobby with multiple couches and a tiled path right through the middle like a red brick road.

"Can I help you?" the curly-haired red-headed girl asked without a trace of a smile.

"Yes, we're here to check in," Lynn said, also without a smile. "Honey Smith."

The girl looked down her nose at Honey. "Can I see some form of identification?"

Honey flipped her backpack around and pulled out the College ID she'd received in the mail two days ago. "Here."

She grinned just like she had when Bernadette had snapped the photo while the girl looked between the ID and her. With a stoic face, the girl finally handed the ID back, then slapped a key on the counter along with a colorful box slightly smaller than a shoe box. "Here's your key, and your welcome package. The room is 302. Your roommate is already there." She pegged Honey with a fierce glance. "We don't want any trouble, wolf."

"Are there a lot of witches in this dorm?" Honey asked. That would explain why she smelled so many different kinds of magic.

"We're all witches, except you."

She grinned. She couldn't help it. "Really? That's awesome! I love witches." She stuck her hand over the counter. "It's nice to meet you," she squinted at the name tag, "Gerry."

The girl didn't smile, but she did squeeze Honey's hand. Suddenly, instead of a serious college girl, Honey was shaking hands with what looked like a cross between a troll and a wolf. She blinked and the girl was in front of her again. "You can do illusions! Cool!"

The corner of the girl's mouth twitched. "You're like an eager little puppy."

Honey flashed her an even bigger grin. "Thank you!"

The girl shook her head. "Just don't chew up the furniture. It's new."

"Yes, Ma'am."

Still grinning, Honey tucked the gift box under her arm and headed down the hallway past a frowning Lynn. Honey pretended not to see the nasty looks the witches waiting for the elevator gave her when she turned into the stairwell. She smiled at everyone that passed her going down although most didn't smile back. That was okay. They didn't know she was a witch too.

63

Lynn grabbed her arm and pulled her into the hallway just outside the stairwell when they reached the third floor, then said in a low voice, "Honey, I'm sorry. I didn't realize this was a witches' dorm. You can't stay here."

"Why not?"

"It's too dangerous. The witches might take exception to you being here and find some way to harm you."

"Where will I stay then?"

Lynn started rubbing her chin with her index finger - a sure sign she was thinking. "I could ask around and see if any of the other members of the board could house you, or you could wait a semester to start."

"No. I don't want to wait. It will be fine Luna."

"Honey, as your guardian, I am responsible for your safety. This isn't safe."

Why was she so worried about witches? "Lynn, witches aren't any more dangerous than wolves. They are people just like us. My best friend growing up was a witch. It will be fine."

"You had friends?"

She'd meant her mom, but she wasn't going to tell Lynn that. "Occasionally. I did take a lot of extracurricular classes."

Lynn let out a long sigh and looked down the hall where a couple of girls were carrying on a very animated conversation. "It would be easier if you can stay here. I'm sure a room will come free in one of the other dorms by the end of the semester. If you can last until then…"

"I can."

Lynn lifted a finger and shook it at her. "But if they start picking on you, I want you to call me. I'll rent an apartment and live with you myself for a few months if I have to."

"I'll be fine Luna, I promise."

Honey grabbed the suitcase and started moving down the hall before Lynn could change her mind. In just three steps she was in front of room 302. A girl was standing in front of the open door in the middle of the room contemplating one of the desks.

Honey knocked on the door. "Hello?"

The girl whirled around and Honey realized her hair wasn't black – it was dark blue.

"You're a wolf. Why are you here?" The girl asked with wide eyes.

"I'm Honey, your roommate."

"No. They said I didn't have a roommate."

"Who said," Luna Lynn demanded behind Honey.

The girl swallowed. "The dorm people when I called a month ago to ask. I wanted to coordinate sheets and see if my roommate was bringing a mini-fridge."

"I did not bring a mini-fridge," Honey stated, "and my sheets are blue."

"That will work then. Mine are also blue," the girl said cautiously.

"Is that your favorite color?" Honey asked.

The girl flicked her short hair. "How could you tell?"

Honey liked her already.

"What is your name?" Lynn demanded.

"Blaze Underwood," the girl squeaked.

Lynn was scaring her. "This is Luna Lynn, my guardian. She is pleased to meet you, but her son is also moving in today and she wants to be there for that, so she will be on her way." Honey grabbed Lynn's arm and gave her a not-so-gentle shove toward the stairs.

"Honey," Lynn started.

"I'll be fine Lynn. I'll bring over your suitcases once I've emptied them."

Lynn looked doubtful but she said, "Okay." She took exactly one step to leave, then spun around and produced her cell phone. "Blaze, can I have your number in case I can't get a hold of Honey for some reason?"

"Of course Mrs. Lynn, I mean Luna, I mean Luna Lynn."

"Luna is fine."

"Wow, she's fierce," Blaze noted after Lynn had left.

"She's just protective."

"Because she's a wolf?" Blaze asked.

Honey shrugged and nodded toward the cluttered bottom bunk. "Did you claim the bottom?"

"If you don't mind."

"I don't."

She unzipped one of the suitcases and pulled out the sheets. Moving around so often had taught her to always pack the first things she'd need on top. She wanted to ask Blaze what kind of magic she could do, but she didn't know if that was considered rude. Other than her mom, she'd never met another witch. Mom always kept her well away from them.

She caught a whiff of lemon while she fought to put the sheet over the far corner of the mattress. She dismissed the random smell as room freshener until she turned around and saw a small cactus floating toward the window.

"You can do telekinesis!"

The cactus fell to the floor and the little pot shattered.

"Oh, I'm sorry." Honey jumped off the bed and scrambled to help Blaze clean up the mess.

"You can jump off beds without breaking anything," Blaze commented.

Honey looked back over her shoulder to make sure the bed was as short as she remembered. "I was standing on the ladder."

Blaze scooped up the little cactus and started fussing over it like it was a precious pet. Honey focused on collecting the pieces of the clay pot. She wished she could try and fix them with her own magic, but she knew better than to reveal herself. "I have a water bottle we could cut in half and make a temporary pot if you can move the dirt into it with your magic, or I could find a broom."

"I can move it."

After she'd set all the broken pieces of pottery on the windowsill, Honey dug out a pair of scissors and started cutting her empty water bottle in half. It was the first thing she'd bought at a gas station the day after she'd run away from the fire.

"You're nicer than I thought a wolf would be," Blaze commented.

"Have you met many wolves?"

"There were some in my high school but we didn't really interact."

She gave her new roommate a big grin. "Well, I'm truly glad I got to meet you then."

"I'm surprised they put a wolf and witch together."

Honey jammed the top of the water bottle upside-down into the bottom so the 'pot' had a way to drain and offered it to Blaze. "How would they know?"

"You have to specify on the residential application form."

"I don't remember seeing that form." Lynn must have filled it out, but why would she put down that Honey was a witch? It must have been an accident. "How would that work anyway? Wouldn't the humans think it odd if there were options for wolf and witch?"

"I hadn't thought of that. Maybe there's magic involved."

"Must be," Honey agreed.

It only took her a few minutes to unpack everything. She was eager to explore the campus and visit the bookstore. Mom's stories about her time on campus had always intrigued her. She knew she could find used books for a good price in the bookstore, but that the supplies were always overpriced. Lynn had offered to buy her books online, but Honey had told her she wanted to look in the bookstore first. Lynn had shook her head, but then she'd given Honey a cash card with several hundred dollars to buy whatever she needed.

"Do you want to explore the campus, Blaze? I need to go to the bookstore."

Blaze was placing the pencil holder in different locations on her desk using telekinesis. "Everyone and their dog will be there." She looked up and slapped her hand over her mouth. "Oh, I didn't mean it that way."

"What way?"

She gave Honey a puzzled look and shook her head. "Never mind."

Honey suddenly felt very overwhelmed. She hadn't realized how much Lynn's support meant until that moment. She was on her own again. "I guess I'll go by myself then." She turned away to hide the tears in her eyes and collect the empty suitcases.

Blaze reached out and grabbed Honey's arm, then almost immediately dropped it as if she was going to attack her. "I didn't say I didn't want to go."

"Really? Let's go then. Oh," Honey lifted one of the empty suitcases. "I need to take these to my guardian first and I wanted to sneak a peek at the suites in the new dorm."

"Ooo. I do too. They looked so elegant online, not like these," she waved her hand around, "jail cells."

"Yeah, but ours is a lot cheaper and has more character."

Blaze rolled her eyes. "Whatever makes you happy."

Blaze took one of the empty suitcases. The new dorm wasn't far at all – just up the sidewalk. Unlike the colorful vehicles of all makes and sizes unloading in front of their dorm, most of the vehicles in front of the new dorm were large, dark SUVs which were slowly losing their contents to a bevy of exuberant males. They were so busy clowning around with each other, Honey didn't think they'd noticed her and Blaze at all until they turned to go into the dorm. Then the wolves started elbowing each other and shooting them grins like they'd never seen girls before. Honey noticed several sniffing the air, then she realized why. She stopped and turned to Blaze.

"Calm down. They can smell fear."

"You didn't tell me this was a dorm for wolves."

"Is that a problem?" She looked around. Blaze was small and there were a lot of big guys around. Maybe she felt intimidated. "They won't hurt you. I promise. I won't let them."

"No offense, but all of them have about twice as much muscle as you."

"But not at much brain."

She snickered, but still smelled afraid.

Honey leaned forward so the wolves trying to eavesdrop wouldn't hear. "Besides, can't you just throw them across the yard if they try anything?"

"Maybe, but they're big and there's so many of them."

"Seriously, don't be afraid. I read the rules. If anyone hurts you they'll get kicked out. They're just full of energy because they get to move in today. Think of them as a bunch of puppies."

"Very muscular puppies," Blaze said as a particularly chiseled specimen sauntered by.

Blaze said it loud enough that he heard her, but by the way the corner of his mouth lifted, he wasn't offended.

Honey turned around and started walking again. Blaze moved up to her side and leaned over and whispered, "Why are they all so muscular? Is it because they are wolves?"

"It's because they exercise a lot because they are wolves."

A tall boy stopped to hold the door for them. Blaze rewarded him with a smile and earned a lopsided one back. She still smelled nervous, but the acrid scent of fear was gone.

Inside it looked like a hotel lobby instead of a dorm. There were wolves everywhere tossing balls, sprawled out on couches, wrestling.

Blaze fanned herself. "Oh my gosh, this must be what it's like to walk into a Chippendales' show."

There was furniture around but it was all contemporary. Honey had a feeling Blaze was referring to some other kind of Chippendales but before she could ask, a haughty voice made every head turn in their direction.

"Honey, what are you doing here?"

"Is he your boyfriend?" Blaze asked in a stage whisper, which would have been fine if it wasn't suddenly so quiet Honey heard someone's pen drop.

"Him? No!" She pushed the suitcases at him. "Here, these are for your mom. Tell her I'm going to the Student Union with my roommate to look around."

Brayton's demeanor suddenly became much friendlier. "I think my mom wanted to go with you. Didn't you say you wanted to see my suite?"

Honey squinted her eyes at him, trying to see into his devious brain. She'd lived across the hall from him for two weeks and he'd kept his door firmly closed when she was around. He'd even slammed it a few times when she got close.

"Please. She's driving me crazy." He lowered his voice almost to a whisper. "She's talking about repainting the walls and going with a nautical theme. If you can pull her away, I'll owe you."

"You should ask him what he'll owe you," Blaze said in Honey's ear.

"I don't want anything from him, but I will help him." She grabbed the handle of one of the suitcases and started toward the elevators, "Come on, we've got a mamsel to save."

"Mamsel?" Blaze asked.

"Male damsel in distress."

Blaze laughed.

Brayton was behind her so she didn't see his reaction, but Honey thought she heard a growl.

Unlike her dorm, his dorm had a whole row of elevators. Even with all the people moving in they barely had to wait, and the elevator was fast. A few seconds later they spilled out onto the second floor.

The hallway had a custom-designed carpet just like the fancy hotel Honey had been to once. Brayton's room was just a few doors down from the elevator. The bigger-than-normal door opened into a living space larger than some of the apartments Honey and her mom had lived in.

"Wow," Blaze said.

Bag-dumping bully, whose given name was Malcolm, was sprawled all over a couch. Rhys, the not-so-quiet bully, was humming tunelessly in the kitchen while he put things away in the over-counter cabinets.

"Who's your fourth roommate?" Honey asked.

"He's not here yet. My room is this one," Brayton walked over to the first door on the left and pulled it open. "Mom, Honey is here."

Lynn was holding a light blue pillowcase up to the wall. "Honey, what do you think of this color?"

"It's nice."

"It would look good on the walls, don't you think?"

"Mmm."

What did Brayton expect her to do? Maybe she should just say it. "Luna, Brayton doesn't want you to decorate his room. He's eighteen and he feels he's old enough to decorate it himself."

Lynn lowered the pillowcase. "Is that true Brayton?"

Brayton stopped glaring at Honey and faced his mom instead. "Yes."

"Well why didn't you say so? Do you have a theme picked out?"

"Mom, I don't need a theme."

"But you're going to live here for the next year at least. You need an environment that's conducive to studying."

Conducive to studying – she could work with that.

"Luna, I have lived in many places decorated and painted many different ways. None of them aided my studying. In fact, some of them were distracting. This room is fine, in fact, it's more than fine. All he needs are a few strings of fairy lights and a maybe a plant or two."

"Fairy lights," Lynn said contemplatively. "How many strings?"

"No. Just no!" Brayton exclaimed.

Ha. She'd made Brayton worried. "I was kidding. Luna, you are great at room design, but don't you think Brayton needs to find his own style? He might prefer the hunter cabin theme like your husband's office over a nautical one. Did you ask?"

The look of horror on Lynn's face was priceless.

"Oh, not that. Please not that."

"I promise Mom, no hunter cabin," Brayton said, stepping forward to gently tug the pillowcase out of her fingers. "Why don't you go shopping with Honey while I unpack. You can come back by when I'm done."

"Are you sure? I can help you unpack. I promise I won't try to decorate."

"Mom."

Honey wanted to explore the Student Union by herself, or with Blaze at least, but she didn't mind shopping with Lynn. In fact, when she wasn't trying to hit every store in the mall, Lynn was fun to shop with. "Come on, Luna. We're going to the Student Union. Maybe you can find him a first day of school gift, like a fancy new pen or a notebook."

Lynn had already bought him at least ten such gifts, but that never stopped her from buying more.

Lynn frowned. "That's right. You don't have your books yet." After hesitating another moment, she marched to the desk and picked up her purse. "Come on. We better get there before they're all gone."

Brayton waved his hand to get her attention and mouthed a 'Thank you' behind his mother's back.

# 9

## *Honey*

Five am. Monday morning Honey turned off her watch alarm five seconds before it started beeping. She'd been awake since four, but she didn't want to get out of bed too early and wake Blaze. Blaze had gone to a coven meet and greet and hadn't gotten back until 11 pm. Honey couldn't stay in bed any longer though. It was finally time to get ready. She climbed down off the bed as quietly as she could and grabbed her shower caddy. Since she'd worn her exercise clothes to bed, she only had to run to the bathroom, brush her teeth, and put on the new running shoes Lynn had insisted she buy.

Outside, it was still dark, but the campus was well-lit by functional yet unimaginative light poles all around the dorms. She set out on a jog along the course she'd plotted on Saturday when she'd located all her classes. The training field was half-way around campus, but she still managed to be fifteen minutes early. She wasn't the only one there early, but most people didn't start showing up until about two minutes before it was time to start. By then, she'd already stretched and was finishing her warm-up lap.

Brayton showed up exactly one minute before they were supposed to be present. He looked like he'd been awake all night. To Honey's surprise, he plopped down next to her on the bleachers where everyone had been instructed to sit. She hadn't seen him since she'd dragged Lynn away. Maybe her act of kindness had softened him up a little.

"Good morning, Brayton."

He slowly turned his head and focused his sleep-blurred eyes on her. "Why are you so chipper?"

"Why do you look like you haven't slept?"

"I didn't. I think."

"Party?"

"Uhh."

"Good Morning! Welcome to WOLF. I'm Captain Young," a medium-sized man said from in front of the bleachers. "Most of you look like you had a pretty rough night. You guys feeling okay?"

He received a collection of moans and grunts in response.

"Aw, you poor little freshman babies. Can't handle your liquor. Well too bad! Get up. Start running. I want two miles out of you in less than 16. Go."

Sixteen minutes? This class was going to be easy. Honey popped up and followed the guy with the green headband who'd stood up just ahead of her. He'd been as early as she was. Keeping to his pace, she finished in fourteen minutes and had to stand and wait while the rest of the group slogged over the line where Captain Young was waiting with a big stopwatch. Brayton stumbled over the line just before Captain Young started shuttling people into another group. The last person to cross the line immediately hunched over and threw up.

Captain Young shook his head at the sick one. "I've separated you into turtles and hares. The turtles here are going to give me sixty perfect push-ups. The hares, you," he nodded at Honey's group, "only have to do thirty, but any of you slower than the turtles will join them and you do not want to be a turtle today. Go."

Green head-band guy and her were again two of the first to finish. The instructor kept barking out exercises until about half of them were turtles and half of them were hares. Brayton somehow remained a hare.

"Hares over here. You get to be the first people to try out the new obstacle course. Turtles, start running. You're going to run for the rest of the practice. Maybe next time you'll get to bed on time and bring your A-game."

The turtles groaned. Green head-band guy and Honey grinned at each other. Captain Young led them to a monstrosity of beams and walls and bars and ropes. It wasn't as colorful as the obstacle course in a show Honey had watched in a hotel one time, but it still looked fun. Captain Young led them around it and gave a brief explanation of what they were supposed to do.

"All right, who wants to go first?"

Honey raised her hand as high as she could.

Brayton tried to pull it down. "What are you doing? You don't volunteer for something like that."

"Girl with the gray shirt. Yeah, you," Captain Young said when Honey pointed to herself, "and the guy next to her. You're up. You can race each other."

Brayton groaned. Honey flashed him an excited grin and got into position.

"On your mark, go!"

The first obstacle was a tall wall. Honey ran at it and used her speed and her wolf claws to get to the top, then threw her legs over and made a perfect landing on the other side. She launched herself out of her crouch directly toward the monkey bars. Four rungs in, she heard a thump that could only be Brayton reaching the ground. She swung from the last bar to the first set of tires they had to step through, high-stepped her way through them as fast as she could, then shimmied up the climbing rope and hit the bell. Brayton's grunts had turned into a continuous growl behind her. Grinning, she slid down the rope, ran across the balance logs, and swung over the mud pit. After nailing that landing with a flip, she ran forward to another balance beam that led to some bars that they were supposed to go over. She flipped her legs and hips over them like she'd done in gymnastics, then worked her way over a series of logs like they were pummel horses, and she was done.

Captain Young was waiting for her at the end with his big stopwatch. "Nice job. What's your name?"

"Honey."

"What pack?"

"Mooney."

"Ten points for Mooney both for doing a good job and for volunteering. Give me two more miles and you're free to go."

"Yes, Sir."

At least a minute later, Brayton staggered across the line and fell over into a muddy heap. Captain Young squatted down in front of him. "Hello Mr. Turtle."

Despite taking a shower and dropping by the cafeteria to grab a muffin and a banana for breakfast, Honey made it to her eight-o-clock calculus class with plenty of time to spare. She only had four classes on Monday, not including WOLF, three before and one after lunch, so she was done by 2. Her homework was done by 3. Blaze came back from her classes at 4. They went to dinner together at 5.

The cafeteria was packed and noisy and full of smells – some delicious and some not-so delicious. It was a warm day, but by the aged smell of the sweat, she guessed some of her classmates had not made it back to their dorms in time to shower after WOLF. On top of the body odor and the food smell, there was a hint of magic which teased her nose and made her want to sneeze.

After ten minutes in a very long, very boisterous line, she and Blaze finally reached the front. Honey was so tired of all the meat she'd been served the last two weeks that she piled her plate high with salad and some kind Chinese-like stir fry with lots of vegetables.

"Where do you want to sit?" she asked Blaze when they stepped out of the line and paused to survey the rowdy tables.

"Um, I was going to sit with some of the people I met last night. It's probably better if we don't sit together. It might cause a scene."

The excited, giddy feeling Honey had had all day deflated like a popped tired. "Oh. Okay." Blaze was the only person in the whole room she knew. The chaotic scene before her suddenly turned from a room full of people having fun to a room full of strangers she'd have to pass to find a seat. If she wasn't so hungry, she would have dumped her tray and left.

Blaze nudged her elbow. "You know what? Who cares. No one will notice in this mess. You are my roommate and if they have a problem with that then they're not worth knowing."

"Are you sure?"

"Absolutely."

Her roommate's smile looked genuine. Honey decided to take her up on her offer. "Thanks Blaze."

"Well, I couldn't leave you standing there looking like a lost puppy. Hah. Get it?"

Honey rolled her eyes. "Very funny. That's not going to get old or anything."

She let Blaze take the lead. Her roommate had skills. She shimmied and twisted through the crowd like a slippery superhero. She even managed to avoid three wolves who spilled onto the ground in front of her seemingly on accident. At long last they made it to a table in the back of the room where the light was dimmer and the people were calmer. It also smelled a lot better – less sweat and more magic. All flavors of magic. Honey took a deep breath and nearly gagged on the scent of skunk. It disappeared even while she sniffed her sleeve to see if she needed to find some tomato juice.

"Hi," Blaze said. She turned enough that the three people at the table could see past her to Honey. "This is Honey, my roommate. Do any of you mind if she joins us?"

"She's a wolf," said a boy with dark hair that was sculpted to stand in a peak at the top of his head.

"No kidding," Blaze said, sliding into a seat and kicking the leg of the empty chair next to her to indicate where Honey should sit.

"Demon dirt. My repelling spell didn't work," the peaky-haired guy said.

"You're a spell-caster?" Honey asked as she sat.

He slumped in his chair. "Apparently not."

"I did catch a very strong smell of skunk," she said encouragingly.

"But you're still here."

"Honey, that's Daegal," Blaze said, pointing at the spell-caster. "The blond girl is Sabine and the rainbow head is Panas."

"It's nice to meet you."

"Really?" the blond girl said suspiciously. She wasn't just blond, she was white-gold blond with just enough wave that her hair caught the dim light perfectly, making her hair shimmer.

"Really. I love your hair."

"I'm not giving you a makeover."

"Okay?"

"That's a lot of salad," Panas said. His hair was a stripy mix of blue, green, purple, and red. "I thought wolves just ate meat."

"Nope. I like salad."

"Why are you sitting with us? Don't wolves always stay in a pack?" Daegal asked.

Honey shrugged and picked up her fork to have somewhere to look. "I don't know."

"You don't know why you're sitting with us or you don't know about wolves?" Sabine asked sharply like she was an investigator and Honey was the lead suspect.

Honey lifted her head and told her the truth. "I'm sitting with you because I like witches."

"You like witches?" Daegal repeated as if he'd never heard of such a thing.

"Yeah, my best friend was a witch." She quickly looked down again so they wouldn't see the tears in her eyes.

"How is that possible?" Panas asked.

The wolves had accepted her ridiculous explanation without question. Maybe the witches would too. "I was a lovechild. My parents hid me from the pack so I made friends outside of it."

"Is your friend here?"

"No, she's…" She couldn't finish and barely held back a sob.

Blaze squeezed her shoulder. "It's okay Honey. You don't have to say anything else. Guys, Honey isn't like the rest of the wolves. She's nice. She helped me re-pot my cactus when I dropped it."

For once she had a napkin. Honey wiped her nose, then lifted her head to smile up at them and change the subject. "So, what kind of magic can you guys do? My friend was a healer. Her magic smelled like spring sunshine. Blaze's magic smells like fresh lemons."

"You didn't tell me my magic has a smell," Blaze frowned.

Honey shrugged. "It smells nice."

Panas threw out his hand and a small flame appeared.

Honey scrunched my nose. "Smells like hot asphalt."

She suddenly got very cold and smelled fresh snow, but there was something else. She'd smelled it along with the skunk smell too.

"Throw a different one at me Daegal. Each spell smells different, but I think I can smell your magic too."

"Why are you not frozen?!" he grunted.

Now she was very hot, like beach on the equator hot. The spell smelled of hot sand and, she sniffed again just to be sure. "Popcorn. Your magic smells like unbuttered popcorn."

"You were supposed to melt."

"I don't think you can melt a living thing. I did get very hot." She shook herself and calmed her atoms so they cooled down. Shoot. Could they tell when she used her own magic? Her mom had never mentioned it.

"I'm not going to show you what I can do. I don't trust you," Sabine said airily.

"Hey, whoa, you're a," a voice came from somewhere above her. Honey looked up to see a tall boy with stylishly messy brown hair with bleached ends. Cool hair must be a witch thing. "Beautiful woman." He crashed down into the seat beside her and leaned his chin on his fist to stare into her face. "I love green eyes."

"This is Esme," Blaze said.

"He likes girls," Panas added.

She tore her eyes from Esme's mesmerizing gaze. "How can you guys tell I'm a wolf? Do you smell it?"

Panas looked at Sabine who shrugged. "We feel it," he answered. "You smell magic as different scents, we feel magic as different tingles. Wolves feel furry."

"You can smell magic?" Esme said. "What does mine smell like?" He placed two fingers on her temple. Abruptly she was in a beautiful park with golden sun streaming down on a blanket with a large picnic basket. Esme was laying on the blanket, propped up on his elbow and watching her with a strange smile that made her want to back away. Except for Esme, it reminded her of one of the many parks she'd visited with her mom and dad and how they'd never take her again. She thrust his hand away and caught a nasty smell.

"Rotten eggs." She looked down quickly, but not fast enough to prevent a tear from rolling down her cheek.

"Ooo. She got you," Panas teased.

"I'm sorry I upset you. That was supposed to be pleasant," Esme said earnestly, grabbing her hand.

Honey squeezed his hand and pulled hers away. "It's all right. Thanks for trying."

"What did you show her?" Sabine asked.

"A picnic."

Honey could swear she felt Sabine's gaze boring into her head. Was she able to read minds? Maybe sitting with witches wasn't such a good idea.

Two more girls came up to the table. One had lush firetruck red hair. The other had blacker-than-black hair that faded to green and the green lipstick to match.

"Hi guys, how did your first day go? Did you see what happened in…" the redhead started but was cut off by a sharp elbow from her friend who nodded at Honey. The redhead's smile morphed into one of horror. "O.M.G., who let the dog in?"

In as flat a voice as she could muster, Honey said, "Ouch."

"She's cool," Esme said. "She's Blaze's roommate."

"Bad luck," the redhead said at Blaze. "Come on Nimue. Let find somewhere to eat that's a little less hairy."

Blaze might have said she didn't care, but Honey saw the worry on her face when she turned to look after them.

"I better go. I have homework to do."

"Liar," Sabine said before Honey could stand. "You've already got your homework done, don't you?"

"Just the part that's due Wednesday."

"Stay and finish your salad at least. We promise to behave."

"Do you mind," Honey asked Blaze.

Blaze turned away from watching the two girls now talking and pointing toward them from another table and shook her head with a reserved frown. "No. Stay."

"Those two aren't our friends," Sabine said. "They were being nosy. They'll tell everyone that we had a wolf sitting with us so we'll be ostracized, but there's a good chance it will end up making us popular because we dared to cross over to the other side."

85

"Why is there so much animosity between wolves and witches?" Honey asked, finally taking a bite of salad. She knew her mom and dad had hidden her because hybrid children were looked down upon. But she hadn't realized wolves and witches hated each other so much.

"You don't know?" Daegal asked.

"No."

"It's been this way forever," Panas said. "All those witch hunts – the wolves started them. All the stories about how monstrous wolves are – told by the witches."

"But why? We're both magical. The only difference is wolves all have the same power."

"Yeah, but we're raised completely different. Wolves have tight packs and traditions. Witches are creative and often live alone," Sabine said.

"I think it's silly."

"Honey!" a familiar voice snapped behind her, "What are you doing here?"

She spun around and had to lean back to see Brayton's face, he was so close. "I'm eating."

"They're witches!"

"So?"

"You're a wolf."

"So?"

"Wolves don't eat with witches."

"Says who?"

"Says me."

"That is the stupidest argument I've ever heard. Go away Brayton." She turned her back on him. All of a sudden, it felt like every hair on her head was being pulled out by the roots. The jerk had grabbed her ponytail.

86

"You are a part of my pack. Stop embarrassing us. Get away from them."

As soon as he had pulled her clear of her chair, she grabbed the hand on her hair with both of her hands to prevent him from yanking it and harder, then twisted to face him. She kneed him as hard as she could where it counted, which freed her hair, then kicked him in the chest to send him flying across the room.

Heart racing from the sudden adrenaline, she turned her back on the ensuing commotion and plopped back down in her chair. "Jerk."

Daegal's mouth was hanging open and Esme's eyes were wide. Panas was leaning back with a smirk to watch whatever was happening behind her.

"Who was that?" Sabine asked.

"Head bully, aka the alpha's son."

"You just sent the alpha's son flying across the room?"

"He pulled my hair first."

"All right, which one of you did that? You know violence between the races is forbidden," another familiar voice asked behind her.

Great, she was going to end up going to college all of one day too. She spun around and stood. "It was me. They didn't do anything."

Three beefy wolves were displaying their muscles behind her. She recognized the middle one.

"Honey?"

"Captain Young."

"What happened?"

"Brayton pulled my hair and I fought back."

87

"He pulled your hair?"

"He grabbed her ponytail and dragged her out of her seat," Sabine said behind her, "like a caveman, or cavewolf, I guess."

"Is he your ex or something?"

"No." She was tempted to call him a big bully, but she behaved. "I'm his mom's ward and he thinks that gives him the right to boss me around."

"You're Luna Lynn's ward?"

"Yes."

"And do you all agree that she was defending herself?" he asked the table.

"Yes," the whole table and a few people from nearby said in almost-unison.

"I guess he deserved as good as he got then." He pointed his finger at her nose, making her go cross-eyed. "No more fighting Honey, except on the field."

"Yes, sir."

She stayed standing until Captain Young had led a hunched and limping Brayton away, then slid gratefully back into her seat. "Sorry about that, and thanks for backing me up."

"Are you kidding? That was excellent. You just did what we've all dreamed of doing and got away with it," Daegal grinned.

"How did you kick him so far," Blaze asked.

I shrugged. "Martial arts classes."

"Ever play volleyball," Panas asked contemplatively. "I bet you can really jump."

"I can."

"You're on my team."

# 10

## Brayton

His balls still throbbed even though they should be well on their way to healing. Malcolm, Rhys, and Cici were waiting for him when Captain Young finally allowed him to leave the study room he'd taken him to, to 'cool down'.

"Still hurting man?" Malcolm winced as he limped out the door.

"Can't say you didn't deserve it," Cici said behind Malcolm.

He stomped forward and stepped into her space. "What did you say?"

She stared him down unflappably. "You heard me. You pulled her up by her hair. You wouldn't do that to a guy."

Cici was always going on about women's equality.

"Should have known you'd take her side." He limped past her.

"You know she's right," Rhys said.

He did and that made him even angrier.

He hated Honey.

It was her fault he'd started off on a bad foot at practice. He'd been looking forward to training on campus for years and she totally ruined it by being so damn chipper and raising her skinny little arm like an eager six-year-old. He wasn't sure how she cheated, but he knew she had. She not only beat him, but she made the best time of the day. There was no way. Out of all the wolves there, someone had to be faster. She'd used another spell, and now he knew where she was getting them from.

"Hey, isn't that her?" Malcolm nodded toward the volleyball courts.

Without consciously deciding to do it, he stepped off the sidewalk in her direction.

Rhys grabbed his arm. "Let her be, man."

Brayton shook him off. "I'm just going to get a look at who she's playing with. I think she's getting spells from them to use against us."

"Why would she do that?" Cici asked.

"Because she's a rogue," he said as if that explained everything. In his mind it did. He just couldn't quite get the words together to explain it properly with his mouth.

"I think you're just peeved that she bested you twice today," Cici said smugly.

"She cheated."

"Not from what I saw."

Cici could be a real pain sometimes, but she was an excellent fighter and one of his best friends. That's why he had picked her to someday be a beta.

It was a beautiful evening with a cloudless sky, the perfect temperature, and a very light breeze. Several students were sitting on the benches waiting for their chance on the courts. He stopped downwind underneath a cluster of trees so his prey wouldn't see him. The stench of magic was so bad it nearly drove him away. There wasn't a single wolf there except for Honey.

Why on Earth had her mother given her such a ridiculous name? Even thinking it made him cringe.

"She's pretty good," Rhys commented when Honey dove for a ball and managed to not only save it from hitting the sand, but pop it up high enough for a rainbow-headed boy to whack it over the net.

All of them were pretty good. Along with rainbow-head, she was on a team with a boy whose longish brown hair was bleached on the tips and a girl with blue hair who looked somewhat familiar. Everyone on the other team also had strange hair except one girl whose hair shone like white gold.

"What's with their hair?" Cici said. "That one chick has half-pink and half-blue. I mean, come-on, make up your mind."

Honey was intently watching the ball while dusting the sand off her front from the dive. She suddenly sprinted forward, only to trip and fall flat on her face.

"Graceful," Malcolm snorted.

Instead of looking embarrassed, Honey lifted her sandy face and yelled to the pointy-haired guy on the opposite side of the court, "That one smelled like horse manure."

"Too bad it wasn't real," the guy yelled back.

"Did he just throw a spell at her?" Rhys asked.

Any other wolf would have known better than to let the witch get away with it, but Honey just dusted herself off.

"We gotta do something about her," Malcolm said. "She's gonna have the witches thinking they can walk all over us."

He was right, but what could they do? He'd already tried talking to her. Okay, he may have lost his temper a little. He found talking to her hard. Any other wolf his age was appropriately submissive, but she didn't know the meaning of the word.

That was the problem. She didn't know her place. His mom hadn't helped by showering her with gifts and giving her a free ride to college. It was no wonder the girl thought she was a princess.

The players changed positions. Honey was now close to the net. Someone on the other team hit a high ball right toward her. It should have been too high for her, but she went for it. Her piercing green eyes zeroed in on the pointy-haired boy a split second before her arm moved too fast for human eyes to see. He tried to dive out of the way, but the ball hammered him in the shoulder and knocked him flat.

They heard his whimper all the way under the tree.

"Damn," Malcolm said in awe.

As soon as she landed, Honey ducked under the net and ran to the boy's side. Brayton didn't hear what she said, but the boy nodded and she offered him a hand.

"Oh, yuck, she touched him," Malcolm groaned.

Cici elbowed him and nodded to the blond girl who was retrieving the ball only a few feet away. The girl squinted at them suspiciously, then jogged directly back to Honey and nodded their way. When Honey looked up, Brayton jerked his head, politely, to indicate he wanted to have a chat. She turned her back on him.

No one turned their back on him.

He couldn't eject her from the pack without his parent's approval, but he could do the next best thing.

"Let's go. If she wants to play with witches, let her play with witches. My parents may have accepted her into the pack, but as far as I'm concerned, she's shunned. Let the rest of the pack know."

"Brayton, I don't think…" Cici started.

He cut her off. "She turns her back on me, she turns her back on the pack. She needs to learn respect."

"Brayton, I'm not sure…"

He turned on her. "I have made my decision Cici. Are you one of my beta's or not?"

"Yes, but part of my job is to keep you from making a mistake. She's a rogue. She probably doesn't know anything about how a pack works."

"You're right. She is a rogue. She doesn't belong with us anyway. Maybe she'll finally get the message and leave."

# 11

## Honey

Tuesday was her first ever lab class in a real laboratory. She was so excited she didn't even realize what was missing until she'd pulled her notebook and her pen out of her backpack and looked around.

There were no wolves.

There was no tell-tell hint of magic.

Every. Single. Student. Was human. Even the teaching assistant was human.

The girl at the next bench gave her a friendly little wave.

Honey waved back. The girl scooted over to sit beside her.

Sadly, she and Evie didn't get to blow anything up. The entire lab was about lab safety.

On the plus side, she got to wear a lab coat.

Wednesday morning her plan was to sleep in ten extra minutes, but she was again awake before her alarm went off. Two hours of volleyball the night before hadn't been enough to tire her out. She really liked playing with witches though. They were always sending her curve balls, literally and figuratively.

She showed up to practice ten minutes early and started jogging. Green-headband guy started doing the same thing a few minutes later but he was way behind her. They were waiting at opposite sides on the same row of the metal bleachers when most of the others arrived. Brayton looked a lot better this time. He even had enough energy to climb to the very top of the bleachers.

"Okay children," Captain Young said condescendingly. "Today we're going to see how combat-ready you are. You all should have had some self-defense classes throughout high school, so let's see how well you learned. But first, two miles in under 16. Go."

She decided to take it slow so she would have plenty of energy left for fighting, but today it seemed like everyone wanted to go fast and she was in the way. After the third person pushed her, she decided to just run her hardest. There was no way she was going to end up a turtle.

Her mom wasn't the fastest, but they had run in the occasional race. As long as she kept her speed around 5 minutes per mile – a safe twenty-five seconds longer than the women's world record pace for a 5K – she could run with humans. Here, she suddenly realized, she didn't have to worry about the humans. She could break the record if she wanted and no one would think anything of it.

She'd already lost a little time, but she could see how fast she could finish and then have something to beat. She took off. She easily passed the people who had shoved her and was soon one person behind the lead. The lead, oddly a big, beefy guy – it was normally the small skinny guys who were the fast runners – did a double take when she pulled ahead of him. He lasted about half a mile, then fell behind. She crossed the line and for once, had to bend over to catch her breath.

A pair of well-worn sneakers appeared in front of her. "Honey, that was supposed to be a warm-up run," Captain Young scolded.

She grinned up at him. "I'm warm. What was my time?"

"Ten minutes, one second."

"I thought I'd done better than that. I'll do better next time."

"Uh-huh. Why don't you go for a short cool-down run while we wait for everyone to finish. A SLOW cool-down run."

"Yes, Sir."

The number of turtles was quite a bit smaller than Monday.

After they'd done fifty push-ups and fifty sit-ups, Captain Young split them into groups based on their packs.

"I want you to take turns sparring within your pack. I'll be around to observe. Go."

Honey was glad she wasn't called first because until that moment, she had no idea what type of fighting her pack did. It looked like a type of judo. She could do that. She'd lost track of all the different martial arts classes she'd taken starting at the age of three at her dad's insistence. Her mom didn't like fighting but had faithfully taken her to classes when her dad wasn't there. Her dad must have known she'd need to fight someday.

Every person in the pack went and some went twice, but Brayton never called on her even though she raised her hand every time after the first round. If she didn't know better, she would have thought he didn't see her. She really wanted to try too. The only wolf she'd ever gone against was her dad and she suspected he took it easy on her. Otherwise, she never went full-out because she had to be careful not to be too strong or too fast around humans.

Captain Young came by and talked to his helper who was observing their pack, then stepped up. "All right, give me two volunteers and show me what you can do."

Brayton again ignored her hand and picked two of his bully squad. Captain Young watched and nodded when Rhys pinned Malcom. "Very nice. Now I'll pick some random people. Honey, you and the little blond here."

"No, not Honey," Brayton said. "She doesn't have any training."

"And yet she handled herself very nicely the other night. As the future leader of your pack you need to know both the strengths and weaknesses. Let her fight."

The little blond was fast – at least when she ran – but she was timid when it came to fighting. Honey didn't have time for timid. Brayton wasn't picking her because he didn't know what she could do. Now was her chance to show him.

It took a single swipe to the legs to take the timid girl down.

Captain Young looked pleased. Brayton, well, he looked like Brayton.

"You." Captain Young pointed to a girl about the same height and build as Honey with brown hair and eyes. She wasn't bad and she wasn't timid. The take-down took three seconds.

"Something a little harder then," Captain Young looked around and settled on Cici.

Cici was very good – she had to be as the only girl on the bully squad – but she favored her left and she wasn't expecting the kick Honey threw to her face.

To Honey's immense pleasure, Captain Young looked impressed. Brayton looked shocked.

"Maybe your pack shouldn't train more of your wolves. You're up." He pointed to a taller wolf with lean muscle and no fat. From watching all the previous fights, Honey knew he was very good. She was surprised he wasn't on the bully squad, but maybe he was too nice.

She quickly reevaluated that assumption. He launched himself at her with a growl. He hadn't done that in his earlier matches. He must not have liked her beating up the girls in his pack. She stopped holding back and took him down with one of her favorite moves – the flying scissors to the neck Black Widow style. The gasp and whispers when several people recognized the move was more than enough reward for all the hours she'd put into it with her training dummy.

"Very good Honey. That's enough for now," Captain Young said.

"No," Brayton said, uncurling his arms. "It's my turn."

"Brayton," Captain Young started.

Brayton held up his hand, "No. You said I should know the strengths and weaknesses. How better to find out than to fight her."

Brayton attacked Honey like he was a bulldog and she had been teasing him with raw meat all day. All she could do was defend. He was bigger than her which meant he had a longer reach. Any hit she got in had to be fast and she had to move quickly to avoid getting hit back. He landed a kick on her shin and a punch to her back. It shocked her. No one ever got a hit in except her dad and his rarely hurt. She had to do something. She was not going to let a bully beat her. She threw a punch to his face. When he didn't step back, she took advantage of his distraction to get her legs in position around his waist and thighs for a scissor throw. It worked except he twisted as he fell and his elbows into her ribs with all his weight. She felt some ominous cracks and didn't try to get up after that.

"Honey. Honey, are you alright?"

She opened her eyes. Captain Young was on one knee beside her. The other wolves were standing around in a circle looking on. Brayton was still glaring. It hurt to look at him, not physically, but inside. She turned away and focused back on Captain Young.

"I think my ribs are broken, but otherwise, I'm good."

He didn't look relieved. "Of course, you are." He glanced around. "The rest of you, go run five miles. You can leave after you're done. Honey, lift up your shirt, and let me see."

She had a sports bra on, so it wasn't weird to let him see her side. He touched the already bruising skin as gently as he could, but she couldn't hold in a hiss.

"Yep. Broken. Let's get you to the doctor for an X-ray. I want to make sure all the pieces are where they're supposed to be."

"I have a Calculus class at 8. Attendance is mandatory."

"Mr. Xavier, right?"

She nodded.

"I'll let him know you were injured during practice. If he holds it against you, you can show him the X-rays. Can you get up?"

"I think I'd rather stay here."

He stepped over her to her good side and put his arm under hers. "Come on little fighter. I know you can do it. You did great, by the way. Who taught you to fight?"

"I took classes and my dad," she forced out as he helped her to her feet. Breathing was painful. One of his assistants drove up with a golf cart, for which she was exceedingly thankful. As they drove off the field, she saw the rest of the pack running along the trees on the opposite side. Some of them looked her way but none of them looked like they cared. Brayton didn't even bother to look.

# 12

## Honey

The campus doctor worked quickly. Honey got the feeling he'd had his job a long time and was well-practiced because she was X-rayed and bandaged within an hour.

It was too late to make Calculus by the time she got back to her dorm, but she didn't want to get on Mr. Xavier's bad side, so she dropped by his office during lunch to turn in her homework. Thanks to Captain Young's warning, she had pictures of her X-rays on her phone when Mr. Xavier asked for them.

After her last class, she crawled into bed and let herself cry. She missed her mom so bad her heart hurt nearly as much as her side. Her mom would have tucked her into bed and brought her, her favorite food – butter pecan ice cream – even as she took away the pain and helped her heal. If she closed her eyes she could imagine her mom's gentle fingers pushing the hair back off her forehead, which made her cry even more.

She must have fallen asleep, because when she next opened her eyes, it was dark and Blaze was breathing steadily in the lower bunk. Her side felt better – she healed as fast as normal wolves – but she'd skipped supper and between the healing and the fighting and the lunch she barely ate, she was starving. It was 11:40 pm and there wasn't a single snack in the room.

Leaving Blaze to her slumber, Honey stepped out into the hall. After checking the shared kitchen on their floor for anything edible – a total waste of time – she stumbled down the stairs in search of a snack machine. The lovely scent of pepperoni started a flood in her mouth. All she could think about was pepperoni while she followed the scent through the lobby. The sight of the empty boxes in the recycling bin nearly made her cry again. She needed food. She was beginning to feel like she had in the mall. A harsh glow caught her eye. Right, there was a snack machine next to the front desk. Somehow, she'd remembered to grab a cash card and her room key. She was saved.

Nope. The stupid machine didn't work.

She may have hit the machine and said some choice words that would have cost her a weekly movie or two if her mother was there, but her actions were no longer registering with her head. All she could feel was how hungry she was. Honey vaguely noted the girl at the front desk looked scared when she detected the faint hint of pepperoni again, and it was fresh. Streetlamps passed by, then an elevator, and the next thing she knew, she was under a table scarfing down a piece of pizza with an empty box on the floor between her legs and a very full-feeling belly. She threw the remaining half-piece of pizza she was still working on into the box and leaned back against the wall with a sigh. Why did this keep happening to her?

"Where is she?" a male voice asked.

"Under there," another one answered. Honey sniffed. Why did it smell like males and why were they afraid?

A pair of nicely shaped, rather hairy legs approached her table. They stopped several feet away and the body and the head associated with them appeared as the owner squatted to her height. She didn't recognize him, but he looked nice enough. He had dark hair, dark eyes, and a kind smile.

"Hello under there."

"Hello."

"I'm Jack, the Resident Assistant on this floor."

"Hello Jack."

"Care to tell me why you are eating a stolen pizza under the table?"

"I was hungry?"

"Mmm. Mind coming out from under there?"

Her face felt greasy and a quick swipe by her mouth came back red. It was bad enough she'd stolen some stranger's food. She didn't want to face them with the evidence all over her face. "Can I have a napkin first?"

"Sure." He tossed a whole pile at her.

She took her time scrubbing her face and wiping each and every finger while trying to remember what had happened. It was pointless. She finally gave up, pushed the box out of the way and crawled into the light. Jack stood, so she did too. He was tall and slim and looked a little older than the four wolves watching them warily near the door. The room appeared to be the living area of a suite like Brayton's, but smaller.

"You're young. Do you go to school here?"

She lifted the lanyard on her neck to display her student ID. "Yes."

"The guys said you stormed into their room and started eating their pizza and when they tried to stop you, you growled at them and disappeared under the table with the box."

"I'm sorry. I didn't mean to." She dug out the cash card she had in her back pocket and laid it on the table. "There's at least $25 on there. Will that be enough?"

"That's good you want to pay for it, but it's not okay to steal other people's food," Jack said like she was a three-year-old.

She nearly growled at him. "You think I don't know that? I told you I didn't mean to. I got too hungry and the vending machine wouldn't work and I smelled the pepperoni and then I don't know what happened."

"You don't remember coming in here?"

"No."

"Did you come up the elevator or the stairs?"

"I don't know."

"Has this ever happened to you before?"

"Once. I got too hungry then too."

"Okay, let's back up. When did you last eat?"

"Lunch, but I didn't have that much. I was in a hurry and I missed breakfast because," she lifted her shirt to show her very colorful side, "there was an incident at training this morning."

Jack winced appropriately.

"Oh, you're that girl," the sandy-haired boy said.

"We did combat today and someone had to get carted off in the golf cart. That was you?" the shortest one with brown hair and light-brown skin asked.

"Yeah."

"What happened?" the first boy asked.

"I took my opponent down with a scissor throw and he landed on me with his elbow and broke a couple of ribs."

"Ouch."

"They're better now, but I slept through supper. I'm really sorry I growled at you and stole your pizza."

"That's okay. It happened to me once too," the first boy said. "Luckily, my mom always keeps the fridge well-stocked. I came to with my face covered in frosting."

His friends laughed, so she did too, or tried to. Her side hurt too much to really laugh.

"I better get back to my dorm."

"Hey, what's your name?" the first one asked.

"Honey."

He gave her a lazy grin. "I like it. I'm Nathan, that's Luca," he pointed to the short one. "Walter is the beanpole with glasses and Liam is the one next to him."

Liam had dark brown eyes and cocoa-colored skin.

They all smiled at her kindly, but it was late, and she was feeling awkward about standing in their suite after what she'd done.

"I guess I'll see you at training."

"Come on, I'll escort you out," Jack said. "Visiting hours end at midnight."

It was very uncomfortable in the elevator under his intense gaze. She had to try really hard not to squirm. It

105

wasn't until they were at the front door that he finally said what was on his mind.

"What pack are you with?"

"Mooney."

"I'm surprised one of them didn't check on you when you didn't show up to eat."

"Why would they?"

"They're your pack. Packs take care of one another."

"Oh." She'd heard that, but she barely knew anyone in the pack. She shrugged. "I'm new. They don't know me."

"Don't you have any friends?"

"Yeah, but they didn't know I was hurt."

"Weren't they at practice this morning?"

"No."

"Why weren't they," he shook his head, "never mind. I don't want you terrorizing my dorm again. Fill your room with snacks if you have to but stay away from our pizza."

"Yes, sir."

# 13

## Honey

The Friday WOLF class was moved from 5:30 am to 9:00 pm so they could all run together as wolves under the nearly full moon in the tree-covered land near the training grounds. Honey had never run with a pack or even with her dad under the moon because he always ran with his pack to keep them from suspecting anything. Wolves didn't have to transform during the full moon like a lot of fantasy books claimed, but it was one of their most honored traditions according to her dad, and a great pack bonding exercise. Witches also had a tradition of community activities under the moon, but theirs usually involved a bonfire and magic. Instead of running, she and her mom had their own coven meeting around a small fire in a little metal fire pit. Her mom would cook s'mores and Honey would practice her magic by attempting to make the marshmallows evenly tan, not black, without the aid of rotation.

The bonfire at the training grounds was nothing like the little fires her mom and her had built. It was huge. The flames were taller than she was. People clustered around it in groups and sipped from colorful canned beverages. There was beer and what she suspected was even stronger stuff in the coolers, but she opted for a water. She'd tasted her dad's beer once. She didn't understand why wolves bothered drinking it. It was nasty and bitter and wolf metabolisms were so fast that they had to drink a lot to even feel it.

After watching everyone on Wednesday, she now knew who was in her pack. None of them had ever approached to say hi, but except for WOLF, she didn't have classes with them and she was usually with the witches in the evenings. Maybe they were just waiting for her to introduce herself. She decided to start with a couple of girls chatting near the end of the row of coolers. One of them glanced her way when she approached. Honey pulled up her friendliest smile. Instead of smiling back, the girl grabbed her friend's elbow and pulled her into the crowd on the other side of the fire. Huh. Maybe they were friends with someone she'd defeated on Wednesday. She searched the crowd for another promising target. Oddly, all of her pack members were suddenly extremely busy talking with their neighbors and none of them were facing her way. Okay. She understood. They'd all been raised together and she was a stranger. It would take time for them to get used to her. She walked away from the fire and found a seat near the bottom of the bleachers.

"Hey Honey," a smooth voice said.

She turned to find the blond from last night smiling down at her. "Hey Nathan and, um the rest of you. Sorry, I don't remember your names."

"Luca, Walter, and Liam," Nathan said.

"Thank you. Sorry guys."

Nathan slid onto the bench beside her, close enough that their arms touched. "You look better. How are your ribs?"

"Still sore, but I feel much better."

"Want a beer?"

Remembering what her mom had said about boys and drinks, she held up her water. "No, I'm good."

"It's a beautiful night," he said, turning to gaze up at the moon.

"It is," she agreed. The other three boys were still standing around. It was making her more nervous than she already was. "Why don't you guys sit down? Don't worry," she said when one of them, Liam maybe, looked warily at the seat beside her, then at her, "I had plenty for supper."

He chuckled and said in a surprisingly deep voice, "I'm not afraid. I figured you were saving seats for your friends."

"Ah, no." It wasn't worth it to explain that they were at their own party – a witch party. "So which pack are you guys from?" she asked when Liam sat down on her other side, but without crowding her like Nathan was.

"The Little pack."

"Really?" The Little pack was actually the biggest pack in Indiana. Many of their wolves worked in the coal and mining industry.

"Yeah, and no making fun of the name," Nathan said.

"It's a great name. Very deceptive," she said.

"Like yours?" Liam teased.

She elbowed him gently. "I had a bad day. I promise I'm not usually like that."

"Uh-huh."

"Who are the other people in your pack?" she asked.

Liam started pointing people out, then Nathan started calling them over. Luca and Walter joined in and suddenly if felt like they had a true party going on their side of the fire. There weren't any s'mores, but someone had brought small sausages they were roasting on sticks and handing out. It was fun and unlike with the witches and the Mooney pack, she felt almost accepted.

The sun disappeared and the moon took center-sky. Captain Young stepped up on a large log in front of the fire. "All right folks, you know what time it is. There are tents set up behind the fire for you to strip in if you are uncomfortable doing it out in the open. There are tables for your clothes too. Boys on this side," he waved both arms to his right like he was directing a plane. "And girls on this side," he waved to the left. "Any peeking perverts will get an immediate F in the class. Since this is replacing our Friday class, I want you to use this as a team-building exercise. I have hidden something very special in the woods. The first pack to find it and bring it back here will earn ten points."

"What is it?" someone yelled.

"Well, you know, I can't just give out points willy-nilly. Part of the exercise is figuring out what it is. The hint is 'white'."

"That could be anything," Nathan mumbled.

"Yeah, white flower, white shirt, white moon," Walter added.

"Hey, why don't you run with us," Nathan said to Honey.

Luca punched him on the shoulder. "Because it's a pack building exercise and she's not part of our pack."

"I doubt anyone would notice," Nathan said.

"Can't you just follow the rules for once?"

"I would like to," she said truthfully, "but Luca's right. I should run with my own pack this time." Should she tell them it was her first time? Maybe they would have some tips.

Nathan rubbed his shoulder against hers, then popped to his feet. "All right. See you after."

There were two problems she had to overcome before she could run with the pack. First, she had to find someone in her pack and make sure she knew what their wolf looked like so she could identify her pack once they were all changed and two, she couldn't change in the tent. Her dad had told her never to let anyone see her change into a wolf, especially not other wolves. Other wolves had to strip and generally took several moments, perhaps painful, to morph into their wolf form. Somehow, she had always been able to change instantaneously with her clothes on.

She saw the first girl she'd fought with on Wednesday heading for the tent. As nonchalantly as she could, Honey moved around the fire, then dilly-dallied outside the entrance to give the girl enough time to start to undress. She didn't plan to undress herself and she didn't want to hang around like a stalker.

"Honey."

"Captain Young." He'd come just as she was about to enter the tent. She was going to miss her chance.

"How are your ribs?"

111

"Much better."

"Still sore though?"

"Yes."

"Take it easy, okay. No five-minute miles."

"Yes Sir."

"Good girl."

Honey slipped into the tent. Her target was gone. There were plenty of other girls going through the tent though. She started working on her shoe, pretending it was tied in a knot. Finally, a girl she knew was in her pack walked in. Honey watched through her hair while the girl transformed, noting the pattern of white patches in the girl's dark gray fur. She could find her again, and maybe even follow her if she hurried. After making sure no one was paying attention, Honey walked between the table and tent, looked down like she'd found something on the floor, then dropped. A few seconds later, she sprinted out from under the end of the table and out the back of the tent in wolf form.

There were so many wolves! She had the strongest urge to pounce and chase them the way she had always played with her dad. Some of the wolves were doing exactly that. She also realized all her worries about finding her pack were silly. In her wolf form, the scents she didn't pay much attention to as a human added a whole other dimension to the world she could sense with her nose. The members of her pack stood out to her like they'd been colored with a highlighter marker even though she didn't know their individual smells.

A white wolf, not of her pack, came up and rubbed his shoulder against her. She sniffed. Nathan. A black wolf bumped her from the other side – Liam. From their demeanors, Walter was the tall dark gray one and Luca the small brown one. Nathan butted her with his head, but not on her ribs. She butted him back. Someone nipped her tail and she spun to see Walter tripping over his back feet to get away and Luca jumping back and forth like he was laughing. She gave a playful growl and started after Luca but suddenly a big gray grumpy wolf who smelled like Brayton's body spray was in the way. He nudged her hard right in her sore ribs. A whimper escaped before she'd realized it was coming. Brayton gave her a look that said, 'serves you right' and jerked his head toward the rest of the pack. Oops, they were waiting for her.

She followed Brayton and waited on the edge of the pack as he faced everyone else. It looked like he was talking to them except he wasn't making any sounds. He gave a final nod and the whole pack abruptly started splitting up and heading off in different directions. What was going on? Did they have assigned groups they always ran in or was it just whoever you were standing close to? She decided to try following the group closest to her. Just before they reached the trees, the last wolf turned and chomped his teeth at her. It must be assigned groups then. She ran for the next group in case that was hers, but a female in the back growled at her. By then the other groups had disappeared. She could have followed them with her nose, but what was the point? The Mooney pack was either full or snobs or they simply didn't want her around. Maybe she could run with the Little pack? Oh, they were gone. The only people left in the field were Captain Young and two of his helpers. She'd been looking forward to running with other wolves. She sniffed. Nope, she wasn't going to cry. She could run just fine by herself. She'd never run under a full moon before. It would be an adventure.

She took off after the moon, half-way pretending she was trying to catch it. At first her side hurt with every step, but after about a half a mile, the pain faded into something she could ignore. Not long after, she reached the bank of a wide river. She followed a trail along its edge until she reached a high point where she could look down over the trees and the land on the other side like she was queen of the world, then stopped. It was lovely even through the tears crowding her vision.

Her parents were watching her, she knew, and they were finally together where no one would judge them. She prayed that everything would turn out all right and could have sworn she felt her dad's nose resting on her shoulder and her mom's hand on her head.

After a good cry and a long pep talk, she noticed the moon had moved quite a bit since she got there. How long did pack runs last? She should have asked. She got to her feet and turned to go back, but a strange sound stopped her. Tilting her ears and following her nose, it only took a few seconds to find the source – a kitten! The poor thing was all dirty and cold and she instinctively knew it had either lost its mother or its mother had lost it. She didn't particularly want to carry a dirty animal in her mouth, but she was afraid she wouldn't be able to find her way back in human form. Very, very carefully, she picked the kitten up by the scruff of its neck with her sharp canine teeth and started following her own scent back toward the bonfire.

When she was sure she could find her way without her nose and that no one was around, she transformed back into a human and scooped the kitten up with her hands.

There were still a few wolves milling about in human form, so either they were packing up or no one was back yet. The still-burning fire indicated it was the latter. Captain Young spotted her and jogged over before she'd even reached the flames.

"Honey, is something wrong?"

"No. I found a kitten. I think he's hungry," she showed him the fluffy little thing who had begun purring in her arms. "He's white too, if that counts," she said.

"Huh. So he is. What are you going to do with a kitten? Pets aren't allowed in the dorms."

"I don't know. Do you know someone who could take him?"

Captain Young gently lifted the kitten so he could inspect him by the light of the fire. The kitten gave a plaintive little mewl. "My daughter will love this. My wife, on the other hand, will probably kill me."

"You could get her a present too."

"She has been wanting an espresso-maker."

"You should get it for her," Honey grinned while trying to imagine Captain Young's wife. She was probably pretty and nice like him.

He put the kitten in the crook of his arm. "Where's the rest of your pack?"

"I don't know."

"Did you get lost?"

"No. I wasn't sure what to do so I just followed the moon for a while."

"Didn't Brayton give you instructions before you left?"

"No."

"Has he always acted like this toward you?"

"Pretty much."

"Here," he handed the kitten back to her. "Keep an eye on him for me and see if you can find him something to eat and drink. The others should be back soon."

She grabbed another bottle of water and a couple of small sausages. The kitten lapped the water out of her hand but seemed unsure of how to eat the sausage. She finally broke it open and let it lick the little bits inside off her finger. After he'd finished almost a whole one, he curled up in her lap and fell asleep. She was halfway through picking the stick-tights and other debris out of the kitten's long white fur when a shadow fell over her. It should have been impossible since the fire was to her side and the wolf was in front of her, but somehow, Brayton made a shadow.

He was still in wolf form and, based on the way he was glaring and pacing, upset about something. Maybe he'd noticed she hadn't run with his pack, although there was no reason he would, unless she was supposed to run with his group. Oops.

"Hi Brayton. Sorry I didn't go with your pack for a run. I couldn't figure out what I was supposed to do so I jogged to the river. Guess what I found though." She scooped the little kitten out of her lap and held it up so he could see it better. "Isn't he cute?"

Most people, when presented with a warm, little sleepy bundle of white fluff would experience a softening

116

of their hearts. Not Brayton. She looked up to see what he thought and saw a claw coming right for the little guy. She turned so her arm was between Brayton and the kitten and felt her skin split as his claws sliced through the muscle of her upper arm.

She was more shocked than anything. She looked down at the blood welling out of the lines on her arm, then up at Brayton. "You would kill a kitten?"

For a moment, she thought he looked a little shocked too, then he lifted his paw again and she ducked to cover the kitten.

# 14

## Brayton

What had he done? He'd only meant to push the kitten away but somehow he'd clawed Honey. The slash marks across her pale skin gaped open like long red mouths full of pulsing blood. Pressure, you were supposed to put pressure on a wound. He lifted his hand to do just that, but it was still a paw. Honey hid her face from him and bent over the kitten like she expected him to kill it.

"I'm sorry. I didn't mean to. I'm going to change. I'll be right back," he sent telepathically.

He ran for the tent. Naked guys were laughing and whacking each other with their shirts but all he could see was Honey's shocked expression and the hurt in her eyes. It was almost worse than the way she'd lain so pale and still after he'd rolled away from her on Wednesday. At least she'd deserved it that time – there was no doubt she knew who was in charge now.

A crowd had gathered around her by the time he jogged back. One of the guys she'd been sitting next to before the run had his shirt wrapped around her arm. His dark skin glistened in the light from the fire as she nodded to something he said. Brayton had the momentary urge to push the guy out of the way and take over, but he shook it off. It didn't matter who helped her, as long as she got help.

"OMG man. That was bad," Malcolm said, thumping his back. "You slashed a chick with kitten. I think that's worse than taking candy from a baby." In Malcolm-speak that meant he thought slashing her was cool and it ranked even higher than candy-stealing.

Rhys didn't say anything, but Brayton could feel his disapproval burning the back of his ear.

Cici punched him. "What were you thinking? I saw the whole thing. She offered you a kitten and you sliced her open like Freddy Krueger."

"Who?" Malcolm asked.

"You know, *A Nightmare on Elm Street*," Cici said. "The guy with razors on his glove."

"Oh, right. Yeah, it was like that."

"It was an accident."

"It didn't look like an accident," Cici said.

"I was just trying to…"

"Brayton Mooney."

He looked up to see Captain Young bearing down on him with, of all things, the kitten in the crook of his arm.

"Yes, Sir?"

"I leave for five minutes. No, less than five, and when I get back, the young woman I left watching over my daughter's new kitten has her arm sliced open nearly down to the bone. Can you tell me please what Miss Smith was doing that required such a reaction?"

"I didn't mean to. It was an accident." He sounded lame even to himself.

"Scratching her would have been an accident, maybe. Gouging that deep requires some effort."

"Really, I didn't mean to. We were talking, well I was talking and she was ignoring me, then she gave some lame excuse about why she didn't run with the rest of the pack like she was supposed to and then she thrust a kitten in my face. I just wanted her to put it down and focus. I guess she thought I was going to hurt the kitten because she turned her shoulder toward me and I sliced her arm open. It was just a bad angle."

"Kinda like what happened on Wednesday when you broke three of her ribs?"

"I...I what?" He broke her ribs? He thought he'd just winded her and she was playing it up.

"Oh, you didn't know? You, the future alpha, didn't bother to check up on a member of your own pack after you nearly punctured her lung? Did it ever dawn on you that perhaps she couldn't run with you because her ribs were still sore? Did anyone in your pack look for her when they realized she was missing or did no one even notice?"

Dissing him was one thing, but his pack...no. "They...Look, she's new, okay. She's never run with us before."

"Explain."

"She just joined the pack three weeks ago. She's a rogue, a lovechild. Her parents hid her. Nobody knows her."

"Where are her parents?"

He shrugged. "Dead, she says."

120

"How did she end up in your pack?"

"My mom is trying to 'save-the-rogues'," he probably shouldn't have rolled his eyes. "We found Honey at a homeless shelter. She claims she got a perfect score on the SAT so Mom decided to send her to college with me. She's very good at convincing people she's some poor little helpless thing. Looks like she's got you fooled too." Oops, shouldn't have said that.

The muscles along Captain Young's jaw undulated as he clenched them, but his voice was strangely still when he started speaking again, kind of like water before a big snake jumps out and bites you on the face. "Do you remember the first time you ever ran with your pack?"

"Sure."

"What was it like?"

It was one of his fondest memories. His dad had acted as excited to run with him as he'd been to run with his dad. His dad had even let him lead the pack for a while. "It was great."

"And you, Cici right, how was your first run?"

"It was good, better than I imagined it would be."

"What did you like about it?"

"Finally being old enough to stay out late, being with my friends, being with the pack, no, being one with the pack."

"Huh. How about you boys, would you agree with Cici?"

"Sure," Malcolm and Rhys said at the same time.

"From what you just told me about Honey, this was her first time ever to run with a pack, is that correct?"

"I guess, I mean, if she's telling the truth," Brayton agreed.

"Okay, and how do you think she'd describe her first ever experience running with a pack?"

"Well, she…," he started.

"No. Think about it. Assuming she is what she says she is, she didn't know what to expect, had no idea what to do, was hurting, and then got injured again by the boy who's supposed to be her future alpha. Worse, not a single wolf in her so-called pack stepped up to help her. Those guys," he waved behind him to where Honey was being helped into the golf cart by a sandy-haired boy and the dark-skinned boy who was still sans shirt, "jumped right in even though she's not their responsibility."

"Who are they?" They probably didn't know she preferred witches.

"That's not the point." Captain Young studied him and petted his kitten just like the bad guy in the old James Bond movies. "I want a thousand-word essay Monday morning at the start of practice explaining why you dislike Honey so much. If you don't have it ready, don't bother coming. Attendance is mandatory by the way. Unless you have a doctor's note or a really, really good excuse, if you miss a day, you lose a letter grade. Understood?"

Warning him was superfluous. Writing the essay was going to be easy.

"Oh, and if I don't like it, you get to do it again," Captain Young added.

That was the catch. He was never going to like it. Honey already had him wrapped around her little pinky.

"Yes, Sir."

"Good." Captain Young spun on his heel and walked toward the fire, still petting the little kitten.

Malcolm punched Brayton and started talking before Captain Young was safely out of range. "Man, you got off easy. I thought he was going to make you wash toilets or something."

"Looks that way."

It was Friday night of a full moon after his first full week of college and thanks to Honey, he felt so tied up inside, he couldn't even enjoy it. He needed something stronger than beer. "You guys want to get out of here and find a real party?"

"You know, what he said was right," Cici said. "If any one of our pack was hurt, you'd check on them, even if you didn't like them, because they're pack. You might not like her, but Honey is a member of our pack now. We should check on her first."

"I'm sure she's fine. Those other wolves are with her. We can check on her in the morning."

"You're just going to leave her with a bunch of strange wolves?"

"She slept in a homeless shelter. She can take care of herself." It was a lame excuse but he didn't want to have to face those sad green eyes again.

"Do you know where she's staying?"

"Yeah. She's in that ancient girl's dorm next to mine."

"You guys go ahead. I'll make sure she gets home."

"Just leave her."

"No," Cici said. "Captain Young was right about the run too. You assigned her to my group. I should have made sure she followed. That's like basic rule number one, don't lose anybody, and I failed. I'll see you tomorrow."

# 15

## Brayton

*Why I hate Honey*
*By Brayton Mooney*

Why couldn't he get past those two lines? Why couldn't he remember any of those sentences he'd crafted Friday night in the bar? He rubbed his temples again, not that it helped to either craft sentences or to lessen the headache that threatened to split his head in half. Why was this so hard?

"Done yet?" Malcolm asked cheerily from where he was perusing a car magazine on the couch.

"No. Is anyone else still feeling last night?" He rubbed his hand across his forehead. Whatever was in that blue drink had a punch.

Rhys tossed him a bottle of water. "You're dehydrated."

"Thanks, Mom."

He downed half the water, then slammed his laptop closed. "I'm going to clear my head. I can't think with this headache."

"Told you that last drink was a bad idea."

"Shut it Cici."

She rolled her eyes and went back to doing her homework.

"Why are you here anyway? Don't you have your own table?"

"Yeah, but Liliana has material all over it."

"You mean a tablecloth?"

"No. She was pinning a pattern to it. She said it was her Halloween costume."

"It's like, the first of September."

Cici shook her head and slumped back over the large textbook she was reading.

Brayton grabbed his wallet and slipped on his loafers. "I'll be back in a bit."


Maybe a walk was a mistake. The sun was brutal. He could feel the intense rays shooting through his eyeballs and lasering a hole through his brain. He veered into the little convenience store that was a part of his dorm and came out with a pair of expensive cheap sunglasses with the school logo on the frame and the biggest soda they had.

His options were well-manicured, tree-lined sidewalks between stately buildings of pale brick and stone or a gravel path through a little park behind the dorms. He turned toward the park. He hadn't explored it yet, but he'd seen students and even some people from the community jogging on the gravel path, which made him suspect it made a big circle around the park. The center of the park was populated with trees that must have been planted when the school first opened based on their size. There was a pond somewhere too. He couldn't see it, but he could hear and smell the ducks from where he stood.

He followed the outside trail until he found one that led to the center. His head was already starting to feel better. He passed a group of people sitting on the grass having what looked like a prayer service and a guy with his books spread around him like it was exam week instead of the first week of school. More than a few girls had found sunny spots between the trees and were laying on towels to soak in the rays even though they were fully clothed. He sniffed. Witches. He looked them over, not because he was interested, but because he thought Honey might be with them. Maybe he could use that. *Why I hate Honey – because I had to search through the witches to find her.* No. That led to questions like why he was looking for her in the first place.

Why was he searching for her? He directed his eyes back to the path and continued forward.

It was shadier here. The trees were old and broad and formed a thick canopy with their crisscrossing branches. They were probably here even before the school was built.

He could see the pond now. A little stone bridge was on one end over the small creek that drained into it. On the opposite bank, a couple of small children were throwing bread crumbs into the water, much to the delight of at least ten ducks. The quacking and squealing made his head pound. He turned onto another path to get away from them, and then an even smaller path because his nose was pulling him that way.

It wasn't a scent so much as a tingle, but eventually he did catch a scent, a wolf scent, one that belonged to a certain wolf he'd been thinking of since he started working on the essay. He realized who he was following about the time she came into view sitting against the trunk of an old tree.

She opened those bright green eyes that had followed him in his dreams all weekend and let out a cautious, "Hi Brayton".

It looked like she dropped a couple of inches right before she spoke to him, but that had to be his aching head playing tricks on him.

"Hi Honey," stupid name. "What are you doing out here all by yourself?" Why had he asked that? He should just leave.

"Feeling nature. It's peaceful here."

She was right about that. He felt more relaxed than he had the whole week. "How are your arm and your ribs?"

She lifted her arm and moved it around in a circle. "My arm is a little tight, but it's almost healed. There might not even be a scar. My ribs are fine. I can take a full breath again."

*Why I hate Honey – she knows just what to say to make me feel guilty as sin.*

"I'm sorry about that – really."

She held up her hand. "Let's not talk about it anymore, okay." She closed her eyes and took a deep breath, then let it out very slowly.

"Are you meditating?" That was something witches did.

"No," she said without opening her eyes. "Feeling nature. Sit down and breathe in for a minute. Something smells really good here."

He didn't know why he obeyed her. Probably because it was better than going back to the dorm to stare at the screen. Ooo, maybe being in her presence would give him some ideas.

He sat down on a mossy piece of ground several feet away and closed his own eyes. Sniffing, he caught the musty smell of old leaves, exhaust from distant cars, ducks, dogs, flowers – maybe that's what she meant. There was a faint smell of honeysuckle and roses. Mostly though, he smelled her. Her scent filled the space beneath the tree.

*Why I hate Honey – first, her name is ridiculous. Second, she smells like her name and makes me want to…*woah, hold on there. He most definitely did not want to hug Honey. He cracked an eye open, half expecting her to be laughing at him, but no, she was sitting with her eyes closed and her legs crossed as serenely as she had been when he found her, except for the lone tear trickling down her cheek.

Damn. Should he go? Should he stay? Should he say something? That was the problem with girls – they always had some emotional issue going on – all except Cici. The only time he'd seen her cry was when she broke her arm falling out of a tree when she was thirteen.

"What's wrong Honey?" stupid, stupid name.

Her eyes flew open, surprising him again with how green they were, then they were gone after she wiped her cheek and looked down. "I was thinking about my mom. She would have liked this place."

"It is nice," he agreed. No way was he going to ask about her mom. That was sure to bring on more tears.

*Why I hate Honey – she cries too much.*

Technically, it was the first time he'd seen her do it, but he'd smelled tears on her plenty of times. Two nights ago, for example, right when she was showing him that damn kitten, she'd smelled like she'd taken a bath in them.

And that's when he had his first ever epiphany.

It truly was like a light bulb went off in his head. Why hadn't he realized it sooner? Honey didn't know how to be in a pack. She might be smart, but her stupid parents hadn't taught her what was important. His mom had been so busy dragging Honey on shopping trips, she hadn't taught her anything either. His stomach twisted oddly. Did she realize she was shunned? Did she think the members of his pack were just unfriendly? His brain quickly shifted to a shinier track.

"Honey…"

She looked up and shot him a wary little smile before pushing herself to her feet. "I need to go study. I'll see you around."

"Sure."

He didn't chase her. He didn't want to scare her and he wasn't sure what he wanted to say anyway. Starting tomorrow though, 5:30 in the morning, things were going to change. He'd take her under his arm and explain how things worked or have Cici do it. He'd un-shun her too. No, that would be weird. People would ask questions. If she hung around with him and his group, people would figure it out. At least he knew how to start his essay now.

130

*Why I hate Honey – I don't. I hate the monster she brings out in me.*

# 16

## Honey

She both wanted to and didn't want to go to practice. In the end, there wasn't much she could do about it since attendance was required. She went early again, because she did like to run and it was nice when it was just green head-band guy. She really should ask him what his name was.

She never got the chance.

Green head-band guy was waiting for her on the bleachers when she got there. He popped to his feet and stuck out his hand. "Hi, I'm Greg."

"Hi, Honey. I mean my name is Honey."

"I know. Can I warm-up with you?"

"Sure." It wasn't like he hadn't before.

"So what pack are you in?" she asked after they'd jogged about a quarter-of-a-mile.

"Mason."

"That's one of the western packs, right?"

"If by western you mean western Indiana, then yes."

"Mmm, a smart-Alec."

"Who is this Alec of which you speak?"

She laughed.

"You're pretty fast. I saw you whiz by me on Wednesday but I couldn't escape the pack or I would have raced you," he said

"Really?" She glanced over at him. He was definitely built like a runner but looks could be deceiving.

"You're looking at me with much doubt."

"No. I was wondering how good you are. You look like a runner and we are wolves after all."

"Your words hold much wisdom, Grasshopper."

"Thanks?"

He nudged her with his elbow. "Hey, maybe we can have a race across the field before anyone else gets here."

"Sure."

Racing Greg across the field was nearly as fun as racing Brayton through the obstacle course. No, it was more fun, because she didn't have to think – she just had to run. He was fast, but they started at an all-out sprint and he tired before her. She slowed down a little, but at the end, she couldn't help herself. She blasted forward again into a round-off and three back-handsprings. She would have done more, but her ribs and her arm were still stiff.

"Wow," Greg said. "I think you nailed that win home."

She grinned at him. "It's called sticking the landing."

"It was pretty impressive. Much better than what I can do."

"Let me see."

He proceeded to do what was either a cartwheel or a handstand, then landed flat on his back.

She offered him a hand. "You nailed that landing."

133

"Ha ha."

"Wanna race back to the bleachers?" She asked after she pulled him up.

"Can I have a head start?"

"How much?"

"Count of three?"

She pushed him toward the seats. "You have two."

He beat her, but barely. People were starting to arrive but she wanted to do more than stretch her legs. She started doing the series of stretches they always had them do at the start of gymnastics. She finished with a handstand into a front walk-over.

Greg rolled his eyes at her when she rejoined him at the bleachers. "Show off."

"Feeling better I see, Honey."

She spun around. "Good morning, Captain Young. Did your daughter like the kitten?"

"Loved it. I caught her putting a dress on it this morning. I explained to her it was a boy kitten. She said he was enriched. I think she meant enlightened. She's only three, so I'll cut her some slack." He waited for their laughter to tail off, then commented. "You must have taken gymnastics."

"Yes."

"That explains how you got through the obstacle course so fast. I'm going to have to find you a harder one."

"Honey!"

Nathan stopped close enough to rub his shoulder against hers. He liked to touch people, she'd noticed. When he and Liam had taken her out to breakfast and then the grocery store on Saturday, every time he'd handed her something, his hand had brushed hers. She wondered if he realized he was doing it. She introduced Greg to him and Liam, then to Walter and Luca who were right behind them.

"Get your two miles in, boys. We have strength training today," Captain Young ordered.

"I'll go with you. I still have another mile to do," she volunteered.

"Me too," green head-band guy, nope, Greg said.

Everything was going well. This was what she'd thought running with a pack would be like, laughing and teasing and just enjoying the day and each other, then Brayton showed up. He was waiting for her when they finished the two miles. She tried not to let his presence get to her, but she couldn't help being wary. Unlike in the park when they'd been alone, she couldn't freeze him if he tried something. Too many people would see.

Brayton was standing near the back of the bleachers with Malcolm, Rhys and Cici. "Honey, come over here. We need to talk."

"Isn't he the guy who clawed you?" Liam said.

"Yeah. He's my pack's alpha's son."

"We've got your back," Nathan said, touching his elbow against hers.

Her new friends clustered around her. She felt like a famous celebrity with a bunch of bodyguards.

"What's up Brayton?"

"Who are these guys?" He demanded.

"Oh, these are my friends." She pointed and named each one of them and realized Greg had followed too.

"They're not from our pack."

"So?"

"You can't just run with another pack. You belong to our pack. That's part of being a pack. We're like family. We do things together."

"Can't I do things with other families?"

"Sure you can," Nathan said, touching his elbow to her arm again. "We've basically decided to adopt you anyway. Right guys?"

"Yeah." "Sure." "Uh-huh." They all sounded sincere. She had to look down to hide the sudden tears in her eyes.

"Wait, what if I want to adopt her?" Greg said. "I saw her first."

"Yeah, but she stole our pizza," Luca said. "Girl steals your pizza you get first dibs."

Her face heated. "Guys, I paid you back."

"What kind of pizza," Greg asked.

"If you gentlemen and ladies are finished with your two miles, get out here and do your sit-ups," Captain Young yelled.

"Honey!" Brayton said. It was a demand that she stay.

"Captain Young is in charge. I have to obey him," she replied, not apologetically.

# 17

## Brayton

"Mr. Mooney, you have something for me?" Captain Young asked, strolling past Honey and her misfits as if there was nothing at all abnormal about a girl and five guys.

Brayton handed him the essay. Captain Young glanced at the title, then at him, but Brayton couldn't decipher his look. "This should be an interesting read. Run."

Honey had walked away from him, again. Yeah, she had an excuse, but he had a plan he wanted to share with her. He'd thought about it all evening yesterday after he'd finished the stupid essay. He'd be her teacher. He'd find a dry erase board and explain pack hierarchy and what was expected of each level, then go into pack runs and strategies depending on the purpose of the run. It'd be like a class. She'd love it.

"What pack were those guys from?" Brayton asked after half-a-mile.

"Four of them were from Little," Cici said, "I don't know about the one with the green headband."

"What is up with the headband? Where do you even buy one of those?" Malcolm scoffed.

"Want one for yourself, do you?" Cici snickered.

"No!"

"You think she's safe with them?" Rhys asked.

"They seem like nice guys," Cici responded. "I waited at Honey's dorm Friday night to make sure she got home all right. The talkative one and the dark-skinned one who went with her to the doctor brought her home too. Then Saturday, I went to check on her and saw her coming from the store with them. They carried her bags in for her. I think they meant it when they said they'd adopted her."

"What did they mean she stole their pizza?" Brayton asked. It wouldn't be good for the pack reputation if that got out.

"I don't know," Cici said. "They live in your dorm. Maybe you could ask around."

He thought about the way Honey had been laughing with her new friends while they were running. She'd looked happy, something he'd never inspired in her. It was the wrong pack, but at least it was a pack and not a coven. She'd pick up the basics just by being around them, then when she ran with their pack at the next moon, he'd make sure to give her special attention so she'd have an enjoyable experience. Once she saw how great their pack was, she'd start to make friends in their pack. His mom would be happy, Honey would be happy, and he wouldn't have to feel guilty anymore. It was a win-win-win.

# 18

## Honey

After only a little wheedling, she talked her Little pack friends and Greg into joining her at supper with her witch friends. It was tense at first, especially when Panas complained how letting in one dog led to a whole pack, but Sabine scolded him and said if Honey kept bringing cute pack members, she was allowed. Nathan took that as a cue to turn on the charm. He easily won over all the female witches and soon her two groups of friends were taking up two of the round cafeteria tables every evening and were by far the rowdiest people on the witch's side of the room. The boys even started playing volleyball with them which encouraged a couple of other wolves from other packs and a few other witches to join in.

To her relief, Brayton left her alone. She rarely saw him or anyone else from her pack except in WOLF and at supper. Her classes had few to no wolves – probably because she had enrolled so late – and Captain Young didn't make them do any more within-pack exercises, leaving her free to do everything with the Little Pack.

Luna Lynn didn't call, but she did text every few days to see how Honey was doing. Honey didn't tell her about her ribs or the scratch. They'd healed and she didn't want to cause any trouble. Lynn had initially ordered Brayton to come home every other weekend and bring Honey with him, but he never asked and she never approached him about it. She liked Lynn, but she couldn't imagine riding in a car there and back with just Brayton to talk to.

Time passed quickly. This month's full moon was on Saturday. There was another run planned, but it wasn't required for WOLF class, so Honey decided not to go. She'd rather be by herself than chase after a bunch of wolves who'd made it clear they didn't like her.

"You're not going?" Nathan whined when she told the boys an hour before they were supposed to report to the field. They were in their living room scarfing down food after a Taco Bell run. She was still amazed by how many tacos the boys could eat in one sitting. "But you have to go. I want to see your wolf again."

"I can show you my wolf here. It won't be any fun to run if I can't run with you guys."

Nathan tapped his chin a few times, then a very determined look came over his face. "I have an idea."

"Oh no," Walter groaned.

"Is it legal?" Luca questioned.

"Two ideas," Nathan said.

"What?" she asked.

"First, you could just join us. One of the gammas leads the pack runs for the college students. He'll probably never notice."

"What's the other idea?" she asked.

140

"We could go to the city. All the other wolves will be with their packs. We won't have to wait in line for anything."

"We won't get to run with the pack," Luca pouted.

"We run three days a week," Nathan argued.

"Guys, just go without me."

"No," Liam said. "Nathan's right. It's Saturday night. We haven't once gone downtown since we've been here. Now is the perfect night."

"I don't want you to get in trouble," she argued.

"We won't," Walter said. "Some of the other students won't be there either. They went home for the weekend."

"Where would we go?" she asked.

Nathan was already searching on his phone. "There's this place called 'Howl at the Moon'."

"That will either be dead or really crowded tonight," Liam said.

"We should probably consider what we wish to do," Walter said solemnly. "We don't need to eat and none of us are twenty-one, so we can't get into any human bars."

"We can go into college bars. Some of them are run by wolves," Nathan muttered, tapping on his phone.

"Can we dance?" Honey asked. Her mom had gushed about how much she enjoyed high school dances and she was always dancing around the house. "I've never been to a dance place."

Nathan looked over his phone with a grin. "Can we dance? Do you want pop or country?"

"Not country. Please not country," Luca whined.

"What's wrong with country?" Her dad had liked country. It wasn't bad.

141

"He doesn't like line dancing," Walter said.

"Line dancing?"

"Like this," Walter said, tapping his phone to start a song, then putting it on the table as he stood. "This classic is called Cotton-Eyed Joe."

"What does cotton-eyed mean?"

"No one knows," he said mysteriously. "Now imagine there's a whole line of people standing next to me all doing the same moves I am."

He tapped his heel on the floor, then his toe, then slapped his ankle, took a few steps, and spun around.

"Then you just repeat."

"And repeat and repeat and repeat," Luca moaned.

"You don't have to dance with me. Come on, Honey, try it." Walter waved at the floor beside him. "Yes, yes that's it," he cheered after she managed to do it correctly one time. "Now you can add things to make it fancy."

"It's still not fancy," Luca said flatly. "It will never be fancy."

"How about this place," Liam said, showing his phone to Nathan. "They have dancing."

"No alcohol!" Walter slapped the phone away. "We are responsible college students."

"We can't feel it anyway," Liam argued. "I don't know why anyone drinks it."

"Taste man, taste. There's nothing like a good, thick lager." Nathan sighed longingly.

"Do you even know what that is?" Walter scoffed.

Luca inspected Liam's phone. "That place features local bands. I think we should go to a place with a DJ so at least the music will be good."

Liam pulled his phone to his chest. "I didn't realize you were such a music snob Luca."

"I'm not, I just think Honey's first dancing experience should be as good as possible."

"Here. We'll go here," Nathan said, flashing his phone around too fast for anyone to properly see it. "I'll drive."

"You don't have a car. We will take mine," Walter said grandly. "I have room for five people."

"And at least a dozen clowns," Luca told Honey out of the side of his mouth. "It's his grandma's old car. The thing's a boat. He drives like his grandma too."

"Better to go a little slower and get there in one piece than go fast and get smeared all over the blacktop," Walter stated.

"You're a wolf. You'd heal in like, a day," Luca said.

The guys were great, but not always the fastest at making decisions. Honey wrapped her arms around one of Walter's. "I'd rather not have to heal. Thank you for offering Walter. I'd love to take a ride with you."

Walter patted her arm. "The lady has spoken. Let us be off."

After a very leisurely ride into the city – the guys hadn't been kidding about Walter's driving – Nathan directed them to a much nicer part of town than she'd seen when she was there before school. He refused to tell them exactly where they were going until they were right in front of the door. It was loud, gaudy, and definitely not for families with children, but the place served wolves and the wolf bouncer let them in.

Honey's first impression was of dark wood floors and an open space mostly free of bodies but it was hard to tell anything with the flashing blue and red lights.

"These lights are going to give me a seizure," Luca complained before she could.

"Then we'll sit where it's darker," Nathan said, "Come on."

They walked around a decent-sized dance floor, past a long bar where a smattering of people sat drinking, wound their way past several tables, and finally reached a booth in the back corner.

"This is perfect," Nathan proclaimed while sliding into the sticky booth. "We can see the dance floor and we have easy access to the bar."

"Maybe for you," Luca scoffed. "I don't want to watch the floor. I want to be on it. Come on, Honey."

"I thought you didn't like dancing," she said as he snagged her hand and dragged her toward the floor.

"I like *real* dancing, not that stuff Walter calls dancing."

He truly was a dancer. He knew all the moves she'd ever seen and some no one had ever seen before. Walter joined them and started doing a passable robot. Liam was a swayer. He shifted from one foot to the other, occasionally matching the beat, while cheering on Luca. Nathan was – she saw him gulp down a bottle of something before he joined them. Grinning, he started waving moving his arms up and down in front of him and rocking from side to side. He looked very loose. A couple of human girls danced and giggled their way closer, so Honey invited them to join in.

144

Mom was right. Dancing was a blast. Then her mom's favorite song came on and grief settled on her shoulders like a lead blanket. She didn't want to disturb the guys – Nathan was flirting with two of the girls and Luca was having a dance off with another one – so she mumbled an excuse about water and turned to the bar.

"Hey, you all right?" Liam asked by her arm just as she stepped off the floor.

"Yeah. It's my mom's song." Saying it totally broke her. Liam pulled her to his chest and put his head on top of hers as she sobbed.

"Hey, it's all right Honey. Let it out. It's a good song. Did you and your mom dance to this one?"

She nodded. She wanted to tell him that they didn't just dance. If the song came on, they stopped everything and danced and sang, but words weren't possible right then.

He grabbed a handful of tiny napkins and passed them to her.

"Thank you." It came out as a whisper, but he heard her.

"Here, sit down for a moment." He pressed her toward one of the bar stools in front of the bar. They were near the end so there wasn't anyone else close by. She slid onto one of the stools and took a sip of water the bartender put in front of her without her even asking.

Liam glanced around and leaned forward on his own stool. "Honey, can I ask you something?"

He looked very serious.

"You already did."

He rolled his eyes. "I'll take that as a yes. Honey, how old are you, truly? And don't tell me you're a minor, I already know."

"Why?" She hadn't told Lynn initially because she wanted to keep her job options open, but once she started making friends, she'd kept it a secret because she wanted to keep her friends. She'd seen enough movies to know that college students didn't hang out with kids four years younger than themselves, not willingly.

"You remind me of my little sister in some ways."

She took a slow sip of water to give herself time to think. "What if I'm really young, like twelve? Would you stop hanging out with me?"

"Of course not. I want to know because, well, I feel protective toward you but I don't want to overstep any bounds. If you were seventeen, for example, I'd be less inclined to step in if a guy was flirting with you than if you were twelve. Are you really twelve?"

"No." She felt bad about keeping so many secrets. She wanted to tell her friends everything but she'd only known them a month. Liam was the least likely to blurt something out on accident and she knew he was a great guy. He'd sacrificed his shirt to help her when she was injured, then had gone out of his way to make sure she had everything she needed so she wouldn't go wild again for lack of food. Although all the guys were great, of her four Little friends, she felt closest to him. She glanced toward the others who were still doing their things on the floor. "Promise you won't tell anyone, not even the other guys?"

"Why don't you want them to know?"

"You are my closest friends. You treat me like one of you. If the other guys or the witches find out how young I am, I don't think they would treat me the same. Also, I doubt they could all keep it to themselves."

"I think you're mistaken about point A, but point B, you might be right. I promise I won't tell anyone Honey, unless it's an emergency."

She crossed her arms and gave him her mom's best no shenanigans stare. "There is no emergency that would require you to divulge this, so promise properly or I'm not telling."

He glared back at her for a moment, but finally caved. "Fine. I promise. Now, spill."

She looked around one last time to make sure there was no one in hearing range, then leaned forward and whispered in his ear. "I'm fourteen."

He didn't even look surprised. Instead, a huge grin spilled across his face. "Really? Wow. That's amazing, and you got a perfect score on your SAT? You're a genuine child prodigy."

"Shh." She waved her hand at him to get him to quiet down. He had whispered, but it was a loud whisper.

"Calm down, nobody heard me."

"Well, they wouldn't tell you if they had, now, would they?"

He laughed. "You've definitely got the angry woman stare down."

She glared harder. He leaned forward and kissed her on the forehead, then put his head against hers. "Your secret is safe with me. Your mom would be very proud of you. Go wash up. I can smell your tears. I don't want the guys thinking I made you cry."

"Thanks Liam," she whispered. She considered kissing his cheek for a moment, but she'd never kissed anyone except her parents and it seemed weird.

The bathroom did not have a pleasant smell. She quickly washed her face, then stepped back out into the slightly better smelling dance club.

A tall wolf with brown hair and hazel eyes stepped in front of her. "Hey babe. I've been waiting for you." She could smell ethanol on his breath, and something else too, something magical, but not a good magical. She glanced up at his face. He was youngish, maybe early twenties, and not bad looking, but his eyes were glassy, and he hadn't bathed in a while.

"Why?"

He blinked. "What?"

"Why are you waiting for me?"

His confused look turned into one that reminded her of the thief in the Disney show where the princess had really long hair. "Because you're beautiful and you deserve a wolf like me."

"Old and smelly?"

His face morphed into something less than pleasant. "Who are you calling smelly when you smell like," he sniffed at her. "Tacos and," he took another long sniff, "old car."

The bottle he held passed under her nose as he leaned forward. Whatever he was drinking smelled like the bad magic too. "What are you drinking?"

148

He held it up so she could see it in the flashing lights. It looked like a beer, but there was a cutout of a wolf on the label and a blue drink inside. "Blue Wolf. Want some?" He offered her the bottle.

She took it and sniffed the top. There was definitely a spell of some kind, but not one she recognized. It was a mix of metal and blood and despair.

"You're supposed to drink it, not sniff it."

"What does it smell like to you?" She offered his bottle back to him.

He sniffed it. "Good times." He threw back his head and drank half of what was left in one sip.

She walked away while he was drinking. He was giving off a strange vibe, and she had a feeling he was one of those guys her mom had warned her about.

"Hey."

The man's fingers wrapped around her elbow at the same time Liam caught her eye. She jerked her elbow away and spun around to face her tormentor.

"It's rude to walk away," Blue Wolf guy said.

"I thought we were done."

"Honey, is there a problem?" Liam asked behind her.

"You're with him?" Blue Wolf guy scoffed. "He's just a boy." He thumped his chest. "I'm a man."

Honey stepped back so that she was closer to Liam. "I like him better though. I'm going to dance with my friends now. Goodbye."

She grabbed Liam's hand and dragged him away, but kept her senses attuned in case the guy followed them. The other boys met her and Liam half-way across the

149

dance floor and immediately put themselves between her and Blue Wolf guy.

"You all right Honey?" Nathan asked.

She squeezed Liam's hand to thank him for his help and released it. "Yeah. I think that guy just had too much to drink."

"What was he drinking?" Nathan asked.

"Blue Wolf."

"Really? I'd heard that wolves could get more than a buzz with that stuff, but I've drunk two and I barely feel anything."

She sniffed the air. She could smell the ethanol on his breath, but not the magic.

"Be glad you aren't feeling it, Nathan. Whatever was in his drink smelled like bad magic."

"Magic to do what," Liam asked.

"I'm not sure. I haven't smelled it before. It smelled like blood, sweat, and despair."

"A spell to cause pain or mental anguish?" Liam guessed.

They had discovered while hanging out with the witches that the boys could tell that magic was being used but not what kind like she could. Liam had a hypothesis, based on her descriptions, that the spells didn't actually smell like she thought they did, but something she was sensing made her brain automatically associate them with a scent that indicated their purpose. It didn't explain why she associated lemons with telekinesis though.

"Maybe we should go," Walter said behind her.

"Are you kidding?" Luca said. "I just got warmed up."

"Is that what you were doing?" Walter teased.

Honey looked around the room. Blue Wolf guy was talking to a girl near the bar. "I think he's moved on. Let's stay a while longer since we're here. Nathan, do you have any of that drink left? I want to see if I can smell the spell in your bottle."

She couldn't smell the spell in any of their drinks. She went back to dancing, although she kept an eye on Blue Wolf guy. He wandered all over the place talking to girls, but none of the conversations lasted long. She felt kind of sorry for him.

"We better go," Walter said, looking at his watch. "It's almost midnight."

"What are you, Cinderella?" Luca snorted.

"No, I'm a responsible adult and it's dangerous to drive when you're tired."

Honey was enjoying herself, but her feet had started hurting and she had the beginning of a headache from the loud music. "He's the one with the car, so he gets to decide," she declared.

"The lady has spoken. Come," Walter offered her his arm, "I will escort you to my chariot."

She wrapped her arm around his. She'd seen Pride and Prejudice. She knew what to do. "Thank you, kind sir."

She took the middle back again on the way home because she was the smallest and fell asleep on Liam's shoulder. Luca fell asleep on her arm. Walter, thankfully, stayed awake. She could have easily slept in the car all night if Liam hadn't poked her and Luca awake just as Walter pulled into the parking lot. She climbed out after

Luca and stretched. It was starting to get cool at night. She shivered after the warmth of the car.

"Where have you been!?"

The streetlight was behind the owner of the angry voice and she'd just woke up, so it took her a moment to identify who was in front of her.

"Brayton?"

He stepped close enough that she could have hugged him if she wanted, which she in no way did. "Yes, Brayton. Future alpha of your pack. Leader of the run tonight. Where were you?"

"We were dancing."

"Where? In Alaska?"

That was a strange thing to ask. "Alaska? Why would we go to Alaska?"

"Ergh!" he growled and wiped his hand down his face. "Why are you so difficult?"

"Why are you always so angry?"

He threw his hands in the air. "Maybe because I've been calling you for the last four hours and you never bothered to respond."

"Oh, I'm sorry. I think I left my phone in the boys' room. What did you need?"

He stared at her like she'd asked him what her name was.

"Other than the fact you were supposed to run with the pack tonight," he said in a strangely calm voice, "you don't need a phone to respond to me."

"I don't?"

"He's talking about telepathy, Honey," Liam provided.

152

"Oh." Because that made sense, not. "I didn't know you were telepathic."

Brayton closed his eyes and started rubbing his forehead with his fingers like he had a headache. Nathan was covering his mouth with his hand like he was laughing for some reason.

"Does telepathy give you a headache?"

Walter snorted. Luca and Nathan bust out laughing. Were they laughing at her?

"What? Gu-uys!"

"Honey, all wolves are telepathic," Liam explained.

"They are?"

"Yes. All the people in a pack can talk to each other when they are in wolf form and you can hear the ones in wolf form when you are in human form."

"Oh. I didn't know."

"Did you hear Brayton talking to you while we were dancing?"

"No."

"You didn't?" Brayton asked, looking through his fingers at her.

"No."

The boys looked at each other and then at her. The Little boys looked confused. Brayton looked doubtful. "Didn't your parents ever talk to you by telepathy?" Liam asked.

"No."

"What about the last moon when you were in wolf form. Did you hear anything during that run?" Brayton asked.

"No. Did you say something?"

153

"I told you to go with Cici's group."

"Oh. Nope. Definitely didn't hear that."

The boys had stopped laughing. "Maybe she's not really part of your pack," Luca suggested.

Brayton leaned forward and sniffed the air around her. "She is. I can smell the mark on her."

"Hmm. Maybe being without a pack for so long has made her telepathically impaired," Liam said, "or maybe she's always been that way. That would explain why her parents never talked to her and why she didn't know about the telepathy. They may not have told her because they didn't want to upset her."

Brayton shook his head. "Ridiculous. All wolves are telepathic. She's lying."

Liam stepped forward far enough that she could have slid behind him if she wanted to. "We can all smell she's not."

"Let's test it then. Honey, transform." Brayton reached up and started to pull off his shirt.

"Here?" she squeaked. "We aren't allowed."

"In the dorm then."

"It's past midnight. We aren't allowed in each other's dorms past midnight."

Brayton growled and pulled his shirt back down. "Tomorrow then. One o'clock. Come to my suite."

Did she want to be alone with Brayton in his suite, no, but she didn't want him to think she was a liar either. "Okay."

# 19

## *Honey*

The second floor of the boy's dorm looked a lot like the third floor, but it didn't feel the same. She'd visited the third floor so much since meeting the guys that all the other boys on the floor knew who she was and would wave or say hello. A lot of them were in the Little pack, so perhaps that's why they were so friendly. Most of the boys she saw on the second floor when she walked down the hall towards Brayton's suite were from her own pack, but instead of smiling or waving, they stared at her, then whispered behind their hands as she passed.

Why they bothered whispering, she didn't know. They knew she could hear them and mostly they just asked what she was doing there. Stupidly, they didn't ask the one person who knew – her.

Four familiar boys were waiting for her by Brayton's door.

"What are you guys doing here?" she asked.

"You don't think we'd let you face that guy by yourself after all the times he's hurt you, do you?" Liam asked, smiling down at her.

Her heart swelled with love for every single one of them and she threw out her arms and hugged them all at once. "You guys are the best."

"We know," Nathan said after he'd untangled himself from Luca and Liam after her epic hug. "Shall I knock or do you wish to do the honors?"

"I can handle a door."

She knocked and knocked again and then again. No one answered and none of Brayton's neighbors had seen him. The boys took it as more proof of Brayton's bullishness but it surprised her that he wasn't there. He might be a bully, but from what she'd seen when she lived with his family, he wasn't irresponsible.

Monday morning, instead of jogging around the WOLF field in human form, everyone changed and jogged around in wolf form. The whole practice was in wolf form, but thankfully, Captain Young stayed in human form to yell out commands and he didn't separate people by pack. He even made them do the obstacle course in wolf form. They were all covered in mud by the time they were through.

Brayton was there, but she only saw him briefly before they were ordered to the tents to wolf out. He had dark shadows under his eyes that made her wonder if something had happened to someone in his family. Maybe that's why he hadn't been in his room yesterday. She purposely placed herself behind the more talkative members of her pack when they walked back to the dorms, but she didn't catch any whispers of disaster.

Brayton looked even worse on Wednesday. Captain Young pulled him aside after he came in well behind where he usually did when they ran. Brayton looked like he was going to puke. From the Captain's body language, Honey gathered he was concerned for Brayton rather than upset. Later, in the cafeteria, Brayton pushed away the full plate that Rhys slid in front of him and instead, rested his head on his hands which were supported by his elbows on the table. His friends all wore matching looks of concern, even Malcolm. The only thing he ate the entire meal was a piece of bread that Cici forced on him.

"What are you looking at Honey?" Nathan asked from across the table.

"Brayton. He looks sick."

Esme glanced over his shoulder. "I didn't think wolves got sick."

"They can, but it's rare."

"Isn't he the one who pulled your hair that one day?" Sabine asked.

"Yeah."

She focused back on her meal. "He had it coming then."

Honey might not like Brayton very much, but that didn't mean she wished him ill. Her mom had once healed a human girl's arm after she fell from a tree, even though the girl was climbing the tree to get at Honey. Her Mom explained later that she did it because healing was a gift from God and He'd made sure she was there to help. Honey didn't have the healing power her mom did, but she did have the ability to see inside, kind of. Maybe she was meant to help him.

She kept an eye on Brayton's table while she quickly finished her own meal. As soon as Brayton and Rhys and

Malcolm got up to leave, Cici had left earlier, she excused herself and followed them outside.

"Brayton."

"What?" He turned toward her and looked so tired and ill that she considered offering her shoulder for him to lean on.

"What's wrong?"

He turned away from her. "Go away Honey. I don't want to talk to you right now."

"My mom was a healer. I might be able to help."

"I've already seen a doctor. They were useless."

"She wasn't that kind of healer. She used...alternative medicine." She hadn't quite figured out how she could help him without revealing her magic, but she had a sudden idea. "Like massage."

"I don't think that will help."

Rhys elbowed him. "It can't hurt. Why not let her try?"

Brayton grimaced and rubbed his forehead again. Malcolm shot him a worried glance.

"Brayton, go back to your suite. I need to get a few supplies. I'll be there as soon as I can," she ordered.

He didn't say no, so she hurried to her own dorm. She knew something about herbs and incense thanks to her mom's business and she knew exactly what to use both to hide the scent of her magic and to help Brayton relax. She just had to find some. Thankfully Gloria, a witch with an amazing green thumb and a room full of plants, had exactly what she needed.

The second-floor hallway in the boy's dorm was crowded with wolves returning from supper and getting ready for various evening activities. They fell quiet and eyed her as she passed, but not a single one of them said hi. Not for the first time, she wondered how she had ended up in the most unfriendly pack of all.

It felt like every eye was on her when she knocked on the door. Why was she risking discovery for someone who hated her? This was a mistake. She turned to leave but Rhys opened the door and actually looked happy to see her.

"Come on in."

She figured she'd have to argue with Brayton more, but he didn't even look up from where he was sitting on the couch, holding his head. He must really be hurting. She sent up a silent request that she'd be able to help him.

From her backpack, she pulled out the small electric hot plate Gloria had loaned her and set it on the coffee table in front of Brayton. Then she went into their kitchen and filled the small pot Gloria had also loaned her with hot water and sprinkled in the herbs. Malcolm watched her closely like he expected her to poison Brayton. Rhys, on the other hand, had the hot plate plugged in when she returned to the living room. She didn't see Cici.

"These herbs will help you relax," Honey said, setting the pot on the hot plate. She could almost feel the pain radiating off Brayton. Something was seriously wrong. The only things she knew of that could make a wolf really sick were rabies and cancer, and she wasn't positive about the cancer.

She touched his shoulder gently. "Where does it hurt the worst?"

He rubbed his forehead.

"Can you sit on the floor? That way I can sit behind you on the couch."

He moved without saying a word. She wanted to hug him, he was in so much pain. Instead, she slipped behind him, put her fingers on his forehead, and started rubbing.

She had never given someone a head rub before, but she'd had headaches. She imagined what it felt like and rubbed the way she would have liked. Meanwhile, she shut her eyes and saw/felt inside Brayton's head with her magic.

The molecules she always imagined when she was freezing someone were all moving the same speed, but some of them were moving in odd directions. Most of them were near the front of his head where he said the pain was, so she focused on them. Maybe if she redirected them, it would help.

Freezing a molecule and then thawing it didn't work – it kept going the wrong way. Maybe if she just applied an opposite force? It took her a few tries, but eventually, she did get one to turn.

She couldn't actually see molecules, else she might have been there for years turning each one. Instead, she only saw about twenty oddly spinning blobs. Fixing them all took her about an hour.

She felt like she'd run a couple of marathons when she finally took her hands off Brayton's temples. Her hands were shaking. She quickly pressed them against the top of her legs so no one would notice.

"Does that feel any better?"

Brayton tipped over onto her thigh.

"Oh my gosh, Brayton!" Had she killed him?

160

Rhys dived in from the side and checked Brayton's pulse, then relaxed. He looked up at her with an approving smile. "I think he's asleep. He hasn't been able to sleep for days. This is good."

"Oh, good."

"What kind of herbs did you use," Malcolm asked, sniffing over the pot, "It smells like magic."

"Common ones, but I did get them and the hot plate from one of the witches in my dorm, so you might be smelling her magic. She may have used magic to grow the herbs." There, that should keep them from realizing it was her magic.

"You used magic herbs on Brayton!?"

"It wasn't like I had time to run to the store," she snapped at him. "Besides, the herbs aren't magic, they were just grown with magic. They won't hurt him."

"How do you know?"

"I have witches for friends."

It had been too long since she flexed her magic muscle. She had to get out of there before she passed out on their couch. She nodded to Brayton who was snoring on her thigh. "You guys want to take him to his bed? I think he'd be more comfortable. *I* would be more comfortable."

Rhys laughed. "Sure. Come on, Malcolm. Let's carry sleeping beauty to his room."

Would it really matter if she just laid down for a while? No. No. She had to get out of there. She reached for the hot plate and burned her finger. Stupid. She didn't have time to wait for it or the pot to cool though and she didn't want to leave Gloria's things with the bullies. She calmed the molecules in the pot and the plate, essentially forcing them to cool, froze the water in the pot, and tossed both into her backpack. Since it wasn't alive, the water should stay frozen long enough to get back to her dorm.

She made herself stand and tugged the backpack over her shoulder. Her legs felt wobbly. Was this the way Mom had felt that one time they'd witnessed a nearly fatal car accident and her mom had partially healed the whole family before the human ambulance came? Mom's hands had been shaking when she got back behind the wheel and she'd slept for nearly twenty-four hours afterward, but she'd drove them both safely home first.

If Mom could do it, she could too.

Step by slow step she stumbled toward the door. Behind her, Rhys and Malcolm were arguing over whether they should take off Brayton's clothes or just his shoes. Honey reached for the doorknob but it disappeared from beneath her fingers, making her stumble forward into Cici. Cici looked as surprised to see Honey as Honey was to see her.

"What are you doing here and what is that awful smell?" She waved her hand under her nose as if the herbs smelled bad. They didn't.

"I was…helping…Brayton." Honey's mind was starting to go all fuzzy. "I…must…go."

To her relief, Cici stepped out of the way. Honey didn't remember going back down the hallway or walking back to her dorm, but she must have because the next morning she woke up in her bed, still fully clothed. She had even removed the pot of ice from her backpack before she went to sleep. Yay her!

# 20

## *Honey*

She didn't see Brayton at all on Thursday, which wasn't surprising because she rarely saw him on Tuesdays or Thursdays, but she couldn't help worrying. Had she put him in an everlasting sleep, or worse, had she killed him? She was so relieved when Brayton showed up to WOLF Friday morning looking much, much better, she nearly went over to talk to him. She quickly talked herself out of it since talking with Brayton could lead to nothing good, and instead headed for the tent to 'change'.

"Honey, wait!"

She turned around and found herself engulfed in a pair of strong arms and the heady scent of Brayton's body spray. "Thank you," he said, then whispered into her ear. "I know those herbs were magical, but I'm glad you used them on me. Make sure the next person knows what they are though, okay? I don't want you to get in trouble."

There was something both nice and disturbing about Brayton's hug. She stepped back out of his arms, then realized what he'd said. He thought the herbs were magical, not her. That was good, but, "You're not going to tell me not to use them?"

"Honey, I think you saved my life. I couldn't sleep, I couldn't eat, I don't know how much longer I could have gone on. If you see someone else in that much pain, help them, just tell them what you're doing."

"Um, okay."

He chuckled. "Go change. Oh." His face took on a look of concern. "We were going to see if you could hear me, weren't we? I completely forgot until now. Come meet me at the bleachers after you've transformed and we'll run together."

Did she want to run with him? No, but she might as well get it over with. Besides, she'd told the boys to start without her. She'd wanted to see Brayton in his human form to make sure he was looking better if he showed up.

Other than Cici prodding Honey in the shoulder with her nose occasionally, running with Brayton and his bully squad wasn't awful. She had no idea if he tried to talk to her using telepathy. She didn't hear a thing. After they finished the warm-up laps, she joined her friends for the rest of practice.

Honey had solved the problem of changing in the tent by draping a sheet over one end of the long tables and pretending she was extremely shy. Most people laughed, then ignored her, so it startled her to find Cici waiting when she crawled out of her little changing area after practice.

"What are you doing?"

"Changing."

"You know, we're all girls here. You don't have anything the rest of us haven't seen." She shook her head. "Brayton wants to speak with you."

Honey stuffed her sheet into a duffel bag she'd found at a thrift store a few weeks ago and followed Cici to the bleachers where Brayton was waiting by the entrance.

"Did you hear anything?"

"No?"

"Not even when Cici poked you?"

"No. What did you say?"

"He called you…" Malcolm started.

"It's not important," Brayton interrupted. "I'm going to ask Mom about this. Maybe she knows a doctor who could help."

"No! That's okay. It's not a problem." She didn't know if a doctor could tell she was half witch but she didn't want to find out.

"Honey, it is a problem. You're basically deaf as a wolf," Brayton argued. "You can't hear or respond to the commands."

"I can hear just fine. You just have to give the commands in a different way, that's all. Don't human commandos use sign language when they're on missions where they have to be silent? Maybe we could communicate like that."

"With wolf paws?" Brayton scoffed.

"Sure." She made a mental note to look up commando commands.

Brayton didn't listen, surprise, surprise. Later that day, Luna Lynn sent a text informing Honey that she had a doctor's appointment for next Friday and that she'd be there to pick up Honey herself. Unfortunately, the time didn't interfere with any of Honey's classes which meant she didn't have a good excuse to turn Lynn down.

The next Friday, Luna Lynn picked her up outside of her dorm. Lynn was in another SUV, but instead of a huge gas-guzzler, hers was a smaller hybrid.

The doctor's office was a short drive away in what looked like a private home in the front. The back yard, though, had been converted to a small parking lot. There wasn't a sign out front, but perhaps that was to prevent humans from going to it accidentally because inside, Honey could only smell wolves. Two pregnant women were in the small lobby: one with a huge belly, and one with a belly just big enough to notice. The slightly pregnant woman had a child of about five with her.

Honey didn't know much about doctors, having never been to one, but she knew they specialized. She thought at first the doctor was for women and children, but while she and Luna were in the waiting room, a large man wearing a flannel shirt came in holding an arm that was clearly and disturbingly broken. Bones were sticking out. She was not upset that he got to see the doctor before her.

Just when she thought she'd be able to talk Luna into leaving so she could make her next class, a woman called out Honey's name. The woman took her height and weight and age, which Lynn supplied, so much for that secret, then left her in a room with Lynn. They were having a nice discussion about her classes when a tall, slim male wolf with curly graying hair, as much inside his ears as out, came into the room.

"Honey Smith, fourteen, healthy female." He peered over his glasses. "Is that you?"

"Yes."

"And you can't hear or send telepathy?"

"I guess not."

"You guess not?"

"I didn't even know wolves could do that until last week."

He grunted and wrote something on his chart, then peered at her over his glasses again. "How long have you had your wolf?"

"Umm." She'd changed the first time at six. Most wolves did it at twelve. Was it safe to tell him?

"Recently?" he asked.

"No."

"Within the last year?"

"No."

"Mm-hm." He wrote something else on his chart.

"All right, we'll do a wave response test. Change into you wolf form, Miss Honey. The nurse will be by shortly to take you to the testing room."

The doctor left but Lynn didn't. She was busy tapping on her phone.

"Umm, can I have some privacy please?"

She waved her off. "Oh, don't mind me dear. We're both girls."

"Please?"

Lynn shook her head, but she put down her phone. "You are a shy one. Okay. I'll be right outside the door."

168

Honey hid behind the examination table and transformed quickly in case Lynn changed her mind and decided to barge in. She didn't. A woman, a nurse Honey guessed, came by and escorted her to a room full of different odd-looking pieces of equipment. The nurse picked up a bowl-like helmet with large holes for her ears and wires attached everywhere else and put it on Honey's head. Next, the nurse plugged the cord coming off the helmet into a computer and started tapping the keys. Honey desperately wanted to ask questions, but it was impossible in wolf form. After several minutes of tapping and a couple of adjustments to the helmet, the nurse took the helmet off and escorted Honey back to the room.

She was nearly out the door when she stopped and looked back at Honey. "You can change back now."

Honey looked at Lynn. Lynn rolled her eyes. "I'll be right outside."

Five minutes later, the doctor came back.

"Well?" Lynn demanded after he'd studied his clipboard for several minutes.

"She can't do telepathy."

"We knew that. Can you fix it?"

"No. She's missing that part of her brain."

Ouch.

"What do you mean she's missing it?" Lynn demanded.

"What she said," Honey added.

The doctor glanced over his glasses at Honey. "Exactly what I said. Now I don't mean there's a hole there. There's brain tissue there, but whatever it's doing is not telepathy."

At least there was something there. That was reassuring.

"How can you tell?" Lynn asked.

"The wave response scanner sends out telepathic waves and monitors for a response. Honey's brain didn't respond at all. Dead as a doornail."

"My brain is not dead!"

"Clearly, or we wouldn't be having this conversation," the doctor agreed with a little quirky smile.

Honey wasn't sure she liked this doctor.

"Now don't be upset," the doctor said when Luna opened her mouth again. "This is rare, but it does happen occasionally. Generally, the child is gifted in other ways." He looked at his chart again. "This says you are a freshman in college already?"

"Yes."

"There you go. No telepathy, but very smart. Every wolf has different skills. She may not be good at patrolling, but with her mind, I'm sure there are many other roles she can fill in the pack."

Luna stared at him for a moment, then started collecting her things. "Well, that was…thank you for your time doctor. I've got to get her back to class so she can use that part of her brain that isn't doing telepathy."

"Of course," he stuck out his hand. "It was nice meeting you Honey."

He winked at her. Why would he wink at her after he told her a piece of her brain was missing? Doctors were weird. No wonder her mom had never taken her to a doctor, well that and she was a magical healer.

170

Lynn didn't say anything else until they'd climbed into the SUV and shut the doors. Then she turned to Honey and covered her hand with her own.

"I'm sorry Honey."

"For what?" Honey tried to sound nonchalant, but she knew what Lynn was about to say. Despite the way the other people in the Mooney pack treated her, she liked being part of a pack.

"I don't think there's anything we can do. Despite his, mmm, oddness, Doctor Ziga is the best wolf doctor in the state."

Okay, that wasn't what she thought Lynn was going to say.

"It's fine."

"Honey, it's not fine. You can't communicate as a wolf. You won't be able to go on patrols or coordinated runs or even hear your friends."

Honey flipped her hand over so she could grab Lynn's and gave it a squeeze. "Luna, until a few days ago, I didn't know wolves were telepathic. I didn't know I was missing anything. I'm disappointed I won't get to try it out, but I can live without it. I have my whole life. Besides, like the doctor said, I still have something there and it's doing something, just not what it normally does. I like my brain and the way it works. I wouldn't want it any other way."

Lynn gave Honey a doubtful look. "Really?"

"Really."

Lynn squeezed Honey's hand, then released it to start the SUV.

Honey had to ask, just to be sure. "Am I still part of your pack?"

"Oh, Honey!" Lynn leaned over and pulled her into a rather awkward hug. "Of course you are. Pack is family. We take care of one another no matter how young or old or injured someone might be." Lynn released her and patted her cheek. "Okay."

The shine in her eyes made Honey's eyes tear up too. "Okay."

# 21

## Brayton

"Mom, it's hamburger night, why would you get a salad?"

"Because I like salads."

"You do not."

Brayton had felt sorry for the students he'd seen in the cafeteria with parents in tow, but oddly, he didn't mind that his mom was visiting. He held up two fingers to the guy at the grill and a minute later, two burgers slid over the counter.

"You're eating two of those things?" Mom mock scolded.

"No. One is for you."

Mom gave him that look, the one that said he'd amused her and she was proud of him at the same time. It made him feel good.

His mom stood by his side and scanned the rambunctious cafeteria while he paid for their meals. He figured she'd complain about how wild everyone was acting – it was really bad because it was a Friday – but she just gave a little sigh and said, "This reminds me of when I went to college. So much fun. I don't want to go back to those days, but I do miss them sometimes."

He nudged her with his elbow. "Come on, Mom. We can sit at my favorite table."

His pack had claimed the southeast section of the wolves' side of the cafeteria. Every wolf from the Mooney pack and a few from others called out a greeting while they walked through the tables. His mom had to be the most popular Luna out of all the packs.

The table he and his friends usually sat at was a bit beat-up, but it was in the perfect location. He had a view of the entire cafeteria. Mom waited for him to choose a seat, then set her tray beside his. Cici, Rhys, and Malcolm dropped into the other seats. Mom didn't. She was busy scanning the room.

"Mom, what are you looking for?"

"Where's Honey? Oh, there she is. I'll be right back."

"Mom…" He started to try and stop her but realized (a) she wouldn't listen to him and (b) she would eventually find out about Honey and the witches anyway. It was inevitable.

Far across the room, Honey smiled up at his mom and cheerfully introduced her friends. Mom did a good job pretending to be pleased to meet them. Other than a little frown right after she turned away, there was no sign she was upset as she made her way back across the cafeteria. He knew better though.

Mom slid into the seat next to him and calmly started stabbing her salad. Calm anger was the dangerous kind.

"What did the doctor say," Brayton asked in a low voice, trying to get her mind on something else. Also, he was curious.

Mom sighed. "Honey is telepathically impaired."

"Can it be fixed?"

She shook her head.

"Impaired?" Cici asked. "What does that mean?"

"It means she can neither send nor receive anything telepathically. Her brain doesn't respond to it at all."

"Wow," Cici said, "How did she take it?"

"Very well actually. I was more upset than she was. I don't think she realizes what she's missing." She looked at Brayton expectantly. "I'm surprised you didn't notice something was wrong the first time you went on a pack run."

He avoided her eyes by focusing on his burger. "It was her first run with us, so I wasn't expecting her to be perfect."

"What happened?" Mom asked. Darn it. Good thing his mouth was full.

"She got lost," Malcolm chimed in. Brayton glared at him.

"Lost? The grounds aren't that big."

"Not lost, lost," Cici quickly explained. "She just got separated from the pack. She was waiting when we returned."

"Playing with a kitten," Malcolm supplied.

"Where did she get a kitten?"

"It belonged to Captain Young's daughter," Malcolm said.

"And you didn't ask her why she didn't just ask for help?" Mom said.

"I did," Brayton ensured her, "But she didn't respond. I thought she was ignoring me."

"Why would she ignore you?"

"You know how some girls are divas? I thought she was like that."

"So, you just walked away?"

Mom knew him too well. Better she learned what happened from him than from someone else.

"No. I lost my temper."

"And?"

"I tried to swipe the kitten out of her hands to get her to pay attention and I ended up clawing her arm instead."

"Brayton!"

Amazing how one word can hold so much disappointment.

"What happened then?"

"Um, well, by the time I changed, one of her friends was already helping her, then they took her to the campus doctor."

"It was deep enough she had to go to the doctor?"

"Yeah."

"Which friend? Someone from our pack at least?"

"No. One of her male friends from pack Little."

"You mean those boys she's sitting with?"

"Yeah."

"Did anyone from our pack go with her?"

"I followed them," Cici said. "I made sure she got back to her dorm."

Mom put down her fork very deliberately and turned her piercing gaze on Brayton. He pretended he didn't notice. "You mean except for Cici, not a single person in our pack cared that the new girl, my ward, had gotten lost and was injured?"

"I don't think they knew," he supplied. "I'm sure they noticed the golf cart taking her away but there wasn't anything they could do by that point."

"No one noticed?! No one noticed that the new girl who hadn't run with the pack was getting chewed out by the future alpha? Baloney! The people in our pack notice everything." She leaned back and snapped at the table full of girls next to them. "Charlize, come here!"

Blond, always perfectly dressed and ready to head the next social function, Charlize immediately pushed away from her table and reported to theirs. "Yes, Luna Lynn, is something wrong?"

"No," Mom said sweetly, "I just wanted to have a chat with you for a moment. Your mother told me you had a first day of school party. How did that turn out?"

"Oh, wonderful!" Charlize beamed. "I think everyone showed up for at least a few minutes."

"Even Honey?"

Charlize glanced Honey's way and wrinkled her nose. "Well, I did invite her telepathically because I didn't know which dorm she was in, but she didn't respond. I didn't realize she'd been shunned at the time, so it worked out."

"Shunned? Who said Honey was shunned?"

Charlize's eyes grew wide and flicked to Malcolm, then back to his mom. "Oh, that's what everyone is saying."

Mom whipped around and nailed Malcolm with her steely gaze. "Malcolm did you tell everyone Honey was shunned?"

"Not everyone, no."

"Why, Malcolm?"

Mom's voice literally dripped with disappointment. A lesser alpha would let his beta take the fall. Brayton was better than that.

"It was my fault mom."

"Your fault?"

"I told him to tell everyone that."

"Why?" Now she sounded both disappointed and hurt. Ugh.

"Because she was playing volleyball with the witches and wouldn't listen when I told her to come over and talk."

"You told her by mouth or telepathy?"

"Neither. I jerked my head like this," he showed her. "Everyone in the pack knows that means they're supposed to come."

Mom closed her eyes and touched the spot between her eyebrows with two fingers. That meant she was either trying not to laugh or not to yell. He hoped she was leaning toward laughter, but he had a strong feeling it was the latter.

"Charlize," his mom said sweetly, turning her back on him, "Honey is not shunned. It's fine to talk with witches. It's fine to play volleyball with them. We have a bad history, but that doesn't mean it has to be that way forever. Spread the word, please, and the next time you have a party and invite Honey, don't use telepathy. She's telepathically impaired and can't hear you."

"Oh! I didn't know."

"Neither did she until today. Be nice to her. She's never been in a pack before. Show her what makes our pack so great."

Charlize beamed so brightly Brayton almost felt sorry for Honey. "Yes, Luna."

"Oh, and Charlize, also make sure everyone knows that Colm, Beta Andrew's son, is now in charge of all pack activities on campus. Brayton has shown that he is not yet mature enough to take on the role."

Charlize's eyes almost popped out of her head at that juicy piece of news. "Yes, Ma'am."

"Mom."

His mom held up her pointer finger. That meant be quiet, but his reputation was on the line. He had to get her to change her mind before Charlize spread the word and everything was ruined.

"Mom."

She turned to him and he cringed. Her eyes were blazing.

"I have never been so disappointed in you in my life, Brayton Maxwell Mooney." Her voice was low enough that the noise in the rest of the cafeteria likely kept the next table from hearing her, he hoped anyway. "You don't shun someone just because they won't talk to you, especially not a little girl who's just joined a pack for the first time in her life and hasn't had a chance to make friends yet. Being shunned can follow someone the rest of their life. Even if she leaves our pack and goes to another,

179

the fact that it happened could follow her and everyone in her new pack will wonder what she did and if she's worthy of joining their pack. Your petty vindictiveness could have very well ruined any hope she has of ever fitting into a pack."

"Mom, you're overreacting. She's just a rogue we picked up off the street. Being a rogue is worse than being shunned. Besides, she's not really pack – she's more like a visitor. She'll find a mate someday and move to a new pack and that will be it."

"So, in that interim, it's fine if she doesn't have a family or any support? Her parents are dead and she's on her own but who cares because she's a rogue and rogues as we all know, are bad people who made bad decisions and are getting exactly what they deserve."

Great, now she was on her soapbox.

"Mom, you know that's not what I meant."

"Then what did you mean?"

"I just meant she's a big girl. We can support her, but I don't think we can expect her to fully integrate into our pack as if she had been born into it."

"Not with that attitude."

"Mom, be reasonable."

"Besides, that's not the issue. I trusted you to watch over and care for Honey. You did the opposite." She pushed her tray away. She hadn't even touched her burger. "I need to get going."

"Mom, about Colm."

"Yes, I really meant it." She pulled out her phone and rapidly typed a text, then showed him her screen. "There, now your father and Colm know too."

"Mom, you can't do this." He'd been looking forward to leading the campus wolves his whole life. It was his chance to demonstrate his ability to lead something other than his high school rugby team. It was the first real pack job Dad had ever entrusted him with.

"I can and I did. Come to me after you've fixed what you've broken and we'll talk." She pushed back her chair and stood.

"I didn't break anything!" Oops. It came out louder than he intended. Every head in the vicinity turned their way.

"Really?" His mom leaned in, grabbed his chin, and forced his head towards Honey. Her whisper was harsh in his ear. "That sweet girl thinks everyone in our pack hates her and she doesn't know why." She moved his chin so he could see the tables around them. "Your pack thinks witches are evil and that it's okay to be prejudice against them. That is not okay, by the way. I don't know why you ever thought it was. And, they think rogues are beneath them and not worth speaking to," she forced his head back toward Honey, "even when they've done absolutely nothing wrong. How am I supposed to help the rogues when my own son sabotages my efforts?"

"Maybe you're not."

She let go of his chin and stood. "Maybe, but I'm going to keep trying because," she tapped her chest, "my heart tells me it's the right thing to do. Maybe it's time you start listening to yours."

He watched, stunned, while his mom walked away from him and back to Honey. Honey turned around with a smile when Mom tapped on her shoulder, but her smile quickly faltered when she looked up into his mom's face. With a loud squeal of her chair that caught the attention of everyone in the cafeteria, Honey stood and hugged his mom as if she were *her* mom instead of his. His mom hugged her right back.

"Man, it's a good thing she didn't find out about the broken ribs," Malcolm said.

"Shut up."

Mom left without saying goodbye.

Brayton forced his burger down while doing his best to ignore all the secret and not-so-secret glances his pack was sending him. The normal laughs and jeers of Friday subsided into whispers while Charlize spread word of his punishment and Honey's situation. Charlize even got up and walked over to squat beside Honey. Honey looked surprised, then confused, then turned his way and very clearly mouthed, 'but why?'

Charlize shrugged, but he knew why he'd shunned Honey – because she didn't belong. She wasn't part of his pack, and if he had his way she never would be. His heart told him so.

He shoved his tray into the middle of the table. "Let's get out of here."

"You're supposed to bus your own tray," Cici said.

"What?"

"Everyone is supposed to take their tray to the conveyor line over there so the people in the kitchen can do the dishes."

"Yeah, but..."

"This is college, not our pack. Here you have to clean up your own messes."

First Mom and now Cici?

She shoved his tray back at him. "I promise it won't hurt you, well, unless you fall onto the belt. Come on. It's only twenty feet away."

"The food is so expensive here, we shouldn't have to clear the table ourselves."

She leaned forward and said quietly. "Just do it. Show everyone that you aren't a spoiled alpha's son who expects everyone to cater to him while he smites innocent girls."

"They don't think that!"

She raised her eyebrows and sauntered off toward the belt with her tray.

"They don't." He said to Rhys when he stood with his own tray.

Rhys nodded toward the table. "Don't forget your mom's tray."

Brayton glanced at Malcolm. Malcolm stuffed the last of his burger in his mouth and shrugged before standing and picking up his own tray. "I agree with you, but Cici scares me."

Picking up both trays, but only because it would look weird if he left his after everyone else had taken theirs, he followed his so-called friends to the belt and then out the door.

As soon as they were clear of the building, Malcolm put his arms around Brayton and Rhys' shoulders. "What shall we do tonight?"

Brayton shoved his arm off. Malcolm was a good friend, but socially clueless sometimes. "I'm not really in the mood."

"Come on, it's Friday. I've been waiting for Friday all week. That girl I met last week said she'd bring some friends tonight."

"The one with all the black stuff around her eyes?"

"That's the one."

"She was scary."

Malcolm snorted. "Your mom takes away your powers and now you're scared of humans? That's just sad."

"I didn't mean I was scared of her. I meant she was crazy in a disturbing way."

"Uh-huh. She said she'd bring one for each of us, even you, Cici."

Cici didn't look back from where she was trudging ahead of them. "Malcolm, I don't want or need your help to find a date."

"We should go," Rhys said, surprising everyone. He never volunteered to go places, he just followed. "It will be more stimulating to discuss how to fix things in a bar than in our dorm."

"I don't know what I'm supposed to fix. Mom's already sicced Charlize on Honey and it's not like I was instructing the pack to hate witches and rogues."

"You could sit with Honey and meet some of her witch friends. That would encourage the rest of the pack to be friendlier to them," Cici shot over her shoulder.

"It's too obvious. Everyone would know why I was doing it."

"So?" Cici said. "You were wrong, Brayton. Man up. A good leader admits when he's wrong and addresses the problem. Besides, I thought you liked her. You hugged her this morning in front of everyone, then you called your mom to take her to the doctor."

"Clearly a mistake," he mumbled. He'd tried to do what was right and his mom had torn him down in front of the whole pack. He wanted to punch something, several times, hard. Not Honey though. He'd probably break her and his mom would never speak to him again. Honey's green eyes looked up at him imploringly in his head and for the umpteenth time he wished he'd never laid eyes on her.

"Yeah. Let's go out."

# 22

## *Honey*

"My roommates and a couple of other girls are going to The Hole tonight. Would you like to come, Honey?"

She was still reeling from the news that the pack had thought she was shunned and that's why no one had talked to her. She hadn't even known what shunned meant until Charlize explained it.

"Do you really want me to or are you just doing it because Luna Lynn told you to ask me?"

"I really want you to," Charlize said earnestly. "I would have talked to you long ago, but shunning is a serious thing. If you talk to someone who's shunned, you might be shunned too. I'm so glad you weren't really shunned."

Honey looked up, right into Liam's warm, concerned eyes. "Can I bring my friends?"

Charlize barely hesitated. "Sure. They cater to both wolves and witches."

"Do any of you want to go?"

"Yes," Nathan said enthusiastically. Liam, Luca, and Walter all nodded.

"We'll have to take a rain check," Blaze said. "We have a coven meeting tonight, but you go and have fun. I'm glad your pack has finally decided to act like a pack."

"It wasn't their fault."

Blaze elbowed her gently. "You are too sweet for you own good, Honey. See what I did there? Sweet, Honey?"

"Yeah, because no one else has done that, ever," Luca snorted.

"Good," Charlize said perkily, popping up from the crouch she'd been in the whole time she was talking to Honey, "We'll meet you all at 7 in front of my dorm. It's easier to walk than to try and find parking."

Ten girls and a couple of guys were waiting when Honey and her friends arrived at the dorm. She didn't really expect the people from the Mooney pack to suddenly accept her, but they surrounded her and the guys and truly seemed interested in getting to know them, especially Nathan. He lapped up the attention.

Several groups of students entered The Hole ahead of them as they approached. Honey was afraid it was going to be too crowded, but it turned out to be very spacious inside. The main room in the front had a live band and a dance floor and tables spread all around the edges of the room. Most of them were already taken. Charlize took the lead and led everyone past the dance floor, past the bar, to a smaller area in the back with three pool tables, another bar, and a jukebox.

She pulled out a chair and indicated Honey should sit. "I know we're a little far from the action, but it's not so crowded here and there's better service."

187

"Once that band starts playing, I'm all about the action," Luca declared.

"Please, no," Walter groaned.

"I think it's a country band tonight," one of the girls commented.

Luca deflated while Walter brightened. "Really? This will be great. I can teach you to line dance Honey."

"Ooo, you like to line dance?" Several of the girls suddenly found Walter much more interesting.

"I can two-step too."

And with those magic words, Walter became the most popular guy at the table.

"I didn't know your pack was so much into country," Liam commented.

"I didn't either," Honey admitted.

"You didn't know Seth Logan was from our pack?" Charlize asked from her other side.

"Who?"

"Seth Logan. He's a famous country singer. He's got several songs near the top of the charts. He played in this bar before he became famous."

"Oh."

"Yeah, we've had several wolves from our pack become famous." She started listing them all and why they were great. Honey was impressed.

The music started. The girl had been right, it was country.

Walter stood and extended his hand. "Come on, Honey. It's line-dancing time. You, too Liam."

# ~ *Brayton* ~

"Do you want to leave?" Cici asked, following Brayton's gaze across the floor to Honey and the dozen or so pack members who'd just walked into the club.

"No."

"You might want to stop growling then."

"I wasn't."

Rhys met his gaze and raised an eyebrow.

"It's country night," Malcolm grumbled, sliding into the seat on the other side of the table.

Cici touched Brayton's arm and he realized he was watching Honey again. "It's not her fault."

"Yeah, it kind of is. If she hadn't..."

"If she hadn't been a rogue who *you* insisted on capturing?" Cici finished for him. "She tried to get away. You were the stubborn one. You were the one who shunned her simply for turning away. It's not *all* your fault though. I shouldn't have gone along with it. None of us should have. We are supposed to advise you and we failed too."

Brayton slammed his fist down on the table. "It wasn't supposed to be like this."

"Like what?" Malcolm said. "You, sitting here watching your pack? You do this all the time."

"I'm supposed to be in charge. I'm not supposed to be the one everyone looks down on."

"They don't look down on you," Cici said. "All of us make mistakes. It just means you're normal, kind of. You

189

will get past this. You will be alpha someday, it's inevitable. Maybe you should enjoy the break and just focus on being a student for a while."

"A student," he snorted as the waitress started placing the drinks Malcolm had ordered on the table. She plunked a bottle of Blue Wolf in front of him. After the headache of the last few weeks, he'd decided not to get drunk for a while, but screw that. He was so tense and angry his head was already hurting. The alcohol might actually do him some good.

He downed that bottle, then a second and third in rapid succession. The music started and he climbed to his feet. Yeah, it was country, but it had a good beat. He could line dance with the best of them if he tried.

~ *Honey* ~

"Watch. It's very easy. One, two, step-step-step, three, four, step-step-step."

"You've very good Walter." She wasn't lying. He was. He had a confidence about him that she hadn't seen before.

"Thank you. Now do it with me."

She tried. She could do the line dance in slow motion, but when Walter went the speed of the beat she got lost.

"Go dance with the girls. Liam and I will keep practicing over here, out of the way."

"You're sure?"

"Yes." She pushed him. "Go."

190

"Do I have to practice?" Liam whined as soon as Walter was gone.

"No."

"Oh, thank goodness." He stopped and leaned against the wall next to Luca.

"Look at them all, stomping away in long blue-jean clad lines," Luca huffed. "Anyone who doesn't do it their way gets trampled."

She stopped in frustration when she realized she'd missed another turn. "How would you dance to this?"

Luca kicked off the wall and approached her with one hand aiming for her shoulder and another for her opposite hand. "May I?"

"Sure."

"First, the basic two-step."

"That's it?" she asked after a minute of basically walking.

"Oh, you want something more challenging?" He grinned evilly. "All you have to do is let me lead. You just be putty in my hands."

She looked to Liam. "Is that safe?"

Liam shrugged.

Luca's idea of more challenging was spinning her until she was dizzy. The whole room was still spinning when Walter stomped over and grabbed her hand.

"That is not how you two-step. Come with me, Honey. I will give you a proper lesson."

Walter was a much better teacher. She didn't even have to concentrate to follow him, and his spins didn't make her dizzy.

191

Walter perked his ears up as the next song began. "Sounds like another line dance. Do you want to try?"

"No. I need a drink." It wasn't an excuse. She really did.

"I can get you one."

"Dance Walter." She spun him toward a cute, petite blond from her pack and left the floor.

There was a large orange cooler full of ice water on the end of the bar, so instead of ordering a bottle of water, she filled a cup and sucked it down.

"Having fun Honey?" Charlize asked, taking a dainty sip out of the bubbling bottle in her hand.

Honey had decided she liked Charlize. She was very positive and only a little bossy.

"Yes."

"So, which one of those boys are you with?"

"With?"

"Yeah, the other girls want to know which ones are available."

"Available for what?"

She gave Honey an amused look. "To date."

"Oh! I'm sure they'd all love to go on a date."

"You wouldn't mind?"

"No, of course not. We're just friends."

"Really? Even Liam?"

"Yes. He's like a big brother. He says I remind him of his little sister."

Charlize glanced over at the wall where Liam was talking with one of the other girls.

Honey nudged her. "Go ask him to dance the next slow song with you. He's not a big dancer like Luca and Walter, but he can handle slow."

"Mm, maybe I will."

Honey drank two more cups of water before her thirst was slated. A slow song, some ballad about a man losing his truck, started and she spotted Charlize leading Liam out onto the floor. For a moment she wished she'd been the one to drag him out there, but she didn't know how to dance country any better than he did.

"Honey, people don't come to bars to drink water," a familiar voice cut into her thoughts.

"Then why is there a cooler full of water with cups beside it on the bar?" she asked without looking at the boy beside her.

"It's for the fools who don't know any better," Brayton slurred.

"Then I'm a fool."

His body heat warmed her side as he leaned against the bar next to her. "You said it." He lifted the blue bottle he was holding like he was clanking it against someone else's bottle then chugged it down.

"Brayton."

"What?"

His breath hit her, and she had to step back from the stench of tortuous magic. "You shouldn't be drinking that."

He had to work to focus his glassy eyes on her. "What, now you're going to tell me what to do? You think that just because my moth-er took away my, my in-chargedness that you can boss me?"

"No." She looked around to make sure there was no one close by that could overhear. "I can smell magic and the drink smells cursed."

He looked at the blue bottle in his hand for several long seconds. "It is cursed. I'm going to be kicking myself tomorrow, but tonight...tonight is smooth."

"Smooth? That doesn't make any sense."

He flung out the hand holding the bottle, nearly whacking a passerby in the nose. "Wanna dance?"

"You want to dance with me?"

He held up a finger. "My mo-ther said I needed to fix things. If we dance the pack will think I like you."

"How will that fix anything?"

"I...It just will. Trust me."

She shook her head. "I don't think..."

"Please."

Did she want to dance with Brayton? No, but he had tried to help her with her telepathy. Yes, he'd shunned her, but now that she understood why her pack hadn't been talking to her, she wasn't upset. She might have never become such good friends with Liam and the gang if it weren't for Brayton. Besides, it was just a dance.

"Okay."

"Really?" He very deliberately set his empty bottle on the bar and offered her his hand. "Come on."

The slow song was still playing. Brayton put his hands on her shoulders and started swaying. It was definitely not the two-step. It didn't matter though because they were on the edge of the dance floor and not in anyone's way. Despite the rancid spell on his breath, she could still smell the body spray or whatever it was that he always wore. He pulled her closer, and to her very great surprise, wrapped his arms around her and leaned his head against hers. His head was heavy.

"You smell good," he mumbled.

"Thanks."

The song ended and something very loud and fast started to play. Brayton lifted his head. "Do you want to dance to this one?"

"I don't know how."

"Mmm." His hand slid down her arm to take her hand. "I could teach you. I saw you dancing with four-eyes."

"How? You only have two."

He looked startled at her little joke, then chuckled. "You are so …young." He reached up and tucked one of her unruly strands of hair behind her ear. "So innocent-looking. Yet you haunt me in my sleep. Why do you do that?"

"I don't."

He gave no sign that he heard her.

"You have the prettiest eyes."

Still holding her hand, he pulled her off the dance floor and back toward the bar. Walter, who was only a few feet away, shot her a questioning look. She shrugged. Brayton was acting strange, but she didn't think he meant any harm.

A waitress passed by so close she brushed Honey's shoulder. Honey smelled magic but didn't have time to figure out where it was coming from because Brayton abruptly stopped and turned to face her. Before she could ask him what he needed, a searing pain shot through her

195

chest. She looked down for the source of the pain and found Brayton's hand wrapped around a knife that was buried hilt-deep in her chest.

It wasn't just the pain that brought tears to her eyes. It was the betrayal.

She looked up into his wide eyes and asked, "Why?"

He didn't look evil or deranged or pleased with himself. He looked as shocked as she did. He released the knife and stumbled back. "I didn't mean to."

He stepped toward her again as she lost control of her legs but Walter grabbed him and yelled across the dance floor at Liam. "Liam, Honey needs you."

# 23

## Brayton

It felt like he'd been lying on the slab of stone that passed for a cot for days instead of hours. He hadn't seen anyone since the wolf enforcer had thrown him inside the small cement room and slammed the door. What if everyone had vanished? What if he was the only person left in the world? Ridiculous, but no more ridiculous than what had already happened. Every time he closed his eyes, he saw the knife sticking out of Honey's narrow chest with his hand on the hilt. It was impossible, yet it had happened else he wouldn't be where he was.

The lock rattled. He rolled to his feet and nearly choked on the bile that surged up into his throat. His headache was back.

The door opened and a different enforcer stepped in followed by his mom and a man he'd seen talking to dad sometimes. His mom looked mad, but not as mad as he expected. She looked more exhausted than anything.

"How's Honey?" He was sure she was fine. She had to be fine, she was a wolf after all. She hadn't looked good though when the paramedics carried her away.

"You have fifteen minutes," the enforcer said and shut the door behind him.

"You stabbed her in the heart. How do you think she's doing?" his mother snapped.

"Her heart?"

His world tilted. He half-sat, half-fell back down on the bed. Wolves could survive a lot of things, but if you disable their ability to pump blood, they could die, just like everyone else.

"Is she still alive?"

"What do you care?"

"Mom, I care. Is she still alive?"

"Why did you do it?" his mom demanded. "Why did you try to kill her? Did you think getting rid of her was going to fix things?"

"No, of course not. I didn't mean to stab her. I don't even know where the knife came from. One moment we were walking across the room and the next, she was standing there with a knife in her chest. You said 'try to kill her'. Is she still alive?"

"Yes. By some miracle, she's still alive."

Mom sat heavily on the cot next to him, but not close enough to touch, and covered her face. He thought for a moment she was crying. She might have been, but he didn't smell or see any tears when she finally rubbed her face and looked up. "This is Colt Delgado, your lawyer. Tell him what happened, and no excuses. By law he can't share anything you tell him."

The lawyer stuck out his hand. "Hi Brayton. Your dad and I go way back."

He shook the man's hand as quickly as was polite. He didn't want a lawyer. He wanted to go back in time and not go out with his friends, or better, go back and not take his mom to the cafeteria. He rubbed his forehead, not that it did anything at all for the pain.

"Something wrong with your head?" Colt asked.

"Hurts. I drank Blue Wolf last night. It's really strong."

Mom pulled out a water bottle from somewhere. "Here. You're probably dehydrated."

"Did you drink enough to get drunk?" Colt asked.

"Yeah. I was pretty toasted." He unscrewed the cap off the bottle and downed it all. It didn't help.

"Your friends said you asked Honey to dance with you."

"I did?" He vaguely remembered talking to her by the cooler.

"And that you hugged her on the dance floor."

"Really?"

"Then you took her by the hand and pulled her toward the bar."

"Why would I do that?"

Colt raised an eyebrow at me. "I don't know. You tell me."

"I don't remember." He closed his eyes. "All I remember was her standing in the middle of the club, looking at me with those green eyes of hers and then looking down and seeing the knife in her chest. My hand was on it but I don't know how it got there. I didn't have a knife with me. I don't carry one."

"It was a steak knife from the kitchen," the lawyer said.

"I didn't have any steak."

"It doesn't matter. Everyone around saw you stab her with it."

"But where did it come from?" He asked, rubbing his head as the guy with the jackhammer inside his skull tried to dig through his temples. "Was I holding it while we danced? Was it in my pocket? I don't even know how big it was."

"Big enough," his mom said.

"Those are good questions. If we can show the attack wasn't premeditated and that he was under the influence, we should be able to get a lower sentence," Colt said.

"Sentence?" Between his head and the visions of Honey and the knife, he hadn't thought that far ahead. He'd only been concerned with what his parents would say.

"Yes, sentence," Mom said. "You've been charged with assault and attempted murder. You're looking at twenty to forty years in prison."

"Prison?"

His head throbbed. The bile he'd washed down came back along with all the water he'd just drank. It splattered on the cement at his mom's feet.

"Oh, Brayton," she sighed. The disappointment in her voice made his heart hurt almost as bad as his head.

# 24

## *Honey*

"You are one lucky little wolf," Dr. Ziga said, scanning the second page of her chart. He hung the chart up on the end of her bed and sat down on the stool beside the bed. "How are you feeling?"

"Better."

"Sore?"

"A little."

He lifted up the gauze on her chest to inspect her wound and the cut he'd made to get inside and stitch up everything that was bleeding. "Looks like you're a fast healer. Your chest will feel bruised for a couple of days though. Nothing strenuous for one week. That means no running, jumping, training, etc. You can walk, slowly. No heavy lifting for one week. That means no heavy backpacks until your chest stops hurting. I'm sure that young man who came with you in the ambulance will be glad to help you out."

"Liam?"

"Mm. Yes. Smart boy to keep anyone from removing the knife."

"He wants to be a doctor."

"Does he?" the doctor stood. "Luna Lynn is here to take you back to your dorm. I heard you already ate half-a-cow so I want you to go straight to bed. If the pain gets any worse, I want you to come back. Wolves can get infections just like everyone else."

It wasn't half-a-cow. It was only three measly-sized burgers.

"Yes, sir."

"And just for fun, you get to leave in this delightful chair with wheels." He waved his hand at the door and a nurse pushed a wheelchair into the room. "The nurse is going to help you dress. I'll send the good Luna to you as soon as she's finished with the paperwork."

"Thank you, Dr. Ziga."

"You are welcome."

She had lied. Her chest wasn't a little sore, it was a lot sore. Pulling on the jeans Luna Lynn had brought for her was excruciating. She had no idea she used so many chest muscles to put on pants. The shirt wasn't much better.

"You sure you're going to be okay, hon?" the nurse asked while she helped Honey into a hoodie. "You can stay another night. Most wolves would."

"I'll be much better by morning. I don't want to miss any classes."

"Your health is more important than a few classes. I'll have the doctor write you a note in case you don't feel up to it tomorrow, okay?"

"Okay."

Honey didn't want to sit in the wheelchair – that was too weird – so she sat back down on the bed to wait.

Several minutes later there was a soft knock on the open door. Luna Lynn peered around the edge.

"Honey, are you decent?"

"Come on in Luna. I'm dressed."

"Good. There's someone who wants to speak with you."

She feared for a moment it would be Brayton, but it was a male wolf she'd never seen before. He had dark hair and a long face but he wasn't bad looking. She guessed he was in his mid-to-late twenties.

He walked forward with his hand extended. "Honey Smith?"

"Yes." She pretended she didn't see his hand by looking up at his face. She didn't feel like having her arm shook.

He dropped his hand and used it to pull a small notepad out of his pocket. "I'm Agent Hopkins, a superhuman investigator. I'd like to ask you a few questions."

"Superhuman? Like superman?"

He blinked at her. "No, wolves and witches."

"Are we human or are we considered a different species? I didn't think humans could procreate with witches and wolves."

"Honey!" Luna said.

"If we can't, then we are technically a different species," she explained.

The agent cleared his throat and looked down at his notebook as if he hadn't heard her. "I'm here to talk about the incident that happened Friday night. Can you tell me exactly what occurred?"

She knew what he wanted, but she was feeling ornery. "I was stabbed in the heart with a knife."

He looked at her over the pen he held ready and said with complete seriousness. "I meant before that. Start with when you arrived at The Hole."

"We walked in, found a table, got some drinks, started dancing…"

"Who's we?"

She started listing as many names as she could from memory. She got all the guys and at least five of the girls before she had to resort to descriptions.

"That's fine," he finally interrupted. "So, you were with a group?"

"Yes."

"What did you have to drink?"

"Water."

"You didn't order anything alcoholic or try someone else's drink?"

"No."

He squinted his eyes at her like he didn't believe her and jotted something down.

"When did you meet up with Brayton?"

"I didn't."

He stared over his notebook at her. "You had to meet him somehow. Witnesses said you were dancing."

"Yeah, but it wasn't planned. I thought 'meet up' meant it was planned."

"When did you talk to him then?"

"We'd been there for a little while and I got thirsty so I went to the water cooler on the bar. I was drinking my third cup when he came and stood beside me."

"What did he say?"

"He told me only fools drink water at a bar."

"Was he drinking anything?"

"Yes. He had a bottle of that nasty Blue Wolf juice."

Agent Hopkins made a note. "Nasty. You tasted it then?"

"No."

"You've tasted it before?"

"No."

He paused with his pen. "Why do you say it's nasty then?"

"Because it smells bad."

He raised an eyebrow at her. "You don't like the smell of alcohol?"

"It wasn't the alcohol. It was the magic. It smelled cursed."

"What magic?"

"There was a spell on the drink. I could smell it on his breath too."

The agent stared at her doubtfully. "You can smell spells?"

"Yes. Can't you?" She knew the guys couldn't identify spells by smell, but she thought they could at least smell them.

"Did you tell Brayton that his drink smelled strange?" Luna Lynn asked.

"Yes. He thought I meant because it had alcohol in it. I think Blue Wolf is supposed to make wolves drunk. He was acting that way. That's when he asked me to dance."

She told him how he'd laid his head against hers and took her hand, then suddenly turned around and stabbed her.

"Did he have the knife with him the whole time?" Agent Hopkins asked.

"I don't know. It wasn't in his hand and I didn't notice anything sticking out of his pockets."

"Did you pass any tables or trays or counters where he could have picked one up?"

"No. There weren't any...wait, we did pass a waitress. I remember her bumping into me."

"Did she have a tray?" the agent asked.

"Um...yes."

"Do you remember what was on it?"

She closed her eyes and tried to remember. "No, I just saw the edge of it."

"Do you remember what she looked like?"

"No. I didn't see her face. She was going the same direction we were, but faster. Her hair was brown and short and curly and she was a little shorter than me, normal sized. There was something else..." She closed her eyes again but after a minute, gave up. "I'm sorry, I can't remember."

"What happened right after Brayton stabbed you? Did he say anything?"

Brayton's white face and open mouth popped into her head. "He looked shocked and then he let go of the knife and said he didn't mean to. Walter grabbed him and then Liam came."

"That's what he said, that he didn't mean to?" Luna Lynn interrupted.

"Yes."

"That means it wasn't premeditated. It was an accident, just like he said," she told the agent.

"Pulling a knife out of thin air and stabbing someone doesn't sound like an accident." He looked down at his notes. "Was this Walter in the group you came with?"

"Yes."

"Did he see it happen?"

"Maybe. He was watching us when we came off the dance floor. I think he was concerned because Brayton was acting so strange."

"Why was he concerned? It sounds like Brayton was just drunk."

"He's hurt me before."

"Yeah, but that was just a scratch," Luna Lynn said.

"And he broke my ribs once."

"He what?" she said.

"When did he break your ribs," the agent asked.

"We were sparring in our morning training class and Captain Young was trying to determine our skill level. After I defeated Cici…,"

"You defeated Cici?" Luna Lynn interrupted.

"Yes."

"Continue," the agent said.

"After I defeated Cici, Brayton volunteered to spar with me. He was mad and very aggressive. It was hard to get close enough to land a hit. I finally took him down with a flying scissor-move. When he fell, he landed on top of me, hard."

"It was just an accident too then," Luna Lynn sighed.

"That's when I met my best friends," Honey said fondly. "I fell asleep after my classes and missed supper. I was so hungry I followed the smell of pizza into their rooms and ate a whole pie. They adopted me after that."

"Were they there last night?" the agent asked.

"Oh yeah – Nathan, Liam, Luca, and Walter."

He flipped several pages back into his notebook. "Liam came with you to the hospital."

"Yes. He wants to be a doctor."

"And they are all from the Little pack?"

"Yes."

"That's my pack." He almost smiled.

"You know them then?"

"I've seen them around. It's a big pack."

All the talking was making her tired. She leaned over on the bed which was still in an up-right position. Maybe she should stay another night.

"One more thing, Honey," the agent said.

"Mmm." The pillow was so comfortable. She closed her eyes.

"How old are you?"

"Not yet eighteen."

"Seventeen then?"

"No."

"She's fourteen," Luna Lynn said.

Honey opened my eyes and gave Lynn a stern stare. "You promised."

Lynn waved her hand at the agent. "He's an officer of the law, Honey."

"A promise is a promise."

"You're only fourteen?" the agent asked in surprise, "and you're in college?"

"She's very smart," Luna Lynn snapped. "Are we done here?"

"Don't tell my friends," Honey told the agent, "I don't want them to treat me any differently."

He nodded. "I won't, but it might come out at some point. Does Brayton know how old you are?"

"No."

"All right. It was nice meeting you Honey." He pulled out a card and put it into her hand. "Call or text me if you think of anything else."

The nurse came in after the agent left.

"Your note, dear," she pressed a piece of paper into the hand with the agent's card. "Are you sure you don't want to stay another night?"

"I'm sure."

The nurse held the wheelchair steady while Honey slid into it, then put the plastic bag with what remained of the clothes Honey had worn to the bar in her lap. Her shirt was gone but her pants and shoes and her student ID were still intact. The sliding double doors at the back of the house-turned-clinic slid open automatically when the nurse wheeled her through the small lobby. Lynn hurried forward to lead them outside. "This way."

She led them toward a large, black SUV. Brayton's dad was waiting beside it along with another wolf Honey recognized as the Beta from her time at their house. Alpha Brandon was brawnier than Brayton, but Honey could see the resemblance in their eyes and their hairline and the way they stood. Alpha Brandon's smile looked sad though, rather than cocky, as he crouched down in front of her.

"Honey. I am so sorry. I don't know what got into that boy's head."

"It's all right. I'll be all better in a few days."

"It's not all right. That's not the way people handle themselves in my pack." He leaned forward and pressed his lips against her forehead in the same place he had before. "And you are part of my pack as long as you'll have us."

"Thank you, Alpha."

He stood and his beta opened the door to the middle seat of the SUV. "Think you can climb up?"

"She'll need help," the nurse said behind her. "It hurts her to pull with her arms."

"Not a problem. Stand up, Honey."

She obeyed and was abruptly in his arms. In two long strides, he was sliding her into the seat. There was another person already sitting in the third row, a young woman with curly, dark blond hair that was valiantly attempting to escape from the confines of a medium-length braid. The woman smiled and gave a little wave. The beta got into the seat behind Alpha Brandon and Lynn climbed into the seat in front of Honey. Lynn pulled down her visor and looked at Honey through the mirror.

"Honey, this is Chloe. She'll be your bodyguard until Brayton is sentenced."

"Bodyguard?"

"Yes. The enforcers are releasing Brayton until his trial. He will continue to attend college, but I don't want him near you, even by accident. She'll escort you to your classes and ensure he stays away at all times."

"Oh." She didn't really want a stranger following her around all the time, but it was probably for the best. "Thank you. Um, where is she going to stay?" Her dorm room was already crowded even though there was just her and Blaze.

"A couple of girls moved out of your dorm. She's going to stay in one of the empty rooms."

"I can't wait," Chloe said cheerfully. "I haven't lived in a dorm since my freshman year."

"Are you in college?" Honey asked.

"No. I graduated last year. I was taking a break before I found a job, but it will be nice to earn a little cash."

The trip was short and Chloe was chatty so it wasn't completely weird to ride in an SUV with the parents of her attacker.

A crowd of people was in front of her dorm when they pulled up. Honey thought at first that they were having a fire drill, until she realized some of them were guys – her guys.

Nathan was the first one to reach her door and fling it open. "Honey! You're home!"

"Very funny."

He gave her an awkward one-armed hug over her seat belt. "I'm so glad you're okay."

"Is this your boyfriend?" Chloe asked beside her.

"One of them. I have several good friends who are of the masculine gender."

"Very nice way to put it, Honey," Walter said, offering her his hand. "May I help you down?"

211

She unhooked her seat belt but didn't take his hand. "Can you lift me down? My chest hurts."

"Of course."

She turned toward him. He put his hands around her waist and swung her down like her dad used to do when she was a little girl. Instead of letting go once her feet were on the ground, he pulled her into a gentle hug. "I'm sorry I couldn't stop him."

She took a deep breath of his familiar, comforting scent. "It's all right Walter. You couldn't know what he was about to do."

"Hey, hey. It's my turn." Luca pulled her from Walter's arms and gave her a hug, then pushed her away and scrunched his nose. "You smell like disinfectant."

"Clean you mean?"

He growled playfully.

"Honey, how do you feel?"

She spun around to face Liam. "Alive, thanks to you." She threw her arms around him, well, not really threw, but she did put them around him and he put his around her.

"I'm glad." He released her to shake his finger in her face. "Don't ever scare me like that again."

"Who's this?" Nathan said in his best hubba-hubba voice, as Luca called it.

She introduced Chloe who had climbed out of the vehicle behind her, then started to make her way into the building. It was not easy. Charlize was there with all the people they'd gone out with the night before and some they hadn't. Several of her witch friends were there too. They all seemed to want to touch her and say they were glad she'd made it back. It was nice, but really, really tiring.

212

Chloe stepped forward after a few minutes and waved her arms like she was parting a river. "Okay folks. Honey appreciates you taking the time to welcome her back, but she just had major surgery last night. She needs to rest."

Honey could have hugged her too.

Luna Lynn, Blaze, and Liam followed Chloe and her upstairs, or up-elevator. Chloe insisted they take it. Honey was glad.

She was shocked at the change to her room when Blaze opened the door. Blaze waved her hand at the mess and grinned at her. "What do you think?"

"I think we're going to have to stand on the beds to get dressed."

She laughed. "It's only temporary. The boys helped me separate the bunks so you wouldn't have to climb up. I'm glad wolves heal so quick though. Not sure if I could stand to live like this for long."

She hugged her, carefully. "Thank you, Blaze, and you too Liam."

Liam patted her on the shoulder. "I'm glad I could help. Now get to bed. Don't even think about going to training in the morning. We'll make sure Captain Young knows what's going on. Sleep in as long as you can."

"I have a note." She pulled it out of her pocket and waved it at him.

Liam grabbed her hand and gave it a squeeze. "I'll tell him. You can show it to him later."

"Thank you, Liam."

He hugged her again and kissed the side of her unwashed head. "Goodnight Honey. Sweet dreams."

# 25

## *Honey*

Honey woke to the mouthwatering aroma of bacon and eggs and a pain on her hip where the jeans Luna Lynn had brought her had pressed into her skin overnight. It had been too daunting to take her clothes off, so she'd gone to bed with them on.

"Ah, sleeping beauty awakes," a not-so-familiar voice chimed. Chloe smiled down at her and waved the breakfast sandwich she was holding above her. "I got us some breakfast."

The sun was up. Lately, it had been dark when she woke every morning and not just on WOLF days. Honey reached for the phone in the handy little pocket she'd found to hang at the head of the bed. "What time is it?"

"7:40"

"I have an 8:00 class!"

"You have a doctor's note."

Honey snatched the sandwich from Chloe and quickly unwrapped it far enough to take a bite. "I didn't hurt my brain."

"Oh, you're one of those."

"One of what?" she asked and nearly lost the piece of bagel she was chewing on.

"Thinks she has to go to every class."

"I like going to my classes."

She finished the bagel in two bites, then rolled off the bed and slowly stood. She figured it would be easier than sitting up first. It worked. She grabbed her shower caddy and the bottle of water Luna had given her the day before and headed for the hallway.

"Aren't you forgetting something?" Chloe asked.

Honey looked down at herself. She was fully dressed. "No."

"You aren't going to take a shower?"

"I don't have time. I'll do it later."

"You might want to do something with your hair then."

"Thanks." She knew her hair probably looked awful, but that's why she was taking her hairbrush.

Considering she'd had a knife sticking out of her chest three days ago, she looked all right. Her clothes were rumpled, her face was pale, and her hair was sticking out in all directions like she'd been standing in the middle of a windstorm, but after she tamed it a bit and pulled it into a bun, she didn't look any worse than the human male who always staggered into class at the last second every Monday. In fact, she looked much better. Her smell ,eh – it could be worse.

She made it to class with two minutes to spare despite Chloe walking so slowly that Honey seriously considered freezing her and carrying her backpack herself. Chloe plopped the backpack on top of a desk then jerked her thumb toward the door. "I'll wait outside. I already sat through this class once. Never again."

"Thank you."

It was an exhausting day, not because she did much other than walk and sit, but because her body was busy healing. Fast healing required a lot of energy. She had a huge lunch, managed to stay awake in the rest of her classes, then fell asleep before she got any homework done. She didn't see Brayton the entire day and the boys brought her pizza for supper, so she didn't have to face him at supper either.

Tuesday, she felt better and finally took a shower. It amazed her how much easier it was to pull on her clothes after a day-and-a-half.

Wednesday, she woke up at 5am and got ready for WOLF. Chloe thought she was crazy and moaned about getting up so early. Honey threatened to go without her if she wasn't ready and informed her it was the one class she had with Brayton and the whole reason she was there. That shut her up.

Captain Young met her at the bleachers. "Honey! You're back. How are you feeling?"

"Better."

"What are you doing here? The boys said you would be out all week."

"I wanted to give you the doctor's note and I wanted to watch."

"Ah, Dr. Zi-ga." He said it like it was two words instead of one as he gave the paper a quick glance. "He's a good doctor." He handed the paper back to her. "You are more than welcome to watch, but only watch. Chloe," he turned to her bodyguard, "you want to help out today since you are here?"

"I'm working," she grumbled.

He chuckled. "Still not a morning person I see."

"This isn't morning. It's still night. It won't be morning for another two hours."

"All right, but if you change your mind, feel free to jump in. Honey, you let me know if Brayton gives you any trouble."

"I will."

"Honey!" Greg jogged to a stop beside her. "You're back." He gave her a sweaty hug. His training clothes always smelled sweaty even when they were clean. She'd grown used to it. It was just part of who he was. "Who's your friend?"

"Chloe. Chloe, meet Greg."

"Nice headband," she smirked.

"Thanks. Honey, want to run with me?"

"Not today. I have the week off."

"Wow. That bad?"

She nodded.

"Okay then. I better get changed. Will you be at dinner tonight?"

"Probably."

"See you then."

"Exactly how many male friends do you have?" Chloe asked, watching Greg lope across the field toward the tent.

Honey shrugged. "You've met all the wolf ones. There are a few male witches I usually eat dinner with."

"Witches."

"Yeah. Blaze is a witch. They're her friends too."

217

"Huh. I thought there was something odd about her."

"Odd?"

Chloe elbowed her. "I meant her hair."

They found seats in the bleachers while everyone did their warm-up run. Honey wished she could run with them. It was cold even with the hoodie she was wearing.

Brayton and his friends showed up at exactly 5:30. He kept his eyes straight ahead. An older wolf, even older than Brayton's dad, was with them.

"Who is that?" she asked Chloe.

"That is Brayton's grandfather, Alpha Braxton."

"His grandfather? He's still alive?"

"Of course. His grandmother too. They're retired and they do a lot of traveling, but they still help out with the pack."

Alpha Braxton followed Brayton to the tent and stood just outside of it like he was guarding it while the boys changed.

"Why is his grandfather here?" she asked.

"He's protecting Brayton from you."

"Me?"

"Yep. The Alpha and Luna didn't want anything else to happen between you two before the trial. They were going to assign a different bodyguard to Brayton, but his grandfather volunteered."

Captain Young walked over and spoke to Alpha Braxton, then nodded toward Honey. The alpha's sharp gray-blue eyes focused on her and she swore she heard him growl. He marched purposely across the grass directly toward her. She would have run if she could have and wasn't frozen in place by his glare.

218

Chloe tugged on her arm. "Come on, let's get this over with. He wants to meet you so he knows who to avoid."

"That's all? It looks like he wants to eat me."

Chloe laughed heartlessly and pushed Honey toward the bottom of the bleachers.

They reached the ground just before Alpha Braxton planted his feet in front of Honey and crossed his arms. He was tall but not quite as tall as Brayton or his dad. She wondered if he'd always been that height or if he'd shrunk the way old people tended to do.

"So, you're the little troublemaker."

How should she respond to that? If she said yes she'd be admitting she was trouble and if she said no he wouldn't believe her. She chose not to say anything.

He uncrossed his arms. "You're Honey, right?"

"Yes."

He leaned forward and took a long sniff, then straightened and frowned down at her. "How are you feeling?"

"Better."

"Why aren't you running with the rest of them?"

"The doctor said to wait a week."

"Doctors are always overly cautious."

She wouldn't know. She thought Dr. Ziga's recommendations made sense though. She didn't say that, of course.

"You stay away from Brayton."

"That's all I've ever tried to do."

He grunted and turned his back on her to stomp back toward the tent.

"That went well," Chloe commented.

"Did it?"

"Yeah. I think he thought you were an evil temptress who had driven Brayton crazy with your seductive wiles, but you're just a kid."

"Thanks."

"You're welcome."

Captain Young split the wolves into groups. Her Little friends sparred on one side of the field while Brayton and his pack practiced on the other. It wasn't until the end of WOLF, after he'd changed back into a human that Honey got a look at Brayton's face. He didn't look good. There were shadows under his eyes again and he had that pucker between his eyebrows that she recognized as pain. Was his headache back?

It wasn't her problem. She turned away before he looked at her and headed for the cafeteria and a mug of hot chocolate.

Friday morning practice was much the same except it was drizzling. She was so cold she asked Captain Young if she could leave early. He said yes, much to Chloe's delight. Honey didn't see Brayton the rest of the day.

Saturday it was still raining. She and Chloe went to visit the guys with a game of Trivial Pursuit she'd borrowed from the front desk of her dorm. She'd just won her third piece of pie – the entertainment one no less, she was really bad at entertainment questions – when someone pounded on the door much harder than was necessary.

Liam answered it.

Alpha Braxton charged in and quickly scanned the room until his eyes fell on her. "What are you doing here?"

"Playing a game."

"In Brayton's dorm!"

"In my friends' rooms."

"I could smell your scent. Get out."

"Why?"

He seemed to grow bigger and completely fill the space. "Because I am the former alpha of your pack and I said so."

Normally she respected older people, but randomly telling her to leave for no good reason when she was in the middle of a game and almost winning was rude.

"Chloe, do former alphas have as much say as current alphas?"

"Yes." Her voice sounded oddly submissive. Honey glanced at her to see that not only was her head down, but everyone's heads were down.

"What's wrong with you guys?"

"He's like, blasting alpha power," Nathan said. "Don't you feel it?"

"I feel mad because he's being unreasonable, but otherwise, nope."

"I could kill you with one swipe of my hand, girl," Brayton's grandfather threatened.

"I could probably do the same thing to you, but I'm not going to. We can finish the game in my dorm, but why is smelling my scent such a big deal?"

He tapped her chest with a finger that was partially transformed so that the wolf-claw was poking her skin.

221

"Because Brayton doesn't need any reminders of what you did to him."

"What I did to him? What did I do?"

"You've driven him insane, that's what."

"He's claiming insanity now? That's," Luna Lynn's sad face and Brayton's exhausted one came to mind. Now that her chest no longer hurt, she wasn't feeling quite as mad at him as she had before. Insanity would explain why he had stabbed her since nothing else did. "that's a good idea. He was acting really strange when it happened. I will testify to that if you want."

She regretted the words the moment they left her mouth. She really didn't want to have anything more to do with Brayton.

"As long as it doesn't interfere with school or anything," she amended, "and I don't have to be in the same room with him."

"Brayton's not insane!"

"You just said he was. Isn't temporary insanity a thing? If he claimed that maybe he wouldn't have to go to jail, assuming he hasn't attacked anyone else." Considering his actions toward her, it wasn't safe to assume. "Has he?"

Chloe gasped.

Alpha Braxton's furry eyebrows lowered so much they nearly hid his eyes. "What did you say?"

"I asked if Brayton has ever attacked anyone else. Am I the only one, or just the only one that's ever been hurt in a public place with witnesses?"

The alpha swelled like a puffer fish. She would have been scared if she didn't know she could freeze him with a thought.

222

"What are you implying?"

"I'm not implying anything. I'm asking a simple question. Has he stabbed or otherwise attempted to murder or harm anyone else?"

"No! Brayton is a good boy. Until he met you, everything was fine, but I can see exactly why he'd want to stab you."

"Why? Because you can't intimidate me?"

He released a low growl that made the hairs on the back of her neck and along her arms stand straight up. Hair started to sprout on his cheeks and the back of his hands. He was changing here?

"You can't do that here. You have to stay human."

Liam grabbed her arm and pulled her toward the door. "Come on Honey. We need to go."

"But…" she didn't know why she was arguing. Alpha Braxton's quickly forming wolf was huge and angry. "…I was winning."

"Just run."

They raced down the stairs and out the door into the rain. They didn't stop until they were inside the entryway of her dorm.

"Oh my gosh," Nathan panted. "I thought he was going to rip out your throat."

"You are either really brave or really stupid," Chloe said.

Honey crossed her arms and looked back at the boy's dorm to see if the monster was following them. "Now I see where Brayton gets his bullish tendencies."

"You were antagonizing him," Walter said.

"No. I was asking a simple question which he didn't want to hear."

"Brayton is his only grandchild," Chloe said softly, "of course he didn't want to hear that."

Honey let her head fall back against the wall. "I know. I just wanted to make sure if I did help Brayton that it wouldn't lead to more people being hurt in the future. Luna Lynn is nice and I don't think she'd hide anything like that, but she's also a mom and sometimes moms can be blind."

"Was your mom blind?" Chloe asked.

"About me? No. She knew me irritatingly well."

"For what it's worth, I've never heard or seen Brayton hurt anyone like he has you. He's let his temper get the best of him a few times in practice fights, but he's never sought anyone out and purposely harmed them."

"Thank you. That's all I wanted to know."

"I wonder if your telepathic disability also makes you immune to alpha power," Liam said thoughtfully, "It's no wonder you drive Brayton crazy. He's not used to people standing up to him."

"Does he have alpha power already?"

"A little," Chloe said. "He'll get more as he gets older. His grandfather's is immense."

"And you were just standing there, looking him in the eye, egging him on," Luca said. "It was terrifyingly awesome. Please don't do that again."

Chloe's phone chimed. She pulled it out and swiped the screen. "I'm being summoned."

"By Alpha Braxton?" Liam asked.

"Yep. Sounds like he's back downstairs if you want to go back to your rooms."

"I'll stay with Honey while you're gone," Liam stated.

"We all will," Nathan said.

"Probably a good idea. I've never seen Alpha Braxton lose his cool like that, ever."

# 26

## Brayton

Grandpa walked through the door of his suite growling under his breath with his clothes in tatters.

"What happened?" Rhys asked.

"Brayton, you had every right to stab that irritating, green-eyed, black-hearted little witch."

"What did she do?" Cici asked.

"She had the nerve to ask me if Brayton had ever stabbed anyone else and the pack had hidden it."

"So, you went wolf on her hide?" Malcolm asked gleefully.

Brayton lifted the ice-pack off his head far enough to see his grandpa. "Did you hurt her?" That would definitely not help his case – or would it? The fact that she'd driven two Mooney men crazy had to mean something.

"No. She ran off before I finished shifting."

"What was she doing?" Rhys asked.

"Playing a game with a bunch of Little wolves and Chloe."

"Oh, those are her friends. She hangs out with them all the time," Brayton informed him. "They're harmless."

"She shouldn't be in your dorm."

"I never go up to the third floor anyway."

"She is not allowed in your dorm," Grandpa said firmly, his alpha power soaking the room. "Text Chloe and tell her to get her ass up here."

"Grandpa, that's not really fair," he tried to argue, but his grandfather's will pounded against him and he was having enough trouble fighting the pain in his head. He let it go.

Chloe showed up while Grandpa was still changing.

"You buzzed?" she asked cheerily.

"Alpha Braxton has declared that Honey is not allowed in Brayton's dorm," Cici said.

"Noted."

"What happened up there?" Rhys asked. "I've never seen Alpha Braxton so mad."

"Honey isn't affected by his alpha power. She stood up to him. I felt like I should be kneeling with my forehead on the floor and she just stood there and looked him in the eye and told him he couldn't intimidate her."

"He said she ran," Malcolm said.

"Only because Liam pulled her out of there when Alpha Braxton started to shift. I seriously thought he was going to slice her to ribbons."

Ice worked a little bit, but Brayton's brain still felt like it was in a fog. "She's not affected by alpha power? Is that because of her lack of telepathy?"

"Liam wondered the same thing."

"No wonder Alpha Braxton was so upset. No one has ever successfully stood up to him before," Malcolm said.

"She wasn't successful," Grandpa growled, stalking into the room clad in a fresh T-shirt and jeans.

None of them disagreed. They knew better.

"How is she?" Brayton asked Chloe. It was the first time he'd been able to ask someone who'd been close to her since they came back to school.

"She's much better than she was Monday. She couldn't even pull her clothes off without help then. She's a fast healer," Chloe said.

"Has she said anything about what happened?"

"No, but I haven't asked. She did say you were acting strange. She volunteered to testify that you were insane before Alpha Braxton went all wolf on her."

"I'm not insane."

"Your grandpa said it first," Chloe said. "Why are you laying there with an ice pack on your head?"

"Migraine. I can't take any medicine for another hour."

"Wolves can get migraines?"

"I'm special," he snapped sarcastically. He was so tired of hurting. Even the pills Dr. Ziga had prescribed only lasted a few hours at a time.

"It's that girl. She caused this," Grandpa growled.

"No. I was having headaches before last week. She knows how to cure them. She helped me." He felt like crying. His one source of relief and he'd nearly killed her. What was wrong with him?

Grandpa snorted. "Well, clearly she didn't do a very good job."

"Maybe I can get you some of those herbs she used. She said she got them from someone in her dorm," Cici said.

"I would really appreciate that." He truly would, and not just because she offered to get them. The fact that his friends were standing by him even though he had clearly been in the wrong meant more to him than he had figured out how to express.

"Herbs or *herbs*?" His Grandpa emphasized the last one with finger quotation marks.

"Nothing illegal if that's what you're asking," he said, except that they were magical and Grandpa would probably consider that not only illegal but grounds for imprisonment.

"Chloe," Cici said, "can you ask Honey where she got the herbs that helped Brayton before?"

"Sure."

"What's she like?" Grandpa asked Chloe. "Anything we can use in Brayton's defense?"

"She's a little nerd and takes her classes too seriously, but that's not a bad thing. She's nice enough."

"Lynn said some of her friends were witches," Grandpa said.

"Yeah. I've met them. They're just kids. They joke around and laugh at stupid stuff like all freshmen do."

"But the fact that she hangs around them is very suspicious. Maybe she bought a spell from one of them and something went wrong."

"To do what, Grandpa?" Brayton asked.

"Love potion. I bet she was trying to win you over. You are the future alpha."

Brayton snorted. Honey trying to win him over? That would be the day. "Honey didn't grow up in a pack, Grandpa. She doesn't know what it means to be alpha and she has never once tried to flirt or even looked like she cared to."

Why didn't she like him? All the other girls did. Of course he hadn't stabbed any of the other girls or broke their ribs or shot them with a tranquilizer dart. His head pulsed and he felt like he might throw up.

"The sooner you can get those herbs, the better."

"I'll ask her as soon as I get back," Chloe promised.

# 27

## Honey

"He was lying on the couch with an ice pack on his head," Chloe said plaintively while blocking Honey's view of the TV. She and the boys had taken over the couches in the lounge on the first floor of her dorm while they waited for Chloe to get back. Honey suspected they were watching the Disney channel, but she wasn't completely sure.

"Wolves don't get migraines," Liam said next to her, "at least I've never heard of that happening. He should go to the doctor."

Chloe rolled her eyes. "He did."

"Did the doctor do anything for him?" Honey asked.

"He has pills, but they wear off."

She truly felt sorry for Brayton. The more she thought about it, the more convinced Honey was that he hadn't been himself when he stabbed her. She wished healing him was as simple as giving him herbs, but if they got the herbs they'd find out she was the one with magic, not the plants. She wasn't sure what would happen, but her mother had spent her whole life hiding her, so it couldn't be good. Surely his head would heal by itself eventually. They were wolves.

"I'm sorry he's not feeling well, but the herbs by themselves won't help much. It's the massage that's the important part."

"They might help though," Chloe insisted.

"Maybe."

Her phone started ringing. No, blasting was a better term.

Walter scrunched up his nose. "What on earth is that?"

"That is the latest from my favorite singer. You like?" Luca asked.

"Why must you keep changing my ring tones," Honey asked, hurriedly swiping at her phone to turn off the noise.

"I'm trying to broaden your musical horizons. Think of it as music appreciation class."

"Uh-huh," she said, putting the phone up to her ear.

"Hello, is this Honey Smith?" a male voice asked.

"Yes."

"Honey, this is Agent Hopkins. Are you available right now? I need a few minutes of your time."

"Sure."

"Great. Can you meet me in front of your dorm?"

"Yes."

"Who was that?" Chloe asked.

"The agent investigating the case. He's out front."

"What does he want?"

"I don't know."

The guys followed her outside. They'd all been interviewed after the incident, but not by Agent Hopkins.

He was standing by the bike rack when they spilled out of the door. His face didn't reveal any emotion while he looked over the boys and then stopped at her. "You look better."

"Thanks."

He indicated Chloe with his head. "Who's your friend?"

"Chloe. Chloe, this is Agent Hopkins."

Chloe put out her hand. "I'm her bodyguard actually."

"Nice to meet you, Chloe."

They shook for so long, Honey and Nathan looked at each other to see if anyone else thought it was odd. Agent Hopkins finally cleared his throat and removed his hand. "Honey, you're probably wondering why I'm here."

"We all are, actually," Luca said.

"I'm sure you are." Agent Hopkins pulled a plastic tube of blue liquid out of his pocket and handed it to Honey. "Can you sniff this for me and see if it has that smell you were talking about?"

"Sure."

She unscrewed the cap and took a whiff, then handed it back to him. "No."

"No? That's Blue Wolf."

"Yeah, but it hasn't been cursed. Not all of it is. Nathan drank some at another club and it didn't smell bad."

"You think someone was targeting Brayton?"

"I don't know. There was a creepy guy at the other bar whose breath smelled the same way."

"Where and when was this?"

She told him.

"All right. I'll get more samples for you to sniff."

"We should come with you," Luca said. "We could help."

"Yeah, no. I don't need a bunch of teenagers to babysit."

"How are you going to get samples?" Liam asked. "Are you collecting random stranger's bottles?"

"No, of course not."

"If someone is cursing particular bottles, they aren't going to give you one if you ask for it," Walter said. "If we came, we could strike up conversations with people and Honey could smell their breath."

"That sounds fun," she commented sarcastically. Nobody paid any attention.

"One of us has to stay with her at all times though," Nathan declared.

"I'll do it. I'm her bodyguard, after all," Chloe stated.

"Good plan. Shall we meet you here tonight at eight or do you want to meet at the bar?" Luca said.

"You're not coming!" the agent protested.

"We'll meet you there then," Luca winked, then grabbed Honey's arm to pull her back inside.

"Do you guys know him?" Honey asked, looking back to see the agent shaking his head.

"He's my cousin," Luca admitted as the door shut behind them.

Chloe disappeared for a couple of hours after making Honey promise to stay with the guys. When she came back, she was dressed in what she termed her 'clubbing clothes' which consisted of tight, shiny black pants, a low-cut silver halter top that exposed her toned belly and pierced belly button, and a short purple jacket. She'd painted her lips a shiny dark burgundy and lined her eyes in black and purple eye shadow with sparkles. Her hair was in two Dutch braids that joined to form a long, curly ponytail at the top back of her head.

Nathan's jaw dropped when he saw her. "Whoa."

Honey felt very under-dressed in her jeans and T-shirt and Chap-stick shined lips. She made a note to ask Chloe how to apply the make-up Luna Lynn had bought for her when they had more time.

She half-expected Agent Hopkins not to show, but he was standing a few doors from the bar when they walked up. His trench coat looked completely out of place compared to the colorful, revealing clothes the students going into the club were wearing. He stepped in front of them well before they made it to the door. "If you're going to insist on helping, I have some rules."

Chloe stepped forward and jabbed a finger in his chest while simultaneously waving behind her back for them to go around. "Shh. You're going to blow our cover," she whispered, then said more loudly, "Who in the world are you dressed as anyway? Sherlock Holmes? Is there a Halloween party tonight?"

Liam grabbed Honey's hand and pulled her to the left. Luca, Walter, and Nathan went right. Agent Hopkins shifted like he was going to step in front of Honey, but Chloe grabbed the lapels of his coat and pulled his face down to hers. He stiffened for a moment, then his arms went around her and he started kissing her back. Honey looked over her shoulder after they had all passed through the door. Chloe and the agent were still kissing.

"Did they know each other before now?" she asked Liam while he paid their cover charge.

"I don't think so."

"She just basically kissed a stranger?" They looked like they were enjoying it, but what did she know? She'd only seen actors in the movies kiss. Her parents never even kissed in front of her.

"You've just witnessed a once-in-a-lifetime event," Luca informed her. "Fated mates acting on their attraction for the first time."

"Fated mates? Is that really a thing?" Her mom had rolled her eyes when Honey asked her about it after she read a fictional book on werewolves.

"For a lucky few," Luca said knowingly. "It tends to run in families. My grandfather and my father both found their mates and I don't plan to settle down until I find mine."

"How do you know they're mates if it only happens to a few?" she waved toward the door.

"Horatio is such a stick-in-the-mud he would never kiss a girl in the middle of the street, let alone the same day he met her."

"His name is Horatio Hopkins?" Nathan snickered.

"Yep."

"Let's get to work while he's distracted," Liam said. "Got your notebook, Honey?"

She whipped out the cute little pocket-sized notebook she'd bought for fifty cents on sale at the beginning of the school year along with a small pencil. The plan was for

Luca, Walter, and Nathan to scout around for Blue Wolf bottles and people who were acting drunk. She and Liam were going to pretend to be doing a survey of the types of beverages college students liked to drink and talk to the people Luca and Nathan pointed out.

Nathan was already headed toward the bar, although that could have been because he wanted a drink before they started. She spotted the orange cooler on the bar and froze.

Liam touched her back. "You all right, Honey?"

The memories were coming so fast. She and Brayton were dancing. He was leaning on her, then they were walking off the floor. A waitress bumped into her but her hair wasn't brown, it was a vibrant red – the kind that comes from a bottle – with waves down to her waist. The waitress smelled of magic, but Honey still couldn't identify what kind. The waitress brushed against Brayton who had been ahead of her and the tray she was holding swung in front of him. Why had she thought the waitress had brown hair? Had she been using a camouflage spell and if so, why?

"Honey?"

She shook her head and the music of that night faded into what was currently playing.

"You okay?"

She blinked up into Liam's worried face. "Just remembering. I thought the waitress had brown hair, but it was red in my memory just now and I smelled magic."

"Walter doesn't remember seeing a waitress."

"She was there. I'm sure of it."

"Well, let's see if we can find some of that cursed juice and solve the mystery."

Chloe eventually joined them, sans Horatio. He went and sat at the bar looking sulky. His trench coat was gone. Occasionally he'd make a move to get up, but Chloe would shoot him a stern look and he'd sit back down. They didn't act like they liked each other at all. Luca had to be wrong.

Lots of people were drinking Blue Wolf but none of them smelled cursed. She didn't see anyone who looked like the waitress either. After an hour of canvasing, they gave up and went to sit in a booth in the back. Chloe went to dance. Horatio shot to his feet but didn't go directly to her. He inserted himself into the crowd a few feet away and wiggled and danced his way to her until she turned to face him. They exchanged words, then Chloe turned her back on him. Honey figured he'd walk away. Instead, he got right up against her back and put his arms around her. Chloe leaned her head back against his shoulder. It was such a private moment, Honey had to look away.

"You wanna dance, Honey?" Nathan asked.

She looked out over the dance floor. They were playing pop tonight and the floor was crowded with people wiggling and bouncing and generally having a good time. She could see where Brayton had stabbed her, but it would be easy to avoid.

"Sure."

# 28

## Brayton

Two am. His head pulsed and he swallowed down the bile again. The relief the pills from the doctor had given him had lasted a grand total of one hour and forty-five minutes, and that was with the herbs Chloe had found and snuck over yesterday evening. He couldn't continue like this. He needed Honey.

Her sad green eyes looked up at him again from the knife in her chest. Would she ever forgive him? Could she? Chloe had said they were going to a club because Honey thought someone had cursed him. He was pretty sure he'd just been drunk. He would have surely smelled the magic if she could, but if that's what Honey believed, maybe she would help him.

The problem was getting past his grandpa and Chloe, but mostly Grandpa. He loved Grandpa but he could be very overbearing and stubborn. Even in his sleep, his snores sounded like commands.

Another pulse of pain. Stupid. He was so stupid. This was his chance. Grandpa was a heavy sleeper; he had to be with those snores. Brayton could slip past the couch where he slept, sneak over to Honey's dorm and...and what. He'd have to get past the front desk and find her room. They'd never let a guy into the girl's dorm this late and he didn't know where her room was. It was hopeless.

He didn't normally cry, but he was so beat down from the pain and lack of sleep and everything, he couldn't stop the tears that escaped the corner of his eyes. It wasn't until he checked the phone again at two-fifteen am. that he remembered he had Honey's number. Mom had made him add Honey as a contact when she bought Honey her phone.

He opened his contacts and found her name but hesitated over the call icon. It was the middle of the night. She was sleeping. She wouldn't want to help him now, if at all. He reached over to put the phone back down, then remembered it was Honey. She'd really hate it if he woke her on a school night, but tomorrow was Sunday. His grandpa was sleeping now, and his head felt like it could explode at any time. He pushed the button.

The phone rang three times. He nearly hung up, then there was a long pause and Honey's groggy voice sounded in his ear.

"Brayton? Hello?"

"Honey. I'm sorry for waking you but my head is killing me and nothing is working. I've tried everything. Will you please, please, please help me?"

"Now?"

"Yes. Grandpa is sleeping. If I can get past him, will you meet me somewhere?"

There was a long pause – a very long pause. He thought she was going to say no. He would have. "Where?"

"Anywhere you want. Honey, I am so, so sorry I hurt you. I don't know how or why it even happened. I wish I could go back in time and undo everything. I'm sorry for the other times I hurt you too. Can you ever forgive me?"

"I'm working on it. Where do you want to meet?"

She was actually trying to forgive him? The vice around his head tightened another notch. Saliva squirted into his mouth and he swallowed several times trying to stop the inevitable.

"Brayton?"

"Hold on."

He lost the battle, but he did manage to hit the trashcan he'd put by the bed just in case. Unfortunately, throwing up did nothing to help his head. He wiped his mouth and picked up the phone from where he'd dropped it on the floor.

"Honey, are you still there?"

"I'm on my way. Bring a blanket and your car keys. I'll meet you in front of your dorm."

His SUV turned out to be an excellent choice. She had him put the passenger seat down all the way and cover himself with the blanket to help him relax. She crawled into the backseat and put her fingers against his temples. Her warm honey scent surrounded him and the next thing he knew, the sun was half-way up in the sky and Grandpa was banging on the passenger side window.

He reached over and turned the key in the ignition to roll the window down. "What's wrong, Grandpa?"

"I've been looking all over for you, that's what's wrong." He sniffed the air. "And why does it smell like that girl in here?"

He took a long sniff. "I don't smell anything." It was the truth, but then he'd been breathing whatever scent she'd left behind all night. He wished he could smell it.

"What are you doing out here?" Grandpa asked.

"I couldn't sleep, so I thought I'd try something different."

His grandpa's voice changed from irate to concerned. "Did it work?"

"Yeah."

"Is your head any better?"

Until that moment Brayton had forgotten about his head. Other than a dull ache, it now felt perfectly normal. Honey had healed him again. He turned his head away and pretended he was searching for his phone while he discretely wiped away the moisture in his right eye. "Yeah."

"Good, let's get some waffles for breakfast." Grandpa tossed Brayton's phone into his lap. "Call your friends and tell them you've been found. I'll drive."

There were several missed calls, all from his friends and his grandpa. "Why did you have my phone?" he asked while Grandpa slid into the driver's seat.

"Because you dropped it on the way here with that girl."

"What are you talking about?"

He jerked his thumb at the phone. "You called her and," he tapped his nose, "it doesn't lie." He started the engine. "What's going on between you two?"

"Nothing."

He leaned over and took a long sniff of Brayton's head. "You smell like her and," he sniffed again. "You threw up?"

"Yeah. It was bad last night." He didn't want to lie to Grandpa and there really wasn't a reason why he should. "I called Honey because I was desperate."

"And she came?"

"I threw up while I was talking with her. I think she felt sorry for me."

He sniffed again. "I don't smell any of those herbs you tried yesterday, well except on you. She didn't use them?"

"No. She said the reclining chair and the blanket were enough to get me to relax. She puts her fingers on certain places on my head and somehow, that works."

"Huh."

Grandpa backed out of the spot and didn't say another thing the whole way to the restaurant. It was pack owned, of course. Grandpa only frequented pack-run establishments unless he had no other choice.

He was in so much pain the night before, Brayton had totally forgotten to put clothes on over his boxers and T-shirt before he went to the car. He tried to talk Grandpa into getting take-out, but he wouldn't hear of it. Brayton finally wrapped his blanket around himself like a toga and followed Grandpa inside. The aged waitress greeted Grandpa like he was a king instead of the retired alpha and would have probably patted Brayton on the head if he wasn't a foot taller than her.

243

The waffles were light and fluffy and the serving sizes were large enough to fill a hungry wolf, which he was. He had two plates to make up for all the meals he hadn't been able to finish the past week. Grandpa kept looking at him like he wanted to say something, but he didn't share.

A group of people were standing in the dorm parking lot when they pulled back in. Brayton dismissed them as a group of college kids about to pile into their cars, then he realized he knew them. Rhys, Cici, Malcolm, Chloe, and all Honey's friends were there, standing next to one of the only empty spaces like they were waiting for him and Grandpa. The wolf with dark skin, Liam, Brayton recalled belatedly, stepped forward when Brayton opened the door.

His brown eyes flickered with anger and he demanded, "Where's Honey?"

"What do you mean, where's Honey?" Brayton asked.

"You called her last night. Her roommate heard her say she was going to meet you at your car."

"We did meet at my car and I fell asleep. That's the last time I saw her."

The shortest of her friends stepped forward, his fists on his hips. "What exactly were you doing in your car and where are your clothes?"

"She was helping me with my headache. I was feeling so bad I didn't remember to get dressed."

"In your car?" the short one growled.

"My car has reclining seats. She wanted me to relax."

The short one kept scowling at him but the blondish one nodded. "Yeah, that sounds like Honey. What time did she leave the car?"

"I don't know. I fell asleep. I didn't hear her leave."

"Well, she never made it back to her room," Liam said. "Her roommate hasn't seen her all morning and she isn't answering her phone."

"I don't know what to say." He didn't. The campus was pretty safe. Other than a few issues between wolves that got out of hand, there was very little theft or other crimes thanks to the wolf patrols.

"Where did you take her?" the tallest of her friends asked. It was strange to see a wolf with glasses. Most wolves had vision and hearing that were better than perfect by human standards.

"We didn't go anywhere. We just sat in the car. In fact, she sat behind me so she could rub my temples. I didn't even sit next to her."

"You weren't even supposed to be that close," Chloe snapped.

"How's your head?" Liam asked.

"Much better."

"So, all you needed was for Honey to rub your temples?" Liam said doubtfully.

The boy was basically calling him a liar. Brayton might be many things, but he wasn't a liar. "Look, I can't explain it. All I know is that I tried everything else and somehow, as soon as she touched my head, it started to feel better."

"Maybe she's your mate," the short guy said.

"Stop with the mate business," Chloe exclaimed. "There's no such thing as fated mates."

"Says the girl who couldn't stop touching my cousin last night," short guy smirked.

"He was touching me!" Chloe's face was so red her cheeks could have passed for ripe tomatoes.

"But you were enjoying it," short guy snickered.

"Did you ask the person at the front desk of her dorm if they saw her come back," Grandpa asked in his no-nonsense tone.

"Yeah," Rhys said. "She saw her leave around 2:20 am. but didn't see her come back."

"Did you track her scent?"

"We tried. There's no trail other than the one between the dorm and where the car was parked."

"Did you smell anybody else?"

"No. Not fresh."

Grandpa stalked back to where Brayton's SUV had been parked earlier and squatted down to sniff the pavement himself. He wrinkled his nose. "Smells like magic."

"I noticed that," Rhys said. "But it disappears pretty quickly."

Still in a squat, Grandpa spun in a partial circle like he was looking for something, but Brayton could tell he was sniffing the air. Even in human form Grandpa was one of the best trackers in the pack.

"It's faint, but the magic goes that way." He nodded toward the dorms.

Brayton squatted next to him to see if he could smell it. The air tingled faintly of magic, but mostly he smelled the scent of Honey when she took away his pain. He stood and followed her scent.

It faded to almost nothing by the time it reached the front of the boy's dorm and he nearly missed where it split, but something made him turn his nose toward the bushes along the side of the dorm. It smelled like it went into the bushes, but the dryer vent behind the bushes was spewing out so much fabric softener scent he couldn't follow it any farther. He would have transformed and inspected the space in wolf form, but there wasn't enough room for his large wolf.

"She might be in there."

"Honey?" Liam called. He started pulling off his shirt.

"I've got this," short guy said. He stripped and transformed into a small brown wolf and slipped between the thorny branches and evergreen leaves.

"She's there," Liam said after several seconds had passed. "Luca says she's sleeping and he doesn't see any injuries."

"Wake her up," Grandpa demanded.

"He's working on it. She's being very stubborn."

"Nothing new there," Cici commented wryly.

"They're coming."

The brown wolf came out first followed by a small red and brown wolf with green eyes. Honey's wolf was one of the smallest full-grown wolves he'd seen, which was odd because her human form wasn't short.

"Transform," Grandpa demanded. "We need to talk."

Honey dove back under the bushes.

"Get out here, you little mutt!" Grandpa growled.

"She's changing," Liam said. "Give her a minute."

Brayton didn't know how she managed to get her clothes on so quickly in such a small space, but a minute later, Honey crawled out in human form.

Her blond friend zipped to her side to help her up. "Honey, why were you under a bush? I've called you like ten times. We were worried."

"Oh. I didn't hear my phone ring." She pulled it out of her pocket and swiped the screen. "Huh. I don't see any calls. Well, that answers that question."

Grandpa stepped closer so that he loomed over her. "Did you use magic on my grandson?" The amount of alpha power he aimed at her was enough to make a grown wolf whimper and cower. Brayton knew, because he wanted to. Honey just looked Grandpa in the eye.

"My mother practiced herbal and alternative medicine. I learned from her."

"I didn't smell any herbs."

"You wouldn't since the technique involved massage."

"I smelled magic."

"I transformed. That's a type of magic.

"I've never smelled a transformation like that before."

"I'm different."

"How so?"

Honey shrugged. "It's just the way I am."

Grandpa growled. Brayton slipped in between them before Grandpa could step any closer. As a future alpha, he was the only one who could actually move. "Grandpa, leave her alone."

"Stay out of this Brayton."

His grandpa used his alpha power on him and he had no choice but to step out of the way.

Honey put her hands on her hips and glared at Grandpa. "So now you're bullying your own grandson?"

"I am an alpha. Our job is to rule the pack. Your job is to submit and obey our rule."

"Humans don't have magic yet they still follow their leaders. Why?" She paused and made a face which Brayton would have called cute if it wasn't Honey. "Well, in some cases I'm not sure, but in others it's because those people are good leaders and have earned the right to lead. I listen to Luna Lynn because she is kind and treats me like a person. You, on the other hand, have only tried to bully me and I don't like bullies."

Brayton knew what was coming before Grandpa even lifted his hand, but there was nothing he could do to stop it. His grandpa rarely had to discipline people physically since his alpha power pretty much prevented people from talking back the way Honey was, but he'd seen him hit a few wolves on occasion. He'd probably break Honey's face with his meaty fist. "Grandpa, no!"

He needn't have worried. Honey ducked and moved so that her dorm was the only thing behind her.

"If you hit me, you will be guilty of assault on a minor. I will press charges."

"We are wolves, not humans. Some laws don't apply to us," Grandpa snarled.

"Then you'll have to catch me first."

She turned and ran with her ridiculous speed to the women's dorm. Grandpa didn't have a chance.

# 29

## *Honey*

She didn't stop running until she was inside the building and half-way up the stairs. That was a close one. She'd nearly had to transform in front of other wolves.

She tore into her snacks, hoping there was enough there to fill the gnawing hole in her belly. Brayton's head had been much worse this time. It had taken her at least two hours to fix everything. Afterward, she'd nearly fallen asleep in the back seat of the car, but knowing what a disaster that would be, she'd forced herself out of the car and as far as the bushes.

There was a knock at the door. "Honey, are you in there?"

She opened the door for Chloe while stuffing the remnants of two pop tarts into her mouth.

Chloe raised an eyebrow at her. "Hungry much?"

Honey ripped open the wrapping on a ClifBar. "Starving."

"Your friends are waiting downstairs. I believe they mentioned pizza."

"Excellent."

Chloe caught her hand when she started to move past her. "Honey, wait. We need to talk."

"About?"

"First, you can't talk to an alpha the way you did Alpha Braxton. That's a good way to get thrown out of the pack. Second, you can't go around meeting with Brayton in the middle of the night without telling someone, especially me. I'm supposed to be protecting you and I can't do my job if you don't tell me what's going on."

"He was too sick to hurt me. I knew it was safe."

"Yeah, but you worried all your friends. Friends will put up with a lot, but good friends don't make them."

She was right of course, but Honey hadn't known it was going to wear her out so much to help him, and she couldn't explain it either, not without revealing her magic.

"I'm sorry Chloe. I appreciate that you are trying to protect me. I did not plan to sleep outside. It just happened."

"Something like that doesn't just happen."

"I got really tired all of a sudden and I couldn't face climbing the stairs."

"Uh-huh."

"So, what are you going to do now that you found your mate? Are you going on another date," Honey asked, blatantly changing the subject.

Chloe spun around and marched down the hall. "That man is not my mate."

Honey grabbed her keys and shut the door behind her before she chased her down. "What's wrong with him?"

"He's...Well, he's of the wrong pack for one."

251

"Does the female wolf always join the male wolf's pack?"

"No. But even if he wanted to join my pack, he's not a good dresser."

"That seems like an easy thing to fix. I thought he looked nice in his trench coat. Kind of like Sherlock Holmes."

"Exactly. I am not marrying Sherlock Holmes."

"You wouldn't be. Sherlock Holmes hardly shows any emotion. The way Horatio looked at you when you were dancing…Let's just say I had to look away."

"Okay, yeah, his looks were intense, I'll admit to that much."

"And you made a really nice-looking couple."

"Did we?"

"And he's an agent, an investigator, so you know he must have some brains."

"Brains, huh?"

"You want to marry someone without any?" Honey asked.

"No. Brains would be good."

"And he's Luca's cousin. Luca is nice. I bet his cousin is too, once you get to know him."

"Is that why you are talking him up – because he's Luca's cousin," Chloe asked while she pushed open the stair door on the first floor.

"No. I'm trying to encourage you to give him a chance because finding a fated mate is something that happens to very few wolves and it would be sad for both of you if you turned your back on him."

"Humph."

The boys all stood when she and Chloe entered the lobby. Liam took three long strides and pulled Honey into a tight hug. "I'm so glad you're okay."

"I'm sorry I caused you to worry," she said when he released her.

"Why were you sleeping under the bushes?" Walter asked, squeezing her shoulder.

"It was dark and cold and I was really tired. It just kind of happened."

Luca got right up in her face and shook his finger at her. "No more antagonizing alphas. You nearly got your brains splattered against the wall." He lunged suddenly and gave her a hug so tight all the air was squeezed from lungs. Luckily, it was short.

Nathan elbowed him out of the way and pulled her in for a much gentler hug, then held her at arm's length so he could look her over. "Hmm, pop-tart crumbs on chin. Chocolate in the corner of her mouth. Yep, I was right. She was digging into her snacks. Let's find her a pizza before she attacks someone."

For some reason, they loved to tease her about how they met. "I'm not going to attack anyone!"

They moved together toward the door. Luca ran ahead and poked his head out. "All clear."

"What did Brayton's grandpa do when I left? Did he try to chase me?"

"About three steps," Liam said. "Then he started mumbling about witches and stomped into the dorm. Honey, why didn't you want him to see you transform?"

She really wanted to ask Liam if transforming the way she did with her clothes on was truly a bad thing. The wolves had accepted that she wasn't telepathic, so maybe they'd accept her odd transforming abilities too. The problem was Chloe. She was nice, but she'd tell Alpha Braxton whatever was said.

"Don't you think it's odd that an old man would want to see me strip naked?" Honey deflected.

Chloe laughed. "That's what you were afraid of? Do you know how many naked people he has seen in his life?" She looked up and down Honey's slim form, "I doubt you would even be a blip on his radar."

"You need to get over your gymnophobia," Walter said.

She knew he probably wasn't referring to gyms, but she said it anyway, "I'm not afraid of gyms."

"No, fear of being naked."

"I don't have a problem being naked, just not in front of old men."

"Or young men or young women, or anyone, really," Chloe added.

It was a perfect lead-in. She took it. "Wouldn't it be neat if wolves could transform without stripping? It would save a lot of time and clothes. Has anyone ever been able to do that?"

"Not that I've ever heard," Chloe said.

"But is it possible?"

"Probably not without magic," Walter said.

"But transforming is a type of magic. Seems like it should be possible to transform clothes if you can transform your body."

They reached Walter's car. Honey had just settled into the middle back seat when a deep voice attached to a pair of long legs just outside the car said, "Chloe."

Who knew so much emotion could be packed into one word? Chloe pretended she hadn't heard and that it was imperative that she climb into the seat beside Honey.

Honey gave her a push. "Go. You need to talk to him. You can meet us at the pizza place."

Chloe crossed her arms and sat back in a huff. "I don't want to talk to him."

Honey really didn't understand her hesitation. Horatio was nice, at least from the short time she'd known him, and Chloe clearly liked him, as in liked-liked him. "Move over then. I'll go with him. I want to talk to him about the investigation anyway."

"No! You are going to stay right here where you can't get lost. What about the investigation?"

"I was just wondering what the plans were for next weekend. I thought maybe we could try that other place downtown."

Chloe mumbled something to herself, then slammed her hand down on the seat. "Fine. We'll meet you there." She scooted back out of the car and stood so that she was face-to-face with Horatio. "We're going to eat pizza and you're driving."

He looked her in the eye for a long moment, then gave a single nod.

"And stop looking at me like that."

"Like what?"

"Like you're going to devour me with your eyes."

Did she realize she'd stepped even closer to him?

255

He put his hands on her hips and said something in her ear that sounded like, "It wouldn't be with my eyes."

Chloe turned her head and they were kissing again, in the middle of the parking lot, in full daylight.

"We'll meet you at the pizza place," Luca said cheerily, then climbed in beside Honey. "Or not. I had no idea Horatio was such a ladies' man."

"I think you mean lady's man, singular," Walter said from the driver's seat.

Her phone trumpeted. She whacked Luca, who was snickering, and glanced at the screen. The text said 'thank you!!!'.

"Who's 'BB'?" Liam asked, looking over her shoulder.

"Bossy Brayton." She sent Brayton a thumbs up.

"You're going to have to teach me that technique that cures headaches with just a massage," Liam said.

"I think it only works on certain types of headaches. I was surprised it worked so well for Brayton, actually." Certain types meaning ones where your molecules were going the wrong direction. Two ideas popped into her head simultaneously, and a couple of questions, but those could wait.

"What do you think was causing it?" Liam asked.

"That is a good question," Honey said. "I know he didn't have any headaches until we started school, at least I didn't hear anything about them while I lived in his house."

"It's something at the school then," Walter said.

"Maybe he's allergic to something," Nathan suggested.

Could someone be allergic to a curse? It would be easy enough to test if they could find a bottle of cursed Blue Wolf. Right, her idea. "Next weekend we should ask Brayton and his friends to go with us downtown."

Luca's head swiveled away from the window where he'd been gawking at some co-eds to gawk at her. "Honey, are you crazy? He stabbed you. You almost died."

"I really don't think he meant to. He had no motive."

"Other than he doesn't like you and doesn't want you in his pack," Nathan said from the front seat.

"We don't have to go together. There is something odd about that Blue Wolf stuff. If he goes, they might serve it to him. We can go in after they get their drinks and I'll sniff them. He can wait on the other side of the room."

"That might work," Liam finally agreed. "But no dancing with him."

"Of course not. I'll stay with you guys." Except when she was scanning the brains in the rest of the crowd. That was her second idea and a question: did the drink mess up other people's brains or was there something else going on with Brayton?

"Honey," Liam said beside her, "What did you mean when you said your transformations were different?"

Shoot. She was hoping they'd forgotten about it. "Just what I said."

"You didn't say anything."

"It's not important."

"Are they painful?" Luca asked.

"No."

"How old were you when you first transformed?" Nathan asked, watching her from the mirror in the visor.

257

She shrugged. "Old enough. Can we talk about something else please?"

"Honey, we're your friends," Luca wheedled. "You know you can tell us anything."

She wanted to. She really did. It would make running with them so much easier. She wouldn't have to go to the tent and pretend to change. She could just walk into the woods with them and step behind a tree while they changed. "My dad said not to let anyone else see me change."

"Why?" Luca asked.

"Because I'm different." Another idea popped into her head. Apparently, she was full of them today. The boys already knew she was different thanks to the telepathy thing. Would that pass as an excuse for why her transformation was different? "Maybe it's related to the part of my brain that doesn't do telepathy."

"What do you mean?" Liam asked.

Was she going to do this? They hadn't even blinked when they learned she couldn't talk telepathically. Her mother had said someday she'd find someone she could trust – someone who wouldn't care that she was a wolch (her term for a part-wolf, part-witch). Maybe she'd found four someones. "If I show you, you have to promise never to tell anyone."

"I promise," Luca said automatically.

"I do too," Nathan said, quickly followed by Liam.

"It can't be all that amazing," Walter said from the front.

"Then it will be an easy promise to keep," Luca said.

"Fine, I promise," Walter sighed.

She closed her eyes and sent up a prayer that everything would be okay and that her dad wouldn't be disappointed in her. A feeling of peace flowed into her chest. It would be okay. She unbuckled her seatbelt.

"You're going to do it here?" Luca squeaked.

She looked at him and transformed. She waited a few seconds, then popped back into her human form. "That's why I don't transform in front of anyone."

Luca's mouth was hanging open. Nathan's eyes were so wide his eyebrows had disappeared under his hair, and Walter was watching her instead of paying attention to the road.

"Walter, look out!" She yelled as the car crossed the line and headed toward a large pickup coming the other way.

He jerked the wheel sharply to the right to get back into his lane.

"How long have you been able to transform with your clothes on?" Liam asked. His look was one of speculation. She should have known he wouldn't be surprised.

"I've always done it that way, ever since I was six."

"You were six?" Luca exclaimed, ending on an impressive high note.

"Yep. My dad was in wolf form playing with me and I wanted to be a wolf to, so I became one."

"I bet you were adorable," Nathan said.

"You used magic." Liam said. It wasn't a question.

"Yep."

"Did you use magic to heal Brayton?"

"Yep."

"And that's why you used the herbs the first time and took him to the car the second time. You didn't want anyone to smell your magic."

She had no idea Liam was so smart.

"Yes, and why I didn't want to transform in front of Alpha Braxton."

"Wait, you have magic?" Luca said.

"Can't you smell it?" Liam replied.

"Oh. Yeah."

"Why do you have magic?" Walter asked.

Again, shoot. Liam had figured it out too fast. She should have transformed downwind instead of inside a car. She still hadn't figured out why her parents had worked so hard to keep her hidden. Witches and wolves went to school together. Was it so surprising that they would have children together?

"I...I'm just..."

Liam took her hand. "You don't have to tell us."

She fiddled with the buttons on the side of her phone with her free hand. "I want to, but I'm afraid of what you might think of me."

Luca took her other hand. "Honey, you're a great person. There's nothing you could tell us that would make us think bad of you."

She looked up and caught Nathan's eye in the visor mirror. "It's true. You're one of the nicest people I know."

Walter looked at her through the rear-view mirror and gave a nod.

"Okay, but this is an absolute secret. You can't tell anyone. Other than myself, everyone who knows is dead."

The word 'dead' tore through the flimsy barrier she had up that kept her sorrow at bay most of the time. The sobs flooded out uncontrollably. Liam put his arm around her and drew her to his chest. Luca patted her back and said things that were probably soothing but she couldn't make out the words. She didn't know what Nathan said or did, but Walter pulled into the pizza place and parked the car, then offered her a napkin from the glove compartment.

"I'm sorry. I'm sorry," she sputtered. She hated crying in front of people.

"Honey, it's okay," Liam said. "We understand. In fact, I'm surprised you've been handling things as well as you have."

"Get it all out," Nathan said. "I'll go in and order our pizzas and get a couple of wet towels so you can wipe your face."

She wiped her nose with the already damp napkin and sniffed. "Thanks guys."

Luca shook his finger at her. "I still want to know your secret though."

"Nathan, wait."

He looked at her expectantly over the front seat. "I'm a...my dad was a wolf, but my mother, she was a..."

"She was a witch, wasn't she?" Liam said when she started crying again.

She nodded.

Luca leaned back against his door. "Wow. I did not see that one coming."

She turned her head to see if he hated her and a huge grin exploded across his face. "That is so cool! What is your power? What does your magic do?"

"Shh. Do you want everyone in the parking lot to hear?"

He mimed zipping his lips, then mouthed, "Sorry."

"I didn't know that was possible," Nathan said.

She looked up at him. "Why wouldn't it be?"

"The offspring of a witch and a wolf is a monster," Walter stated calmly. "That's what everyone believes anyway."

"That's wrong, and it doesn't make sense. We're basically both human with a little something extra. In my case, my little extra is a mix between wolf and witch. I'm a wolch."

"That's what people have believed for years though, and it's such a strong belief that any child born to mixed parents is automatically put down," Liam said. "Marriages between wolves and witches are strictly forbidden."

"No wonder your parents kept you hidden," Nathan said.

"What is your power?" Luca whispered.

"I can manipulate molecules."

"Cool." There was a long pause. "What does that mean?"

"It means I can make every molecule in your body stop moving. You'll be frozen for about thirty seconds and won't remember a thing."

"Cool. Wait. Does that mean I'd be cold, like a popsicle?"

"No. I just slow down the molecules. Nothing crystallizes like it does when it gets cold."

"What about Brayton's head? Did you freeze it?" Liam asked.

"No. Some of his molecules were spinning the wrong way. I forced them to go the other direction. I can't explain why it worked. I just fixed what looked wrong."

"You could have killed him," Liam said.

"No. They're just molecules. They wiggle about all the time."

Liam shook his head. "You can't use your magic on wolves. It's illegal."

"Except in cases of self-defense and when they request your help. Brayton asked for help."

"But he didn't know what you were doing," Liam said sternly.

"He knew magic was involved, just not how."

"Leave her alone Liam," Walter said, surprising her. He never overruled anyone. "She used her magic for good and it sounds like Brayton is none the wiser. We can help her keep it that way."

# 30

## *Honey*

Telling the boys her secret did *not* make it easier to shift at WOLF. The trees were all on the opposite side of the field and the guys preferred the tent so they knew their clothes would be dry and bug free when class was done. Liam was dead set against her going into the trees anyway. He insisted she keep doing what she was doing even though Chloe kept trying to catch her at it.

Liam had changed. He hadn't blinked an eye when she told him her age, but now he no longer smiled when he saw her or chatted spontaneously with her like he had before. Luca was just the opposite. He kept wanting to see her magic, but he gave it different names like bunny and kitty and pencil so no one would know what he was taking about. Nathan and Walter treated her nearly the same, except now Walter took her side more often than Liam.

She texted Brayton her idea to visit the club downtown. He was all for it. As far as she knew, his headache hadn't come back. He looked healthy the few times she saw him. His grandpa, on the other hand, always looked like someone had forced him to eat his least favorite food and then blamed it on her. She kept her distance since she was pretty sure he'd rip her head off the first chance he got.

Friday came.

Chloe wore a little red dress that slipped off one shoulder and flowed down to a skirt so short Honey would have been afraid to sit down in it. Chloe had arranged to meet Agent Hopkins at the club and needed a ride, so Luca had to sit in the front middle of Walter's car between Nathan and Walter. Honey sat in the middle back with Liam on one side and Chloe on the other. She told herself it was promising that Liam would at least still sit beside her, but she had a feeling it was only because Nathan always beat everyone to the front and Walter refused to let anyone else drive his beloved car.

They got lucky and found a space along the street a half-block down from the club. Horatio was waiting for them near the club's front door. By the time Walter had parallel parked his huge car, Horatio was standing on the sidewalk beside them. He looked completely different from the first time he'd met them. Instead of a trench coat and black clothes, he had on a dark blazer that contrasted perfectly with his light blue shirt and tan pans. He also looked like he hadn't shaved in several days, and his hair was tousled instead of neatly combed. If Honey didn't know he was an enforcer, she'd have thought he was a model.

Luca turned around and gaped at Chloe. "What did you do to my cousin?"

Chloe only had eyes for the man opening the door for her. "I sent him a few pictures of what people are supposed to wear when they go to a club."

"Can you send me some pictures?"

"Google it."

Horatio helped Chloe up, right into his arms, just outside the door.

There was no getting out that way. Honey turned to Liam. "We'll have to get out on your side."

"Oh, sure." He fumbled with the handle a second before it opened. He didn't look before he opened it and nearly lost the door to a car speeding by. Luckily, Walter didn't notice.

They'd just made it safely to the sidewalk when a gun shot came from the vicinity of Honey's jacket pocket. She glared at a giggling Luca and pulled her phone out. He pretended his finger was a gun and blew on the tip. There was no way he was getting a hold of her phone himself. Walter or Nathan must be helping him.

"What did Bumbling Buffoon say?" Walter asked, leaning closer to read the message over her shoulder. She'd sent Brayton a text while Walter was parking.

"They're in the front right corner. He said to give him a minute to get his grandpa across the room."

"It will take us at least that long to get through the line."

"Or longer," Liam groused, nodding at Nathan who had run ahead to get in line but was now insisting a couple of scantily clad co-eds go in front of him.

"ID," the bear of a man who smelled like a wolf insisted at the front door several minutes later.

The boys all pulled out their driver's licenses. Honey didn't even have a permit. "Um. I didn't know we'd need it. They didn't ID us before. Will my college ID work?"

He took it from her and scanned it and her as if he could tell if it was fake. "You're in college?"

"Yes. I'm a freshman."

"You don't look like a freshman, Miss …Honey? Honey Smith? That's the worst fake name ever."

"Because it's not fake." She held up her lanyard. "I have a dorm key."

He squinted at her. "How old are you?"

Shoot. If she told him she was a minor, he'd never let her in. "Old enough to go to college."

"Get out of here."

"But…"

"Is there a problem?"

The bouncer frowned at Horatio behind her. "Who are you?"

Horatio whipped out a billfold with a badge. "Agent Hopkins. She's with me." He leaned forward and said very quietly. "I'd appreciate it if you don't blow our cover."

The big man crossed his burly arms. "What are you investigating?"

"An attempted murder. She's a witness. I need her to ID the suspect."

"Strange way to go about it."

"It's a strange case."

"All right, but this is a pack club. If anything goes wrong, you're all banned from all our clubs."

"Now wait a second," Nathan began.

Luca elbowed him in the stomach.

267

"Thank you." Horatio stuffed his billfold into his pocket and herded them all inside.

It was much more crowded and much louder than the first time they'd come. The dance floor was full of people bouncing and rubbing up against each other. There wasn't room to do much else. After they paid, they shuffled forward into the closest open space.

Chloe, who was walking behind her, tapped Honey's shoulder and pointed to her right. Malcolm raised a bottle when he saw them looking his way. He was the only one at the table.

"I'll be right behind you," Chloe said in Honey's ear.

Honey sat at the table and the boys followed her lead. Sitting and sniffing everyone's drinks would be less conspicuous than standing and sniffing, she hoped. She discretely lifted each bottle of Blue Wolf and passed them under her nose. They smelled fine.

"All clean," she told Malcolm before she stood. "We'll find a table on the other side of the floor. Have Brayton text me if you order more Blue Wolf."

"Will do."

Her group stood and wove their way through the tables. There were bottles of Blue Wolf everywhere. She smiled and said hi to every wolf they passed with a bottle in his or her hand. Some of them smiled back and talked to her. Their breath was curse-free.

The only empty tables were the ones near the bathroom. They made a mutual decision to go to the bar instead after Nathan made sure Brayton and his grandpa weren't in the vicinity. There were no seats open at the bar either, but she found a spot to stand near the far edge where she could see all the drinks being served, including the ones the waitresses retrieved while their trays were refilled. Unfortunately, she was too far away to smell them.

"Can you use your sparkly pen?" Luca asked.

"My sparkly pen?"

He grinned. "Or maybe a fan to blow the scent your way?"

"But then everyone would smell the ink."

"You just need to be closer." Walter said. He grabbed her hand. "Hurry. That woman looks like she's getting up."

They managed to slip past all the other patrons lining the bar and made it to the empty seat before anyone else could take it. It was a good seat; right next to the part of the bar where most of the drinks were being served. Walter waited until she was seated, then leaned past her to order.

"Two Coronas please."

The bartender opened two bottles and plopped them down before us. "No Blue Wolf? There's a special tonight."

Walter threw some money down. "My girlfriend doesn't like it. She says it stains her teeth."

"Your girlfriend?" Luca smirked just loud enough behind them for Honey to hear.

Honey grinned and hoped her teeth looked white.

"That explains why there are so many people drinking it," Walter mumbled to her while the bartender moved on to the next person who happened to be Nathan.

"They aren't cursed though."

Nathan stuck the bottle of Blue Wolf he'd just bought under her nose. "Yeah, but they still have more kick than anything else."

"Smells good," she told him.

"Are we close enough?" Walter whispered over the top of his beer while looking out over the dance floor.

"Almost."

"Let me know if you smell anything."

With all the wolf noses around, she didn't dare use her magic. All she could do was sniff the air and hope the movement cause by people rushing by was sufficient to move the air over the bottles waiting for the next waitress her way.

"I'm going to dance," Luca declared after a minute. "You going to stay here, Walter?"

"Well, I'm not going out into that drunken orgy pit." He waved his bottle at the dance floor where Nathan was wiggling his way past two girls.

"What about you, Liam?" Luca asked.

"I'm going to get a drink."

"Your loss."

Luca dove into the dancers. Liam leaned past Honey and ordered a sparkling water. Honey normally didn't drink beer, but she was thirsty and since Walter had already paid for it, she decided to try hers. Liam grabbed it out of her hand before she could put it to her lips and slid the water in front of her.

"Hey!" She actually didn't mind, but she couldn't let his grabbiness go without some form of punishment.

"You are not like the rest of us, nor are you…tall enough."

By tall enough he meant her age. She knew he meant she might not be able to handle alcohol like a full wolf by the rest of the sentence, but Liam's voice and face were mean rather than teasing. It hurt. She turned her back on him so he wouldn't see the moisture that sprang to her eyes.

Her pocket banged.

"What does Betty Boop have to say now?" Walter asked.

"Betty Boop? How did you come up with that?" she teased while she pulled out her phone. She avoided looking at Liam.

"She was a comic strip character in the 1930's."

Walter knew the most random things. Honey shook her head and opened the message. "He says his grandpa knows I'm here."

"We'll just stay on this side of the room then. I doubt his grandpa is going to dance in that mess."

Her phone banged again loud enough that the bartender gave her an odd look. "And that he's looking for me."

"Great." Walter was very good at sarcasm. "Try not to antagonize him."

"I never do."

"Exactly."

Alpha Braxton came into view around the corner of the dance floor before she could even start to formulate a plan to avoid him. She spun in her seat to face the bar and put her back to him. Yeah, that was going to work.

"What are you doing here?" his gruff voice demanded to the back of her head.

She pulled up a smile and spun around. "Oh hi, Alpha Braxton. It's…um," she'd say it was nice to see him but she didn't want to lie. "I'm just hanging out with my friends. How are you?"

"Leave."

His sour breath washed over her and she knew. "You've been drinking Blue Wolf haven't you?"

Walter, who had moved as close to her side as he could, looked at Alpha Braxton, then her. "The sparkly kind?"

"Yep."

"I'll get Horatio," Liam said.

"What's going on?" Alpha Braxton demanded, loudly.

"Let get away from the bar so we can talk in private."

He poked her near her collarbone with his thick finger. "I'm not going to go anywhere with you, little witch. You're going to round up your boy toys and get the hell out of this club."

"Grandpa, you can't order her to leave. It's a public club," Brayton said behind him. Malcolm and Cici were with him.

Alpha Braxton whirled around to yell at his grandson. "Like hell I can't!"

"Brayton, his drink. It's what we were looking for. Is there any left?" Honey asked.

"I'll see," Cici said.

She looked around Alpha Braxton's broad back to Brayton. "Where did he get his drink from? Was it the bar or a waitress?"

"I'm not sure. He got them from both."

The alpha turned back to her. "Stop talking to him."

272

"Is there a problem here?"

Alpha Braxton turned just enough to reveal the bouncer who'd been at the door.

"Oh, it's you," the bouncer said when his eyes fell on her.

"There's no problem, mister bouncer. Alpha Braxton is just loud."

"I am not loud!" Alpha Braxton yelled.

Horatio jogged up with Chloe behind him. "Honey, are you sure?"

"He's the attempted murderer?" the bouncer said, pointing to Alpha Braxton.

"No!" Alpha Braxton and Honey said at the same time, although he was much louder than she was.

Honey turned to Horatio. "I think so. I can smell it on his breath. Cici went to get his drink."

Horatio pulled out his wallet again and held up his badge. "Alpha Braxton, I'm Agent Hopkins. Honey is helping me with an investigation that should benefit Brayton and you might have stumbled onto a clue. Why don't we take this conversation back to your table and away from the bar."

"Investigation? What investigation?" He bellowed loud enough Honey was pretty sure everyone in the club heard him.

"Come with me and I'll explain."

"All right, but she goes in front where I can keep an eye on her. Brayton, stay behind me."

Everyone at the bar and on the edge of the dance floor watched while their group made their way along the narrow path between the seating area and the rail that surrounded the dance floor towards the front door. So much for their undercover operation.

Cici met them half-way, empty-handed. "I'm sorry. All the empty bottles were gone when I got to the table."

"Did you see who took them?" Horatio asked.

"Rhys might have. Who are you?"

"Agent Hopkins. Let's all sit down and have a chat."

The empty bottles might have been gone, but there were two full ones waiting. Both were Blue Wolf. Rhys stood when they got close and probably would have bowed to Alpha Braxton if wolves did that kind of thing. "Sir, the waitress brought you a fresh bottle. I didn't realize you were still working on the other one."

"Which one is his," Horatio asked.

"Either one I guess."

"This one," Alpha Braxton said, snatching up the one farthest away and putting it to his lips.

"Wait!"

He probably would have drunk it all down at once if Brayton hadn't spoken up at the same time Honey did.

Alpha Braxton looked over the top of his bottle at Brayton. "Why? What's going on?"

Brayton held out his hand. "Let me see your bottle for a second."

"I thought you weren't drinking anything tonight."

"I'm not going to drink it. I just need to check the bottle. It might be cursed."

"What?" Alpha Braxton exclaimed, looking with sudden suspicion at his drink. He handed it to Brayton.

Brayton sniffed it before handing it to her. "I don't smell anything."

She took a deep whiff and nearly gagged. "I do." She handed it to Horatio, "Let me see the other one."

It smelled fine.

Horatio sat down with both bottles in hand. "Everyone sit down. We're being too conspicuous."

The burly bouncer loomed over them while they all found seats. "I want an explanation. Now."

"Sit, and I'll explain." Horatio said. He looked toward Rhys. "Rhys, right? Which waitress brought the bottles? Can you describe her?"

Rhys opened his mouth and then frowned. "Not really. She was very, plain. Brown hair, middle-age, middle-height, plain clothes."

"I don't have any waitresses like that," bouncer-guy said.

"Are you the owner?" Horatio asked.

"Manager. What's going on?"

Horatio nodded to the two bottles in front of him. "We have reason to believe one of these bottles has been tampered with, cursed, if you will. Honey says she can smell it."

"Let me see."

Horatio offered both bottles, but Honey noticed he kept a firm grip.

"I don't smell anything."

"Honey is different," Liam said.

"She's telepathically impaired," Walter quickly interrupted, "but she can do other things that most of us cannot, like identify the type of magic being used based on how it smells."

"Really?" The bouncer-manager looked at Honey curiously. "What does it smell like to you?"

"Despair, blood, iron, pain."

He made a face then shook his head. "If what she says is true, it wasn't anyone who works here."

"We have some witches back at the office. I'll have them run some tests on these bottles," Horatio said.

"I'm afraid I can't let you do that," the manager said, reaching for the bottles. "My pack spent years optimizing the recipe for Blue Wolf so that wolves could enjoy a good drink just as much as humans. We are finally beginning to make a profit on our investment. I cannot let the recipe fall into other hands."

Horatio nodded while pulling the bottles out of the manager's reach. "I understand. Would you be opposed to a witch testing it here? The test is only to detect a spell and nothing more."

"I have no way of knowing that."

"I work with agents from your pack. What if they supervise?"

"That might be acceptable."

"Who spelled it though?" Brayton asked.

"Good question." Horatio looked up at the manager again. "Do you employ any witches?"

"No. Most of the employees are from my pack but I do employ a few people from other packs."

"What about at your brewery. Any witches?"

"No. Only my pack works there."

"Is there any way a witch could access some of your brew between the brewery and here?"

"Not that I know of. We use our own trucks to deliver the bottles."

"Okay, so it's got to be someone here, which makes sense since not every bottle is spelled," Horatio concluded.

"You don't even know that's true," the manager huffed.

"It's a working theory. Do you have any employees working here tonight who were working at The Hole three weeks ago?"

"What happened three weeks ago?"

"The attempted murder."

"Oh, right. Some girl got stabbed by her boyfriend. Did she survive?"

"Yes," Honey said. "And he wasn't my boyfriend, but he was acting oddly and I smelled the curse on his breath. A waitress bumped me and I smelled some other magic just before he stabbed me."

"Are any of the waitresses at The Hole witches?" Horatio asked.

"Not that I know of, but I could ask Edgar. He's the manager down there. Why are you here if she was stabbed down there?"

She jumped in before Horatio could. "Because on the night of the last full moon, I smelled the curse on a guy's breath here."

"Did he try to stab you?" the manager asked.

"No, but he was acting weird too. He was waiting for me outside the bathroom."

The manager shook his head. "Sadly, little girl, that's not that weird."

"In any event," Horatio interrupted, "it appears that someone is doing something to some of your bottles at both locations. Can I get a list of all your employees and where and if they were working tonight, last Saturday, and the Saturday of the full moon?"

"Sure, but I'm warning you, if you try to take those bottles out of this club, there will be repercussions."

"Noted. I'm calling the agents I mentioned now. Oh, and don't tell anyone of our investigation."

"Wouldn't dream of it."

Alpha Braxton reached toward one of the bottles while the manager stomped away. "Can I have a sip out of my bottle since you can't take them out of the club anyway? The air in here is so dry it's sucking the moisture right out of my lungs."

"You can tell which one it is?" Horatio asked.

He pointed to the bottle in Horatio's left hand. "It's that one."

"How can you tell?"

"I just can."

"How many of these have you had?"

"One."

"Two, not including that one," Brayton piped up. "Both from the same waitress."

"Do you see her?"

Brayton and Alpha Braxton both looked around. Alpha Braxton pointed into the corner and raised his hand to signal her. "That's her."

"Maybe we won't need that list after all," Horatio mumbled. He handed the plain bottle of Blue Wolf to

Rhys and the bottle of cursed Blue Wolf to Chloe who was sitting beside him. "Don't drink that."

A woman who met Rhys' description hurried over. "Can I get you something Alpha Braxton?"

"Yes, another one of those Blue Wolf specials please."

She glanced at the bottle in Chloe's hand then back to him. "You drank that one fast. You must really like them."

"I do. Can I get one for all my grandson's friends and another for myself, of course."

Her eyes fell on Honey and she frowned, but just for a moment. "Of course. Are you celebrating something?"

"We are. Chloe here just found her fated mate and he was in our pack the whole time. Isn't that amazing?"

Alpha Braxton had lied twice. Every wolf around the table could smell it and even Honey could smell that Horatio and Chloe were not from the same pack. The waitress pasted on a smile that almost looked genuine. "Ah yes! You must have a big pack."

It was a test, Honey realized. She smelled like a wolf but she couldn't *smell* like a wolf.

"It's a good size, but not as big as the Little Pack. What pack did you say you are from?"

"The Little Pack."

"No you're not." Liam said behind her. He and Nathan had finally realized they weren't at the bar and had come looking for them.

"It's a big pack and I'm usually at work."

Liam leaned forward and took a sniff. "You don't have the mark of the Little Pack." He sniffed again. "In fact, you don't have a mark at all."

279

Honey pushed back from the table and walked around to where the woman stood next to Alpha Braxton and breathed in the woman's scent herself.

"I'll get those drinks."

Honey grabbed her arm. "No."

The waitress jerked her arm away. "Let go of me, wolf!"

Nathan and Liam blocked her from backing away.

Honey focused on the spell she suspected surrounded the waitress that made her smell like wolf. The molecules were all locked up tight except for the ones over the necklace she was wearing. That must be why she could smell a very faint shielding spell.

"You are a witch."

"No. Get away from me."

"You're wearing a necklace with a shielding spell to hide your true form."

The waitress flung the sharp edge of her tray at Honey's neck, but Honey got her jacket-covered arm up in time. Alpha Braxton launched out of his seat and grabbed the waitress by the back of her neck, then sliced through her necklace with a sharp claw. Her dowdy look fell away with the necklace and suddenly a lovely redhead stood before them. She would have been lovely, that is, if she didn't have such a nasty look on her face.

Honey smelled the magic in her words when she very firmly said to Alpha Braxton, "Let go of me."

Alpha Braxton immediately released her.

"What's going on Tiffany?" The manager loomed over Horatio on the other side of the table, a piece of paper forgotten in his hand.

"This man is behaving inappropriately. He needs to leave."

"Your spell only hides you from certain people?" Honey asked. "How does that work?"

"Spell?" the manager said.

"What does she smell like to you?" Honey asked.

He marched around the table and took a sniff. "Human and, no. Magic?" he stepped back in surprise. "You're a witch?"

"Yes, I'm a witch. I've always been a witch, you furry-brained, four-legged giant."

"I don't understand."

"Would you have hired me if I wasn't a wolf? No! You wolves promised non-discrimination when hiring except for pack-owned businesses. Funny enough, since the treaty was signed, all wolf-owned businesses have become pack-owned and because of your furry-buddy system, all the best locations go to wolves. The only witch-owned clubs are so seedy you risk getting a disease just stepping into them."

"Why did you spell the Blue Wolf? What's the spell supposed to do?" Horatio asked. He was still seated at the table but Honey noticed he had his phone tilted in Tiffany's direction.

"What spell? What are you talking about?"

Alpha Braxton puffed up like he was about to say something, but Horatio held up a hand and continued with his questioning. "Do you sometimes work at The Hole?"

"Yes," she spat out after a few moments.

"Were you there last week?"

"No, I was off."

"How about the week before that?"

"No."

"And before that?"

"Maybe. That was a long time ago."

"What about the night of the last full moon? Were you working then?"

"She was here," the manager said, "and three weeks ago, she was at the university location. A couple of girls called in sick. I should have realized there was something odd about that."

"You're blaming me for something that's completely normal just because I'm a witch! That's discrimination, right there."

"I interviewed every waitress at that location after the attempted murder, but I don't remember seeing you in either form, nor did I speak to someone named Tiffany," Horatio said. "Can you tell me what you saw that night?"

"A lot of college wolves trying to get drunk."

"What about during the stabbing."

"I didn't see it. I was headed to the bar to get more drinks."

"Why didn't you stay for the interviews?"

"I," she faltered, then a fierce determination settled over her. "I am not like you wolves. I find the sight of blood disturbing. I left."

So far everything she'd said was true, at least according to Honey's nose. She couldn't claim she had much experience picking out lies. Her mother never lied to her. She just didn't answer if it was something she wanted to keep to herself.

282

"Was it you who bumped into me just before Brayton stabbed me?" Honey asked.

"I don't know. Maybe."

"Lie!" Alpha Braxton growled.

"As you're probably aware, wolves can detect lies by smell," Horatio said calmly, "and Alpha Braxton is well known for his skill. Please try again and answer truthfully."

"Maybe is not a lie. I bump into people all the time."

"But you know you bumped into her. There's no maybe about it," Walter said.

"Fine. I bumped into her. I didn't stab her."

"Did you serve some of the special Blue Wolf to Brayton?" Honey asked.

"Who's Brayton?"

"Me," Brayton said.

She looked at him and curled her lip. "Why aren't you in jail?"

"You recognize him," Horatio said. "Answer Honey's question. Did you serve Brayton special Blue Wolf?"

"There is no special Blue Wolf. It's all just Blue Wolf. I get more tips if I call it special."

"Did you serve Brayton Blue Wolf?" Horatio repeated.

"Probably. You can't blame me for his over-indulgence though. Look, I'm sorry you were stabbed, but I need to get back to work."

"No you don't," the manager said. "Answer their questions."

"Were you in possession of a knife when you bumped into Honey?" Horatio asked.

"Who's Honey?"

283

"The girl who was stabbed."

The waitress looked at Honey with a smirk. "Poor thing. Your mom is a Hippie-wolf isn't she?"

"No."

"You recognize her," Horatio stated. "Answer the question. Were you in possession of a knife?"

"I...there might have been one on my serving tray, but that doesn't mean I gave it to him."

"No, it does not," Horatio agreed. "We were just trying to figure out where the knife came from."

"Good. Can I go now?"

"Not yet. We're waiting for a few specialists to arrive. Have a seat."

"We're really busy. I need to get back to work."

The manager shook his head. "Not here you don't."

"Why, just because I'm a witch? That's discrimination."

"No, because you lied to get this job and you used magic on us."

"You wouldn't have even bothered to interview me if you knew I was witch and technically, I didn't use magic on you. I used magic on myself."

"Lie," Alpha Braxton barked.

Honey caught a whiff of magic and finally recognized the scent. Her mom had used it in some of her soaps. "Camphor. Your magic smells like camphor. You influence people. That's your power."

"And your power is to sniff into other people's business?"

"No, but I smelled it right before Brayton stabbed me and I smelled it just now. Who are you using it on?"

"Let her go." Alpha Braxton was looking right at Honey and puffing up like he had in Brayton's dorm.

"You're making Alpha Braxton use his alpha powers to influence everyone," Honey realized.

"Yep, and you can't do a thing about it, wolf." The waitress reached over the table and swiped the phone from Horatio's hand, "And I'll take that."

Honey threw her body on top of the leaning woman and slammed the waitress' head against the table. She simultaneously froze her so it looked like the waitress had been knocked out. If anyone smelled her power, she could blame it on the witch.

Honey looked over her shoulder from where she was holding the waitress down. "Alpha Braxton, are you in control again?"

He shook his head. "What did that witch do to me?"

"Get out of here before she wakes up. If she controls you, she controls the whole club."

"I am not leaving!"

Brayton shot out of his chair, making it crash into the chair behind it, and grabbed the alpha's arm. "Come on Grandpa. Honey's right. You can't fight against the witch's magic."

"I am not running away from a little witch!"

"Please Grandpa. If she tells you to stab someone, you won't be able to stop."

Alpha Braxton glanced down at his grandson, then much to Honey's relief, nodded. "Brayton, you're with me. The rest of you stay here. I want a full report."

"Yes, Sir," Rhys and Chloe replied at the same time.

Honey caught Brayton's eye. "I'm not sure how far her power extends, Brayton. Be careful."

"I will."

"I'll go with you, just in case," Cici volunteered.

"Just go quickly. Before she wakes up," Honey urged.

Horatio had retrieved his phone and was rapidly texting someone. "The witches will be here in a few minutes. They're bringing an inhibitor."

"What's an inhibitor?" Honey asked.

"It will keep her from using her powers on anyone."

"Really? I didn't know that was possible."

"It's just a spell on a stone like the one she was wearing."

The waitress twitched.

"She's coming to. Shall I release her?"

Horatio nodded. "Yes."

Walter had moved so that he was standing where Alpha Braxton had been. Luca and Nathan were at Honey's back. Tiffany shook her head and slowly stood, looking around at all of them.

"What are you going to do to me?"

"You just used magic on an alpha and we all witnessed it. What do you think we're going to do to you?" Chloe hissed.

Tiffany's eye's blazed and Honey smelled a powerful wave of camphor. Somewhere in the club there was a scream. "Sounds like there's a fight breaking out, Max. Better go check it out."

Honey put Tiffany in a sleeper hold so she could knock her out by restricting the blood flow to her brain. At least that's what it looked like. She froze her after a few seconds. "Do you happen to have any of those tranquilizer darts with you?" she asked Malcolm and Rhys while she deposited the waitress in a chair.

"Sorry, left them in my other pants," Malcolm quipped.

The screaming hadn't stopped. "I'm going to see what's going on," the manager said, and ran toward the noise.

Horatio nodded at Tiffany. "Two of you boys, carry her out of here before she wakes up again. I'll text the other agents that you are outside. Honey, you stay here."

"No. I should go in case she wakes up again. I can tell if she's using her magic."

Chloe put her hand on Horatio's shoulder. "I'll go with her. We'll come back as soon as she is inhibited."

A young waitress in a halter top ran up to them. "Which one of you is Agent Hopkins? Max told me to get you. We have a problem."

# 31

## *Honey*

Horatio handed both bottles of Blue Wolf to Liam. "You're with me. Don't lose the evidence."

"Yes, sir."

Walter squatted, then stood with Tiffany draped over his shoulder. "Let's go."

Honey jogged ahead of him to open the door. Luca, Nathan, and Chloe followed him. The people just coming in gave them some strange looks but they didn't say anything. Walter jogged downhill to a park bench a block away with the rest following, then dumped Tiffany on the bench.

Chloe frowned down at her. "Shouldn't she be awake by now?"

Nathan felt her neck. "She's still alive."

Almost like he'd given her permission, Tiffany's head rolled to her shoulder, and then up. Her eyes opened, blinked, then focused on Honey.

"What are you, some kind of assassin?"

"Um, no."

"Special forces?"

"No."

Tiffany lurched at Honey and grabbed the collar of her T-shirt, but just as quickly released her.

"What was that for?" she asked, patting her shirt back in place while Luca and Walter each grabbed a shoulder and pushed Tiffany back.

"Just checking. I thought maybe I wasn't the only one hiding her identity." She looked around. "You carried me outside. Dumb."

Honey smelled Tiffany's magic again right before she leaped off the bench. Honey tripped her, then dove on top of her and banged her head against the cement using a fist-full of hair, not hard, but enough to hurt. "Stop it. Don't make me knock you out again."

"You should have."

Tiffany's magic surrounded her and she banged the woman's head against the cement again, while freezing her. She rolled off the waitress to find her friends just watching. "Geez, don't help or anything."

"You had it," Nathan said.

"Yeah, I had no idea you were so good at knocking people out," Chloe said.

Walter looked at her with a question in his eyes. Honey nodded, to indicate she was using her magic. "Three times in like, five minutes? Is that healthy?"

Honey looked down at the redhead apparently sleeping on the sidewalk at her feet. "Probably not for her. I could smell her magic. What did she do to you?"

"Nothing," Chloe shrugged.

289

"No," Walter said. "I didn't help because I thought someone else would help. Did you all think the same thing?"

"Yeah," Luca said. Nathan nodded.

Chloe growled. "Damn witches."

A black van pulled up beside them and a woman dressed all in black like a ninja stepped out. "Any of you Honey?"

"Yeah, that's me."

"Is that the witch?"

"Yeah."

The woman dropped down beside Tiffany and touched her neck. "What did you do to her?"

"She was using her power against us. I knocked her out so she wouldn't hurt anyone."

The woman moved her fingers around on Tiffany's skin, then called back over her shoulder. "Gene, I'm not feeling a pulse. Get over here!"

Honey was pretty sure she hadn't killed the woman, but she'd never froze someone three times in a row. The woman probably couldn't find a pulse because Tiffany's molecules were still frozen, but it scared her. "Do you have the inhibitor?"

"It doesn't matter if she's dead!"

The woman in black backed up as another woman, this one in a sweater and tights, squatted beside Tiffany. Honey willed Tiffany's body to unfreeze. The woman in black turned her head sharply to look at her, just as Gene said, "What are you talking about? Her pulse is right here."

"Put the inhibitor on her," Honey said. She didn't want to have to freeze her again. "I think she may have caused some injuries inside the bar. There were people screaming."

"Yeah, we know," Gene said. "An ambulance is on the way. Horatio told us to secure the prisoner first. She's all yours, Amber. I'm going to see if I can offer some assistance." She started jogging up the hill toward the club.

The woman in black, Amber, secured Tiffany's hands behind her back with a set of handcuffs. A blue stone encased in silver hung on the chain joining the cuffs.

"Is that the inhibitor?"

"It is."

Tiffany was fully awake now. "Let me go!"

"Are you sure it's working? I can still smell her magic."

"Yeah, it's working." Amber raised her hand like she was going to do something, but nothing happened. "See, I'm too close. I can't spark a fire."

Amber's magic smelled like Panas' magic - like hot asphalt.

"I can still smell it," Honey insisted.

"Huh."

Amber got up and pulled Tiffany to her feet. "By the authority of the Coalition and my position as an Enforcer, I hereby arrest you for illegal use of your power to cause harm or mischief."

"I was defending myself."

"Tell it to the judge."

"If you're not part of the solution, you're the part of the problem."

"And what problem would that be," Amber asked while leading Tiffany to the back of the van.

291

"The wolves run everything. We're basically at their mercy."

"They don't run everything. We co-run the Coalition."

"No, they only allow witches to help to keep us placated. It's like throwing a dog a bone."

The back door swung open with some help from a man inside.

"And how does using your power to make wolves attack each other help the situation?" Amber asked while she helped Tiffany step up into the van.

Tiffany didn't answer. Amber slammed the door, then walked to the still-open front door and pulled out a black duffle bag. Slinging the strap over her shoulder, she looked back at Honey and her friends. "Shall we?"

Back inside the club, the lights were still flashing, but the music had stopped. The waitresses had formed a line to keep the customers sequestered to the dance floor and bar and away from the area near the bathrooms. Most of the customers had their cell phones out and were either calling their friends or taking videos and pictures of the scene, although there was one scantily clad girl who was clearly taking pictures of herself.

Beyond the waitresses, three bodies were lying on the floor. Several others were either sitting on the floor or in chairs. Gene was crouched over a body surrounded by a puddle of red.

Amber strode into the middle of it all and called out, "Hopkins! Where's the evidence?"

Horatio was squatting next to someone propped up against a chair and holding tightly to their arm. He jerked his head toward Liam who was standing to the side and holding onto both bottles with white knuckles. Liam thrust them at Amber. "Here."

As soon as they were out of his hands, he ran to Gene and asked if he could help.

Honey wanted to help too, but it looked like everyone was taken care of. Amber handed the bottles to Walter, told him he better not drop them, and started digging around in her bag. She pulled out a small box with several tubes inside and a black marker. She then handed Honey her cell phone. "I want you to record this."

Luca took it out of Honey's hands. "She's only owned a cell phone for a couple of months. I'll do it."

Nathan pulled his phone out of his pocket. "And I'll do a back-up recording, just in case."

"You guys are not giving me a lot of confidence here."

Luca pushed a couple of buttons and showed Amber the screen. "Light's red. Recording is on."

"Focus on me." She held up the tubes in front of the phone. "Tubes containing spell detection powder. If the solution is spelled, it will turn black." She waved at the bottles. "Evidence collected at The Club on Saturday, one week before the full moon in October. We have reason to believe one of these bottles is spelled or cursed. The proprietors have requested we not take the bottles off the premises for testing, so we are doing it here." She uncapped the marker and wrote 'A' and 'B' on the tubes, then 'A' and 'B' on the bottles. After tossing the marker back in the bag, she took the 'A' bottle and poured a small amount into the 'A' tube and shook it up. Nothing happened. She handed that tube to Chloe, then did the same thing with the 'B' tube. She held them both up and shook them again. "They're both negative."

"No. I could smell a spell on one. Can I sniff them again?"

"Sure."

Honey took a deep sniff and immediately wished she hadn't. The stench was worse. She thrust the offensive bottle away. "It's B."

"The test is negative."

"But none of the other wolves can smell it either. Could it be inhibited in some way?"

She scrunched up her nose. "It's possible. The correct term would be concealed." She dug out two more tubes from her bag, a bottle of powder, and a small tube rack. "De-concealer." She used a little spatula to transfer a few grains into each tube, labeled the tubes, then repeated her experiment. Tube B turned a nasty shade of purple-brown before swirling into blackness. She held them up in front of the cameras. "Positive for concealed spell. Now we have to figure out what kind."

"Cut," Nathan said. "This is getting too long for one video."

Amber rolled her eyes and looked at Luca. "Keep it rolling."

Amber pulled out another rack of tubes. Honey already knew what type of spell it was. She'd only been concerned that the witches wouldn't be able to detect it. She left Amber to her tubes and wandered toward Liam who was watching Gene run her hands over a gaping wound on a girl's neck. Gene's magic smelled a lot like her mom's.

"What happened Liam?"

He pointed to a guy slouching on a chair next to the restrooms with two large guys standing over him. "That guy partially transformed and started clawing and biting people. He nearly killed this girl and that guy over there isn't much better."

Gene took her hands away. "There. I sealed up the worst of it. Tell the paramedics to take it easy on her. I'll take a look at the other one now."

She swayed a little as she stood up. Honey grabbed her elbow.

"Thanks. Stood too fast."

"They're wolves. They're not as fragile as humans. You don't have to go that far with them."

"I know. I've healed a lot of them."

Honey let her go. Liam followed her. Curiosity drew Honey to the almost-murderer like a magnet to metal. The two men guarding him watched her suspiciously while she approached.

One of the guards put out his hand like he was a crossing-guard. "Stop right there, little girl."

"I recognize him." It was the guy who'd followed her to the bathroom, but he looked horrible. He'd lost weight and there were dark shadows under his blood-shot eyes. He lifted his eyes up to hers and she'd never seen anyone so sad and full of anguish.

"Did I kill them?"

"No."

"I didn't mean to hurt anyone."

"I know." She plopped down on the floor in front of him. He reeked of the curse.

"What are you doing?" one of the guards demanded.

"He's not dangerous. He was cursed," she informed them without taking her eyes off the young man. "Does your head hurt?"

"Not now. You said I was cursed?"

"You reek of it."

"That's not curse you're smelling girl," the shorter guard scoffed. "He hasn't seen the inside of a shower for weeks. He's nothing but a lousy drunk."

"What do you mean your head doesn't hurt now?" she asked.

"Blue Wolf takes away the pain."

"You drink it to cure your migraines?"

"Yes."

"There's a witch over there, a healer. She might be able to heal you."

"No. Those people need her. I don't deserve her help."

"You've been hurt as much or more than they have, it's just a different kind of injury. There was a waitress who was spelling some of the Blue Wolf. I think it allowed her to control you more than she normally could. The more you drank, the more you were under her control." Honey wished she could help him, but with the two wolves on either side, she was afraid to even try to look inside his mind. "I will tell the healer you need help. Maybe after she recovers from healing those people she'll be able to help you."

296

He looked down at his blood-stained hands. "No one can help me."

He was so sad. Despite his smell, she wanted to take one of his hands.

"What is your name?"

"Zavier."

"I'm Honey. A few weeks ago, someone else who was cursed stabbed me in the heart. I know it wasn't his fault and I don't hold it against him. Once those people realize you were cursed, they won't hold it against you either."

A hand fell on her shoulder. "Honey, what are you doing?"

"Talking to Zavier." She looked up to see Chloe holding her nose.

"He reeks."

"He just needs a bath."

"Isn't he the one that hurt all these people?"

"He has a headache like Brayton did. He kept drinking Blue Wolf to get rid of it."

"No. I know what you're thinking. As your bodyguard I'm putting my foot down. No head rubs. Come on. We're done here."

"I need to speak to Gene before we go."

"Fine."

# 32

## *Honey*

After class Tuesday afternoon Chloe was waiting for her in the hallway with the biggest smile Honey had even seen on her beautiful face. Chloe threw her arms around Honey causing the other students, who were mostly human, to glance at them curiously. "You did it!"

"What did I do?"

Chloe released her and waved a phone in Honey's face. "All charges dropped. They were able to connect the stuff in the drinks to the waitress."

"That's great. Do they know why she did it?"

Chloe rolled her eyes and fell into step beside her. "Something about using her power to influence our leaders so they'd make the laws fair, but that plan was flawed from the beginning since she worked at college bars. She decided to target the leaders' kids but that only worked if she was next to them, so she decided to get them all arrested while at the same time destroying the reputation of our businesses so the witches could take over."

"Wow."

"Yeah. Crazy, right."

"What about Zavier? Did they drop the charges on him too?"

"Who? The guy who hurt all those people? I don't know. Probably."

"Honey!"

A body hurtled toward her. Before she could step back, she was engulfed in a strong pair of arms and a familiar body spray. It was actually very nice, but also very tight.

"Brayton, I need air."

He immediately released her with his arms but grabbed her shoulders with his hands, kissed her forehead, then put his own against hers. "Thank you. Thank you. Thank you."

"You're welcome?"

He laughed and fell into step on her other side. He acted completely oblivious to the glare his grandpa was trying to pierce her with. Cici and Rhys were there too.

"I guess this means I'm out of a job," Chloe sighed.

"I bet a certain Enforcer could put in a good word for you," Brayton teased while they walked past his grandpa.

"Shush."

Honey pretended she didn't notice the glare now burning her back between her shoulder blades. "You could get matching trench coats."

"And fedoras," Brayton added.

Chloe growled under her breath but Honey noticed the twitch at the corner of her mouth.

"Honey."

She stopped and turned, dreading whatever was coming next. "Yes, Alpha Braxton?"

He grabbed her shoulders and pressed his lips against her forehead just like Brayton had done. "Thank you for saving my grandson. I am…proud…to have you in our pack." He smiled, actually smiled at her. His face went from mean and grumpy to almost kind. "Brayton's mother is planning a celebration tonight. I hope you can be there."

"Sure."

"Good." He nodded toward Brayton. "He can give you the details. I'm going to pack. I think I've had enough of dorm living."

"Are you feeling okay?" She was concerned he had a headache like Brayton and Zavier after drinking Blue Wolf.

He threw back his head and laughed, then patted her on the shoulder. "Never better." He was still chuckling as he walked away.

Maybe he was too old and set in his ways for the curse to affect him? She used the back of her sleeve to wipe off the lingering feeling of the old man's lips.

"What is with you Mooney men and kissing people?"

Cici grabbed her arm from behind and pulled it down. "That's how the alphas accept you into the pack and reward you for service. You've been given a great honor by being accepted by the past, present, and future alphas."

"Oh."

The party was at a fancy steakhouse downtown. Chloe spent two hours getting ready and looked absolutely amazing in a non-club hopping kind of way when she met Honey at her room. Her light blue, gauzy dress flowed into an uneven skirt that fluttered gracefully around her legs and was just see-through enough to make you think you could see something through it but really couldn't. Her hair was an elegant pile on her head with a single blond tendril tumbling down one cheek. Honey felt way under-dressed with her mostly-loose hair and the simple knee-length red dress with white flowers Lynn had bought for her on one of their shopping trips. Chloe said she looked sweet.

Luna Lynn had rented a private room and invited everyone involved including Honey's Little friends, Horatio, and the witches who had helped out last night. Honey rode with her friends. Chloe rode with Horatio, but he didn't come in. Chloe said the Enforcers weren't allowed to attend because it would look like Luna had bribed them to make Tiffany look guilty. Dr. Ziga and a few nurses were there too.

Honey sat with her friends on one side of the table near the end. Luca, on her right, 'mmm'ed with every bite of his bloody steak. Walter kept leaning behind her and poking him, trying to make him stop. Nathan focused his attention on the closest females, namely her and Cici, but Cici wouldn't deign to even look his direction, which made Nathan all the more determined. Liam, on the other side of Walter, ignored them all. She tried not to let his indifference bother her.

She wasn't really paying attention to the conversation farther up the table until she heard Zavier's name and 'it's a shame' in the same sentence. "Are you talking about the Zavier who was at the bar?" she asked.

"Yes," Lynn answered, "He always seemed like a nice boy, like he had it all together. His mother must be devastated."

"He didn't look too good Friday," Brayton said.

"Did something happen?" Honey asked.

"Yeah," Brayton answered. "He tried to commit suicide."

"But he knows it wasn't his fault, right? Didn't his charges get dropped too?"

"It happened on Sunday, Honey, before they finished the investigation," Lynn said.

"You said tried, though. Is he okay now?"

Lynn shook her head. "No. He's unconscious in the hospital. He hasn't woken since he tried to hang himself."

"But wouldn't he be healed by now if he hurt his neck?"

"It took a long time for someone to discover him," Dr. Ziga said. "Even wolves can get brain damage from lack of oxygen, although I'm not saying that's the problem. I'm just stating a fact."

"Did Gene have a chance to look at him?"

"Who's Gene," Luna Lynn asked.

"She was a witch healer at the club Friday. I spoke to Zavier. He said…," she started to mention the headaches, then realized that might be a mistake since no one else seemed to realize Brayton's headaches had been caused by the spelled beer. Her ability fix magic-induced headaches could raise unwanted questions. "He was …despairing. Full of despair. The spell in the Blue Wolf smelled like despair, so I thought if a witch cursed him maybe a witch could heal him."

302

"He was feeling bad about what he'd just done," Lynn said gently.

"I know, but it was really bad – he looked really bad. I think he was feeling the curse long before he attacked those people."

Chloe shook her head regally instead of snorting like she normally would have. "He looked bad because he was a drunk."

"Maybe so," Lynn said, "but I don't think anyone ever plans to become a drunk. Maybe the curse had something to do with it. His parents are betas for the Wolfborne pack and I know he did quite well in college. He has an engineering degree and last I heard, a lovely girlfriend he is head-over-heels for."

Luca swallowed the bite he'd been enjoying with his eyes closed, but without the mmm's. "Maybe they broke up and it drove him to drink."

Luna Lynn shook her head. "I don't know and I'm not going to speculate." She patted Brayton's hand. "I am just glad it didn't happen to you."

Dr. Ziga leaned forward so he could see Honey past all the people sitting between them. "I don't know if a witch healer looked at him or not. I'll ask."

# *Notes from the Author*

Want more of Honey's antics? You're in luck. Honey's got a big adventure ahead of her. It took me seven books to tell the whole story. They're already written and nearly ready to be published so if they aren't online yet, they should be shortly.

Reader feedback is very much appreciated. Please leave a review if you liked the story and tell your friends and your librarian. (That's me marketing. Impressive, right?)

You may have noticed the 'Clean Fiction' logo at the beginning of the book. I love to read but sometimes, okay often, find myself in the middle of a good story and abruptly I'm in someone's bedroom getting a play-by-play. Sex happens but I don't need to be there. I'm not the only one who feels this way. I discovered whole communities on Instagram and a magazine devoted to clean reads. To make it easier for like-minded people to find clean books and to encourage other authors to go clean, I thought a logo on said books would be helpful. So, if you are a writer or know one and would like a copy of the logo, drop me a line. LisaL.author@gmail.com. I'd be glad to share. I have both gold-foil and black-ink versions.